The Relic

The Crypt Trilogy: Book One

Bill Thompson

Published by
Ascendente Books
Dallas, Texas

This is a work of fiction. The events and characters described herein are imaginary and any reference to specific places or living persons is incidental. The opinions expressed in this manuscript are solely the opinions of the author. The author has represented and warranted full ownership and/or legal rights to publish all the materials in this book.

The Relic of the King

V.1.0

Published by Ascendente Books
ISBN 978-0996181600
Printed in the United States of America

DEDICATION

This book is dedicated to two very good friends of mine,
Tom and Belinda Runnells.
Thanks for letting me weave your names into this novel.
Although I used your first names, the characters really aren't you – you're neither old nor owners of an occult bookstore!
Belinda, I thought of your love for England and history as this story came together.

ACKNOWLEDGEMENTS

My books couldn't be finished without the help of beta readers Jeff and Ryan and my wife, Margie, who patiently listens as I read every word aloud (an important element of my proofing process).

Thanks for critical feedback, corrections and comments.

Author's Note:

For ease of understanding, I used US dollars for most of the monetary transactions in this book.

CHAPTER ONE

Moscow, 1994

Sixteen-year-old Slava Sergenko would kill a man this afternoon. It would be his first murder, but there would be more. Many more.

Slava sat upstairs in a building that looked just like a thousand other Soviet-era offices near trendy Novy Arbat Street. It was only a block from the exclusive shops of Vuitton, Cartier, Jimmy Choo and Fendi. In an area where wealthy shoppers could find virtually anything their hedonistic desires craved, this particular place offered something unique. Something carnal. Something bad.

The day was brutally cold and windy. Sleet pelted the faces of pedestrians as an overweight Russian wearing an expensive cashmere overcoat hurried from his limousine to the front door of the establishment. He rang the doorbell. Someone glanced through a peephole then quickly opened the door. Seeing his boss safely inside the establishment, the limo driver pulled away from the curb. He knew from experience it would be several hours before he was called to pick up the wealthy businessman.

"Welcome, Comrade Bodrov. Come in and get warm!"

The man stepped into a large cozy room that looked like the den of a fancy dacha in the country. A corner fireplace held a roaring blaze, and overstuffed couches and chairs were tastefully placed around the room. It was inviting and warm on a frigid December afternoon in Moscow.

A porter took Bodrov's coat. "Another new suit, comrade? It's elegant."

The portly man laughed. "You always notice, Dimitri. I was in London a month ago and I couldn't resist!" Since the porter was the recipient of lavish tips each time Comrade Bodrov visited the brothel, he always complimented the tycoon.

A lady entered the room. Around forty and blond, she was still beautiful although in her twenties she would have been something really special. Bodrov had known her in those days and had followed her career as she gravitated from call girl to madam, and then to become the proprietor of this unique establishment.

She offered her cheek for a kiss and whispered into his ear, "Hello, Andrey. Here to check up on your investment, or looking for a little diversion this afternoon?"

"Both, as it turns out. Let's go to the office and talk. Meanwhile let Slava know I'm here."

She nodded and whispered to the porter. As he left to tell the boy, she and Andrey Bodrov went up a flight of stairs to a spacious office. She closed the door and locked it.

"I presume you want to discuss our finances in the usual way." She laughed, unbuttoning her blouse.

"Absolutely." He removed his suit jacket and hung it neatly on a hall tree in the corner of the room. He unbuttoned his shirt, careful with his gold cuff links. By the time his pants came off and were put on a hanger, she was nude. He looked at her admiringly. Even at forty her incredible figure was stunning. Tall and thin, she could easily have passed for thirty.

Once he was naked, he sat on a couch and said, "Bring me the financials for last month. I have some questions."

The oligarch flipped through the financial statements as she sat on the floor, her fingernails lightly brushing the insides of his legs. He began to become aroused as she worked him deftly up and down.

Bodrov had set the woman up in business after she approached him with a novel idea. The concept was interesting and he immediately saw potential in it. The chance of being caught in a place like this made it dangerous, which was titillating both to him and ultimately its clientele. Although Bodrov's ownership would never be discovered, his monthly visits might be. He was always very careful and he had several means of escape should the authorities ever decide to raid the place. He doubted that would happen – the police were well compensated for averting their eyes. But if the public learned about this particular brothel, even broad-minded Muscovites who customarily ignored the excesses and deviances of others wouldn't accept what went on behind these doors.

So he was careful. His ownership was concealed in layers of corporate shell companies. Only this woman knew the extent of his financial involvement, and she owed her entire lifestyle to his generosity. She was afraid of him – she had seen what he did to people who crossed him – but even more, she wasn't about to change her lavishly comfortable ways. She made a fantastic amount of money in exchange for discreetly running a very unusual place. She'd never betray Andrey Bodrov.

He spent fifteen minutes asking questions about the brothel's income and expenses. She answered while stroking him, pleased with the obvious pleasure he was experiencing from her touch. Finally his questions ended. Her work was complete as well. He was ready.

As they stood, she kissed him on the mouth. "Enjoy."

He gathered his clothes and walked to a door at the rear of her office. Unconcerned about his nudity, he entered an adjoining bedroom and hung his garments on a hook. The other clients in this establishment would have been taken to rooms on the first floor. Only Andrey Bodrov used this very special bedroom. It had been constructed solely for him, and a security team swept it daily for bugs. Its steel-reinforced walls made it a fortress. The bedroom could withstand a bomb and that was exactly why it was built. The tycoon was safe here.

The nude boy stretched seductively on the bed. Slava Sergenko, a sixteen-year-old from Ukraine, smiled as the fat tycoon entered the room. He noticed that the man's penis was erect from the preparatory work in the office next door. It was the same every time. The boss lady got the big man ready and Slava finished the job. But this time it would be different. This would be the best session of the boy's life.

A year ago Slava's father had sold him to the brothel. Although the man had justified it as a financial transaction that would better both himself and his son, the father knew exactly where the boy was going. And he had let it happen for ten thousand US dollars.

The woman who ran the establishment had called Andrey as soon as she made the deal for Slava. He was one of a half dozen boys and girls who made her establishment unique in Moscow – none of her prostitutes were over sixteen. For that reason, wealthy Russians flocked to her discreet doorstep. The place made millions, much of it tax-free thanks to some of her clients who paid in cash. Although most put the two-thousand-dollar fee on a credit card and expensed it through their companies, she and Andrey particularly liked those who paid in hard US greenbacks, the only cash she accepted.

That day Andrey Bodrov had first met Slava he'd spent an afternoon like never before. To say it was different would be a vast understatement; when it was over, the oligarch was hooked. The boy had been on the streets – even though he was merely a teenager, he knew what he had to do to make his clients happy. He was good, but he also was crafty, deliberate, calculating and wise. His wealthy clients didn't know that part. Only fifteen when he arrived, Slava already knew what he ultimately wanted. He just needed to figure out how to get it. And once he had gotten to know

Andrey Bodrov, the answer became clear. He'd bide his time until things were right. And that day was today.

"Come in, darling," the boy said to the man, who was old enough to be his father, maybe even his grandfather. He lay on the bed seductively as Andrey approached.

The man sat on the bed as Slava got up to retrieve a bottle of baby oil. He lay back on the pillow and Slava began to massage him. Andrey's eyes closed and he rubbed the boy's leg. Slava moved one hand lower and lower down the Russian's stomach. At the same time he casually moved his other hand under the mattress where he'd hidden a seven-inch-long darning needle.

As the boy's hand moved to stroke Andrey's penis, the Russian groaned in anticipation. Slava smiled and said, "Are you happy?"

"Oh yes," was the breathless response, the man's eyes closed in ecstatic pleasure.

"So am I." Slava pulled out the long needle and plunged it directly into Andrey Bodrov's heart. His eyes popped open in surprise and he opened his mouth, but no sound came out.

Slava had read an article on the Internet about how to kill someone with a darning needle. Death was instantaneous; there was no blood and only a tiny puncture wound. He had spent time learning exactly where the heart lay within the chest. It had worked perfectly.

"Sleep well, you bastard." The boy laughed without remorse. He pulled the bedcovers up to the man's neck and stepped back. To anyone who looked in, the oligarch would appear to be napping. This was perfect because it gave Slava plenty of time.

Every time Andrey had a session with Slava, the man slept for a couple of hours afterwards. In the beginning the boy would creep quietly out of the room when they were finished. Once he realized how quickly and soundly the Russian fell asleep, Slava began going through his pockets now and then, just to see what he could find. He never stole anything. But it all became part of Slava's master plan.

Now that Andrey was dead, Slava worked efficiently. He got dressed then emptied Bodrov's pockets. Inside his wallet was a fat wad of US hundred-dollar bills, and in his suit jacket a thick bank envelope held a lot more. A silver ring held several keys but only one that Slava wanted – a specially shaped key that he had seen elsewhere. The lady who ran the brothel, Slava's madam, had an identical one. The clever youth had sneaked around sufficiently to learn there was a locked cabinet in the woman's office. She had one key to it and this was the other. He was pretty sure what was inside. If he was correct, it would be his ticket to independence.

Slava took the man's debit card and saw he had carelessly jotted his PIN number on the back. Wealthy businessmen like this didn't expect to get their wallets stolen, Slava presumed, so they weren't careful. Too bad. Andrey wouldn't need his money now anyway.

The boy went to the bed, slipped his hand under the covers, and grasped Andrey Bodrov's left hand. He removed a watch, heavy ring and flashy bracelet. Each sparkled ostentatiously with gold and diamonds, and each went straight into Slava's pockets.

He opened the bedroom door leading into the hallway and listened. He could hear the woman downstairs speaking with another client. The coast was clear. He closed the door, crossed the room and entered her office through the same door Andrey had used earlier. Slava walked to the locked file cabinet, inserted Andrey's key and opened it. He had been correct about what was inside, and he was ecstatic. What he saw made his plan complete. He was free!

In the top drawer over a hundred folders were filed alphabetically by name, a virtual Who's Who of Russian business and society. He recognized many of the names. They were all men, all older, all wealthy beyond the comprehension of young Slava. He opened one folder to see what it contained – a dossier gave detailed information about the client, his sexual preferences and his payment details, including credit card numbers. He glanced at others; each had an identical sheet inside.

A lot of files also contained grainy photos obviously taken by a hidden camera. These would be the brothel's insurance policy against problems with its customers. There were even pictures of naked politicians with young boys and girls. Perfect. Slava stuffed everything into a box he'd prepared just for this day. Although there were a lot of files, each was slim, and they all fit easily in his little box. He didn't bother to close the file drawer.

He glanced at the Russian's watch and put it on his wrist. He had at least an hour and forty-five minutes to get to the bank's ATM and make a withdrawal. Eventually the madam would check on her boss. But not for a while. He needed Andrey Bodrov's money, but it was far less important now than it had been before he'd opened the cabinet and taken the files.

The boy stepped into the hallway, pressed the lock on the knob and closed the door. Without a sound he carried his small box down a back staircase that led to the kitchen. No one was there at this time of the afternoon. He grabbed someone's heavy coat and cap from a peg by the back door, put them on and stepped out into an alley filled with garbage cans. His box of treasured information under his arm and Andrey's plundered possessions in his pockets, Slava Sergenko walked away from this life forever.

That was his first murder. Only the first of many.

CHAPTER TWO

As she worked in her office next door, the woman realized Andrey was sleeping much longer than usual today. And, she mused, Slava must be napping with him. When their sessions were finished, the boy usually left and Andrey dozed for an hour or so. Today she hadn't heard a peep for over three hours. There wasn't a sound from the room next door.

By five it was getting dark and she had to do something. Andrey should have left by now, heading home to his wife and his dinner. At the risk of angering her boss, she decided to take a peek inside.

She opened the door quietly. In the gloom she could see Andrey sleeping. Slava wasn't with him. That was odd; once he finished, he was required to report to her. Time was money in this business, and there was usually another customer waiting his turn. She pulled the door quietly shut and walked downstairs.

Ten minutes later she knew Slava was gone. No one had seen him for hours, and the coat and hat of her handyman were missing from a peg by the back door. Now she had to wake Andrey. She walked upstairs, tried the door in the hallway, found it locked, and entered the bedroom through her office.

"Andrey, darling. Andrey, wake up. It's after five and you need to go."

Nothing. She didn't hear snores. She didn't hear anything. Not a rustle.

She walked to the bed and put her hand on his shoulder. "Wake up ..."

She stifled a scream as she felt cold flesh. He'd been dead so long he wasn't even warm anymore. She pulled the covers back; he was naked, but she saw no wound, nothing to indicate he'd died from anything but natural causes.

This was a dilemma. She didn't know what to do. She felt no sadness – as sexually involved as they'd been, he was not her lover in the emotional sense. She was worried because she was in a jam. Should she call Andrey's wife? Another person at the company he ran? None of those solutions sounded good. She had to get his body out of this place without involving the authorities. That she knew for sure. If she called the police, she might as well get fitted for her prison suit because that was where she'd be for the rest of her life.

Damn you, Andrey. Why did you have to die here?

Suddenly she remembered something. Andrey had a son who worked for him. He'd told her once the boy was in his thirties and his name was ... What was it? Boris? Boris Bodrov? Yes, that was it!

She placed a call to PetroRussia, the huge oil conglomerate Andrey controlled. She asked the operator for Boris Bodrov and soon was speaking to a secretary. The assistant quizzed her for a moment about the nature of her call until she finally said, "It's about his father. There's been an accident. I must speak with him now!"

As she waited, she hoped Boris knew his father frequented brothels. She had no intention of letting him know exactly what kind of place this was, of course. She'd make it sound like the regular kind, with beautiful ladies for sale. Regardless, it would be embarrassing and difficult if the man had no idea about his father's prurient side.

The son undoubtedly didn't know that Andrey owned this place. That would be good for her; she could just keep things going and the money would be hers instead of Andrey's. She wouldn't mention anything unless the younger Bodrov brought the subject up. In the meantime she'd better move the client dossiers locked in the file cabinet. It would be better if they were somewhere else for now. She glanced across the room and gasped.

Oh God, no.

The top drawer of the cabinet was open slightly.

She ran to look and her worst fears were realized.

It wasn't just Slava who was missing from the brothel. The files were gone too.

And that meant soon she'd be as dead as Andrey was.

The porter, Andrey Bodrov's son and two men he enlisted from the oil company had difficulty moving the heavy man's body downstairs. Before moving his father, Boris waited until the establishment closed and all customers had gone. By then rigor mortis had set in; Andrey's body was stiff as a board.

The woman had told Boris Bodrov his father was enjoying the company of a female prostitute when he died. He had no idea that this place even existed, much less that it housed child prostitutes. All the young employees had been closeted away far out of sight. She also now understood he had no idea Andrey owned it. Those were the only positive things at this point.

The public story was that Andrey Bodrov died of a heart attack at home. No one called the police, no one thought to check him for a tiny puncture wound to the heart, and no autopsy was done.

The woman would like to have kept the brothel open for at least a few months so she could accumulate enough money to live comfortably. She had some now, but Moscow was an expensive place to live.

There was no question that Slava Sergenko had taken the files and disappeared. It was also obvious what would happen next. The brothel's customers were going to get a surprise soon. The clever boy would extort money from them, she was certain. Once that happened, she was a dead woman. The first place her wealthy Russian clients would come was to her. They'd demand to know about the files, the pictures, and where they were. They'd torture her to find out what they wanted. She had to leave, and leave quickly.

She took all the cash she had in the place – around ten thousand dollars – and ran. She wasn't smart and didn't really have a strategy. She just wanted to get far, far away. Without proper papers she couldn't leave Russia, so she went as far as she could. She found a nice beachfront flat where she could enjoy the summers and tolerate the winters.

About a year later a couple was strolling the beach in front of a resort near Sochi, Russia, on the Black Sea. Arm in arm and lost in each other, they almost tripped over the nude body of a woman lying on the sand.

The tourists began to scream in horror.

The body was missing its head.

You can run, but they'll find you eventually.

CHAPTER THREE

That afternoon in Moscow, Slava Sergenko had made a fateful, life-changing decision. The authorities might have gone easy on the sixteen-year-old child for murdering the man who'd sexually abused him and sold his body to other pedophiles. He might even have been exonerated for that crime. But he'd gone further – past the proverbial point of no return. He'd sealed his fate and his future by stealing client information from Andrey Bodrov's brothel. The things he stole became both his blessing and his curse.

Those men whose information he now had were all active participants in the child prostitution ring. They also were some of the new Russia's highest-level executives in business, government and even religion. Since the fall of the Soviet Union in late 1991, certain people who previously were at the top of the KGB and the military had become immensely wealthy. The newly elected president of post-Soviet Russia rewarded the Communists who had worked with him. Those people transitioned easily from the USSR to Russia. They continued to be its powerful elite. Instead of holding intelligence or military jobs, they were handed oil companies, telecommunications firms and a thousand other new private businesses required for a country suddenly thrust into capitalism.

These fat cats – these mostly corrupt Russian political hacks – became wealthy beyond anyone's wildest dreams. And it happened literally overnight. As many suddenly wealthy individuals do, they became enamored with wealth, power, excess and impregnability. They were bulletproof. They could do whatever they wanted and no one could stop them.

Until now.

Over a hundred powerful men, customers of an establishment that provided underage children for sex, were being systematically blackmailed.

The plan had taken time to set up. Slava was tall and thin, wise beyond his sixteen years, and armed with an idea that had worked amazingly well. Between what he took from Andrey Bodrov's dead body – money and jewelry – and the ATM at the bank, the boy ended up with nearly forty thousand US dollars. He rented a cheap flat in the suburbs for a month and obtained a new identity. That had cost him a fourth of the cash he had, but it was worth it. Within a week his new passport and identity card showed he was no longer sixteen. He was Juan Carlos Sebastian, a twenty-four-year-old citizen of Spain.

He bought a laptop and began to research which countries had financial secrecy laws. He learned how to set up offshore bank accounts, initiate and receive wire transfers, and move funds from one place to another.

Two weeks later he left Russia, presenting his new credentials at the airport and boarding an Aeroflot plane for Prague. He carried a suitcase that held everything he owned, including over thirty thousand dollars.

In Prague Juan Carlos rented another small apartment like the one he'd had in Moscow. He opened a local bank account and deposited his dollars. He created three more – one in Cairo, one in the island country of St. Lucia, and a third in Paraguay. One country he'd considered but avoided was Cyprus. It was famous for bank secrecy, but almost every one of the Russians he planned to blackmail had accounts there, according to the information sheets he'd stolen. With that much money in that small a country, it was possible someone could pay off a banker. He had to be anonymous. His very life depended on it.

Juan Carlos set up a complicated system of interlocking email accounts, using every trick he'd read about. One morning it was time to make it all happen. He prepared a brief demand letter, entered a hundred email addresses and emailed them individually.

Dear Comrade ________:

My name was Slava Sergenko. I was one of the children at the brothel in Moscow you frequent. I am also the person who killed Andrey Bodrov. I tell you this so you will understand my motive.

I want two million US dollars. You have ten days to comply with my demand. You may not know that Comrade Bodrov took secret pictures of you with his children. I have those pictures and so will the press if you do not do as I demand.

Juan Carlos provided the Cairo bank account, which auto-forwarded the money to Paraguay and finally to St. Lucia. Although he only had photos of half the men, they didn't know that, so almost all of them paid up. He was exhilarated to see dollars – amazing numbers of dollars – begin to accumulate in his bank account within just a few days.

After ten days Juan Carlos Sebastian had $168 million. Eighty-four men had coughed up the funds he demanded. The other sixteen got a second offer – the Slava Installment Plan. Fourteen of those paid fifty thousand a month. Some paid for a year or so and quit, others were still paying. He decided not to pursue them, but he kept everyone's information, including the pictures, just in case.

That accounted for all but two. They committed suicide. One was a prominent cleric and the other was head of the government's education system. Juan Carlos had no tears for them – his only regret was that they got out of paying the blackmail.

CHAPTER FOUR

Prague, Czech Republic

After his windfall from the blackmail scheme, Juan Carlos found himself bored. He had to live under the radar, always watchful. There were a hundred wealthy men who would search the world for the blackmailer, cut his dick off, stuff it in his mouth, and laugh while he choked to death. He could never be ostentatious – he never spent much money although he had millions. He was reluctant to take a job, had allowed himself no friends, and had nothing to occupy his time. He had all the money a person could ever want and no way to spend it without risking exposure. He was bored.

Juan Carlos began to travel extensively throughout the world. He visited archaeological sites on six continents, and he began quietly acquiring rarities. He found a solution to his boredom and a way to spend his money without fanfare. Through research and intuition, he developed an eye for quality and learned to separate the fakes from the authentic pieces. Within a couple of years he had a very private, very valuable assortment of rarities from the world's past great civilizations.

Juan Carlos displayed only a few things in his Prague flat and, with no visitors ever, they were solely for his pleasure. The bulk of his collection was in a safety deposit box in Lucerne, one of several cities where he maintained an apartment.

He loved traveling, but he wanted something else. He wanted the semblance of a normal life. Although he could afford to never work, he wanted interaction with other people. He couldn't allow friends into his very private existence, so he thought of other ways he might get the social interaction he craved.

On a whim one afternoon he answered a help-wanted ad for a bartender in the Princi Palace, Prague's newest and trendiest hotel. His personality and looks got him the job, and soon he was the star of the show every evening as regulars looked forward to seeing him.

Ten Years after leaving Moscow
Summer 2004

Juan Carlos gazed through expansive windows at a park across the street from the Princi Palace Hotel, where he'd been behind the bar the past three years. It was eighty degrees outside. He would have loved to be with one of the beautiful, bikini-clad girls he could see sunbathing. Summers in Prague were his favorite time – the country had become totally Westernized since the fall of Communism, and the girls loved to bask in the sun. The strikingly handsome bartender with his fashionable close-cropped mustache and beard could have dated any girl he wanted. Despite their attraction to his rugged, aristocratic good looks, he kept to himself. He had secrets he couldn't share.

At thirty-four, the age he'd chosen for his passport, Juan Carlos was fortunate – he was free to do whatever he wished. His investment portfolio was vast, his current profession was extremely lucrative, and tending bar was an enjoyable, convenient and simple cover for it. For some time he had run the evening shift in the bar of Prague's finest hotel. He knew his regulars by name, profession and interests. They knew him too – at least the story Juan Carlos had created. And everyone liked spending time with the suave, affable bartender who kept a close eye on his guests and made sure drinks were always full and conversation always entertaining.

None of his acquaintances – customers, employers, anyone – had ever ventured into Juan Carlos Sebastian's personal space. No one knew what he was like outside of the bar, how he lived, what his interests were – anything. That was good, because Juan Carlos certainly wasn't a struggling bartender.

He glanced at his Casio watch. Juan Carlos never wore the Rolex to work – there would be questions if well-heeled customers saw the bartender sporting a watch more expensive than theirs. It was almost five o'clock and staffers from the embassies would begin filtering in sometime around six. The upscale bar adjoined the lobby of the Princi Palace, built ten years ago after the Velvet Revolution transformed Communist Czechoslovakia into the democratic Czech Republic.

There would be a drop sometime this evening; he had learned that a moment ago when he watched the sun goddesses in the park from the window. At the bus stop outside someone had drawn a large X on the schedule sign with a marking pen. That was this week's signal. He'd keep his eyes and ears open tonight.

Right now he set up whisky, wine and beer, wiping clean a streaked glass here and there and prepping lemons and limes. Before long the first customers arrived.

In flawless French Juan Carlos welcomed three girls in stylish pantsuits who took seats at the bar. He knew them well; like many of his patrons, they stopped by after work every day. Mid-level translators from the French Embassy, they were young, beautiful representatives of their native country and enjoyed the bartender's friendly banter in their own language.

Juan Carlos was a natural linguist, fluent in five languages and conversant in several others. He had learned both his native Russian and English in elementary school like every other student in the Soviet Union. Languages came easily to him. He had picked them up as he traveled from place to place over the past ten years.

He set up drinks for the young French beauties as two groups entered from the lobby. They too were regulars – one was Italian and the other from the United States Embassy across the street. The Italians took a table by the window and the three Americans sat at the bar. A cocktail waitress handled the room while Juan Carlos greeted the Americans.

"The usuals?"

The woman smiled, nodded then turned to her male companions. Soon they were deep in whispered conversation. Juan Carlos mixed her martini and brought Czech beers for the men.

Within a half hour the bar was full. Thirty-foot ceilings and plush Oriental rugs kept the noise at an acceptable level. A couple of businessmen, probably Russian, were chatting up the French girls. They bought a round, then another. Juan Carlos smiled – the girls would keep the conversation sufficiently stimulating to get some free drinks, but this situation would ultimately go nowhere for the hopeful men. It was the same way every night – the hotel's guests were easy to spot because they were the only non-regulars in the house. Most of them drank at the bar; a few, like these two, made valiant, usually unsuccessful attempts to snag a date – or more – for the evening.

It was 7:15 before the pace began to slow. The girls were gone, the Russian men were on their fourth Scotches at the bar and the American trio had finished their quiet discussion. After her martini, the woman switched to Pouilly-Fuisse. The men were on their second round of beer, drinking more slowly as their boss sipped her wine. Juan Carlos walked to their end of the bar.

"Staying busy?" he asked her in his flawless Oxford-accented English.

"Always." She was around thirty-five and impeccably dressed in a black skirt and jacket. "The life of an attaché never slows down."

"I can only imagine." Although these three carried the titles and credentials of attachés, it was no secret that in most embassies those persons were actually intelligence agents of one type or another. And Juan Carlos Sebastian knew exactly who these people worked for. He knew this lady very, very well. In fact, he worked for the same organization she did.

A year ago, on a rainy night when the bar was almost deserted, she'd lingered after her associates went home. She'd sat at the bar until closing time then taken the handsome bartender home to her apartment. The next day he had been torn between fear and passion. He regretted letting his guard down even for a moment, but he also hadn't been with a woman in a long, long time. And she wasn't just any woman. She was very good at what she did. Both in bed, it turned out, and at the embassy.

After a few months their relationship moved to a different level. One night she approached him with an idea, a plan to make some significant money. She couldn't have known that Juan Carlos, the handsome bartender, was a millionaire many times over. And the rich, bored bartender was interested in her idea not for the reason she thought – the money – but for the excitement he desperately wanted in his life.

It all began with a small job here and there. Maybe he'd pick up a parcel and deliver it somewhere else. Other times he met a flight at the airport and followed someone to a hotel. He never knew what lay behind the assignments, but they got more and more involved as time went by. Finally one day she offered him what he had seen coming.

They both understood that their situation – the occasional meetings for a night of steamy sex – wasn't a long-term thing. She asked Juan Carlos one night if, in exchange for giving up what had been a lot of fun in bed, he was willing to do a big job, to make over a hundred thousand dollars. And his comic response – "Who do I have to kill?" – received an answer which really didn't surprise him.

I'll let you know when the time comes.

He'd felt no remorse when he killed Andrey Bodrov nearly a decade ago. In his analytical mind he easily separated emotion from fact. Although she had no idea he'd killed before, she told him he was a natural – intelligent, smooth, calculating. The only question was if he wanted to move into something way beyond the norm.

As it turned out, that was exactly what Juan Carlos Sebastian wanted. He transitioned smoothly from being the woman's lover to having her as his handler, and he began doing the occasional wet-ops job for the unnamed agency of the US government she worked for.

Tonight at the bar the American lady signaled for a check as they stood. She paid their bill in Czech crowns, stuck a hundred more in a tip jar on the bar and handed a US twenty-dollar bill to Juan Carlos with a smile.

"This is for you, my old friend. Thanks for the great service. See you in a day or so."

He put the bill in his pocket and bid her goodbye.

By midnight only a couple of customers remained. When they tabbed out, Juan Carlos closed the massive doors to the lobby and cleaned up for a half hour. As always, he walked several blocks, took a Metro, doubled back, walked the streets again, carefully noting pedestrians and cars around him, and finally took another subway to his street. The exercise took half an hour twice a day; it was inconvenient, especially on nights when he was tired, but it was unavoidable. Living a double life was dangerous. He had to be careful. Always.

His four-room apartment was rented in the name of a German company. It was in a nice part of town but not the best – comfort was great but opulence could attract attention. There was no doorman, no concierge to notice his comings and goings. He buzzed himself into the building and took the lift to his fifth-floor flat. A tiny piece of tape was affixed to the bottom of the door, exactly as he had placed it when he left around noon. No one had entered.

He performed his usual walk-through in the dark, listening and looking for signs of anything out of place.

Everything was exactly as it should be – the beautiful golden artifacts in his living room cabinets glistened as moonlight beamed through the expansive windows overlooking a park across the street.

The man called Juan Carlos undressed, showered, poured a drink and set up an ultraviolet light on his kitchen table. He took the twenty-dollar tip the American woman had given him and put it under the lamp. All around the edges on both sides was writing, invisible without the purple bulb. He read the words several times then used scissors to cut the bill into tiny pieces. Those he flushed down the toilet. He sent a text to his boss at the hotel, advising he needed two days off – that wasn't a problem. Juan Carlos was the favorite at the Princi Palace bar. The clientele loved him, and his manager willingly granted a day off now and then.

He went to bed, bringing a plan together in his head. He had a plane to catch tomorrow.

CHAPTER FIVE

Dubrovnik, Croatia

When the afternoon session of the Summit of Former Soviet States ended around four, Sergei Godunov left the large meeting room quickly. It had been a long day and he was ready for a drink. He walked purposefully to the sprawling veranda that wrapped around the Metropol Hotel and took a seat. The beautiful vista of the azure Adriatic Sea stretched before him. It was early enough that he was the only customer. He signaled a waiter and ordered a double Stolichnaya over ice. When it came, he asked for another. As the waiter turned away, he downed his first drink in two massive gulps.

Sergei unbuttoned his collar and loosened his tie. It was warm and he was sweating profusely. There'd been no time today to break away and nurse his addiction. By the time he left his boss and the rest of the Ukraine delegation, his hands were beginning to shake. He'd made it just in time; he wiped his brow as the second drink came. He asked for a third.

"Actually, just bring me two more." Why waste time having the man run back and forth?

It would be easier if they did it like in Russia. There they just bring the vodka bottle and a glass to your table.

But in Croatia things were different. It was nice here, like Yalta on the Black Sea back home. Here the Adriatic was serene and peaceful. Relaxing a little, Sergei reflected that he was a lucky man. Only recently had he begun to enjoy the good life. He made nothing working for the government, but he'd gotten a break. Some Americans from the embassy in Kiev talked to him one night, and within months he had more money than he'd ever dreamed of. Over a thousand US dollars stashed away already, and more to come, just from his American friends. Now Sergei Godunov had gone one step further and become a double agent. It sounded so clandestine – he was a spy! From a simple desk job handling secret transmissions, he'd become an operative not only for the American CIA but also the Russian FSB, the successor to the KGB. He loved every minute of his new, exciting life.

Finishing his fourth double vodka, Sergei paid the tab and walked to the elevators. He was a little unsteady, but he was accustomed to copious quantities of alcohol. It would take more than a few drinks to stop this secret double agent.

He fumbled with the key to his room, opened the door and stepped inside. The curtains were shut, and when the door closed, his eyes took a moment to adjust. He saw a man sitting in the chair across the bedroom and jumped, startled.

"What the hell …" Sergei yelled in his native language.

The response was also in perfect Ukrainian, not a hint of accent. The man was an accomplished linguist, after all.

"Party's over, Sergei. You've been a bad boy. Good night."

Juan Carlos Sebastian shot the man once in the forehead with a silenced Sig Sauer pistol. The bullet exited the back of his head and lodged somewhere near the ceiling. That slug didn't matter; he dropped the gun on the floor and walked out. He stripped off the latex gloves he wore, stuck them in his pocket, took the elevator to the lobby and left the hotel. No one gave him a glance.

CHAPTER SIX

Three Years Later
Prague, 2007

Juan Carlos Sebastian's last day in Prague began uneventfully. It was a Sunday and he strolled the narrow, crooked streets of Old Town, finally ending up in the massive square, its beautiful cathedral looming high above him. At noon its bells began to toll and a series of small doors opened in the spires above the square. Mechanical boy and girl figures emerged and circled around a track, finally returning through another pair of doors. It was a stirring sight and thousands of tourists in the square watched it happen every hour.

The day was gorgeous, and Juan Carlos sipped champagne as he reflected once again on his good fortune. After leaving Russia with a new identity, the sixteen-year-old suddenly became twenty-four thanks to a perfect Spanish passport. His fluency in that language had been helpful; he sounded like a native. So Juan Carlos Sebastian came to Prague, systematically blackmailed one Russian executive, cleric or government official after another, and ended up with nearly two hundred million dollars in bank accounts, real estate investments and stock holdings around the world.

And thanks to smart investing, his money was compounding every day.

There were many, many men who had each remitted two million US dollars. Some of his "installment plan" clients still paid today. Despite Juan Carlos's promises to destroy the evidence against them, he kept the files secure in a safe deposit box. They were his insurance against ever being poor again.

I'm probably the wealthiest bartender in the world. He laughed to himself. He had needed an airtight identity, and with his wealth, he'd created one. Juan Carlos could have lived the life of luxury, but he was young, so he carefully donned the façade of a working man. He didn't need inquiring minds wondering how a youth could afford to live without a job. To the world, Juan Carlos was a bartender.

Actually his work was great. He loved the interaction with customers. The job was fun, it was a great cover for his clandestine activities with the CIA, and he could get plenty of time off whenever work or play necessitated it.

Every time he was out around town, Juan Carlos was on alert. When he strolled or sat at a café, he took in the scenery, noticing anything that might be out of the ordinary – anyone who might be looking for him. There would always be those hundred Russian men who would pay a fortune for his execution, but his identity was secure, the payments to his bank accounts flushed through a set of pipelines, and no danger lurked around him. At least up to this point that had been the case.

Only recently, after years in this identity, did Juan Carlos finally begin to feel like a free man. As usual he kept an eye out for activity around him as he blended with the tourists in Prague's Old Town Square, but he also read the paper, sipped his drink and simply enjoyed the day. If any of his patrons from the bar at the Princi Palace Hotel happened by, they'd see their favorite bartender taking advantage of a gorgeous Sunday afternoon off.

In reality Juan Carlos had let his guard down a little over the past three years. If he'd been as watchful today as he had then, he might have noticed the tourist couple a block away, snapping pictures of the cathedral, the square and Juan Carlos.

Sunday evenings were generally quiet in the hotel's bar and tonight had been no exception. Juan Carlos locked things up at 11:30; although it was early, only a half dozen people had been in all evening. From a briefing report the hotel's front desk sent every afternoon, he knew occupancy was only 20% for tonight, so the chance of a late patron wanting a drink was slim.

He took the usual circuitous route home. Despite his failure to notice anything in the square earlier today, now he was aware of a couple strolling arm-in-arm behind him as he headed to the Metro station. He made a couple of turns, including one that took him around a corner into a cul-de-sac. Half a block before the street dead-ended, Juan Carlos stepped into the shadows of a doorway and waited. Within thirty seconds he saw the couple, still casually talking and smiling, coming down the narrow street. Just tourists, it seemed, but they were absolutely following him. There was no reason for them to be here otherwise. This quiet residential street went nowhere.

They walked past his hiding place then saw the dead-end ahead. The man whispered something. As they turned, Juan Carlos stepped out into the cobblestoned street, blocking their way back.

"*Dobri vecher*," he said in Russian. *Good evening.*

The startled woman reached for her pocket as Juan Carlos aimed his pistol at them. He continued in Russian. "Keep your hands where I can see them."

The man began to move away from his partner, making it impossible for Juan Carlos to keep his gun aimed at them both. In one swift move the man pulled a knife and threw it. Juan Carlos moved just in time, but the knife sliced the sleeve of his jacket. During the confusion, the woman took a small revolver from her pocket.

As she brought it up, Juan Carlos pulled the trigger, his aim a little off but still hitting the shoulder of the hand that held the gun. With a scream she dropped it. In Russian she cursed, "Damn you, Slava Sergenko! You'll die soon enough, you bastard!"

Keeping the gun on the man, Juan Carlos answered her. "Sorry I hit your shoulder. I meant to kill you, but I fired too quickly and my aim was off. Speaking of dying soon enough, obviously you know who I am. Sadly then, my next shot will be in your heart."

A light came on in the house next to where they stood. Someone had heard the noise of the gun and their voices.

Police would be coming soon. There was no time to find out who these people were. Juan Carlos fired two more shots in rapid succession. Each found its mark. The couple lay dead in the narrow street.

It would have been helpful to know who had sent the couple, but things hadn't worked out that way. All he knew was that they had orders to kill him and sadly his time in Prague was finished. Somehow his cover was blown. Juan Carlos, nee Slava Sergenko, had to leave this city and this life he'd come to enjoy. Tonight.

CHAPTER SEVEN

Dresden, Germany/Lucerne, Switzerland

At two a.m. Juan Carlos Sebastian transformed into a new person in the backseat of a taxi he'd hired in Prague. The Spaniard's passport, Czech identity card, driver's license and credit cards went into a manila envelope, then a packet for overnight delivery. He found a FedEx drop box at a large brightly lit truck stop on the German border. Tomorrow the items would arrive at Roberto Maas's house in Lucerne. They'd go into the wall safe until Juan Carlos's services were required again.

The taxi driver had picked up Juan Carlos Sebastian three blocks from his apartment in Prague, and two hours later he dropped Roberto Maas at the Dresden train station. Same person, different identity. Roberto had a passport, credit cards, money, everything he needed. He was a twenty-nine-year-old Luxembourg citizen residing in Switzerland. As he killed three hours waiting for the train to Lucerne, he double-checked all of Roberto's information – he had to know it perfectly because it was his from now on.

Juan Carlos had needed to get out of Prague fast. He had no idea what resources the people stalking him had at their disposal, but it was possible they were already watching the airport and train station. He had to get into Germany.

Dresden was the opposite direction from Lucerne, but it was the closest major city outside the Czech Republic that had rail service throughout Europe.

The taxi's late-night border crossing had been a nonevent. It was his first use of Roberto Maas's passport and it had worked perfectly. A sleepy border guard with a cigarette hanging from his lips gave him hardly a glance. He waved the taxi through and went back to a flickering television in a guardhouse.

After killing the two Russians, Juan Carlos had taken a cab to his apartment. He pulled his emergency suitcase from under the bed; it contained clothes and toiletries for two days. He emptied his wall safe, taking papers for his new identity and fifty thousand euros. Into a backpack went his laptop, iPad and two paper notebooks full of encrypted information. He left everything else – clothes, furniture, books, food – even his collection of artifacts.

After years of safety the encounter tonight rattled Juan Carlos. How did the couple find him? Who sent them? It was likely he'd never know the answer to either question. In all the years since he left Moscow, no one had caught up with him. Not until now. He chastised himself for becoming complacent. That couldn't happen again. He'd have to remain on guard forever.

Tonight he'd had no idea how much time he had or how many others were waiting for him. He spent only twenty minutes at his flat in Prague. Giving the apartment a quick once-over, he walked out and shut the door to this stage of his life. Juan Carlos would resurface again someday when his services as a hired killer were required. But now he was Roberto. Roberto Maas.

The taxi dropped him at the train station in Dresden at eight in the morning. During the nine-hour trip from Dresden to Lucerne, Roberto filled the time making notes. There was a lot to do now.

His flat in Lucerne was fully furnished. A biweekly maid service ensured it was always clean and ready should he suddenly arrive. He sent a text to the service, saying he was coming. That text would initiate a quick cleaning and a fully stocked refrigerator and pantry. The service knew exactly what to buy for his arrival – his list was always on file.

Next he sent an email from the account of the company that owned the Lucerne condo. It advised the security director of his apartment building that a man named Roberto Maas would be arriving later that day. As the train clacked down the tracks, he handled a dozen other tasks and projects that had suddenly become necessary thanks to his dead-of-night departure from Prague. He methodically listed each and dealt with it.

The only things he'd wanted but couldn't bring tonight were the artifacts in his living room cabinets. He enjoyed his collection of ancient things, but especially loved these particular golden objects. They were his prizes – they were unique, one of a kind. He'd arrange for a lawyer in Prague to pick them up in the next week or so. They'd be shipped to a law firm in Geneva and stored at the bank where his other antiques were kept. Once things settled down, Roberto would put them in his apartment once again.

By the time the train stopped at the Swiss border, he was checking his investment accounts at brokers in London and Geneva. When Roberto Maas presented his Swiss passport to the officer, he received a friendly "welcome home" in response. Piece of cake.

As with his other three homes, Roberto's flat in Lucerne was complete – clothes hanging in the closet, everything ready for a visit on a moment's notice. The few who needed a story were told a vague tale of a young man who was fabulously wealthy thanks to an inheritance from deceased parents. He was no different than a thousand other outrageously rich people who maintained homes worldwide, staff standing ready should the master arrive on a whim. Roberto was just a lot younger than most.

A different shell corporation owned each of his homes. The name Roberto Maas showed up nowhere. The only friends he ever cultivated were ones where he worked.

No one knew where he lived or anything about his personal life. And that was good, since up to now the various identities he assumed really didn't have personal lives at all. They were fictitious.

Roberto enjoyed being in Switzerland in autumn. As the taxi maneuvered the broad avenue around the water to the high-rise where his flat was located, Lake Lucerne shimmered in the late afternoon sun. It was gorgeous and the day couldn't have been nicer.

Thanks to his earlier mail, the doorman was expecting him. Roberto merely flashed his passport to prove his identity and took the elevator upstairs. The maids had left the drapes open wide in anticipation of his arrival. He opened his patio doors and stepped outside. Lake Lucerne lay below, fringed by a panoply of trees and bushes in striking fall colors. Sunlight reflected off the majestic snowcapped peaks of Mount Pilatus and the Swiss Alps far in the distance. Not much impressed Roberto Maas, but this was one sight that always did. Of all his homes, this was his favorite, and he was glad to be back.

Roberto walked to the kitchen and opened the freezer. Pleased to find his martini glass and vodka bottle there, he retrieved both and poured the chilled liquid into his frozen glass. He peeled a lemon and created a twist.

The vodka was Stolichnaya Elit. He drank it as a tribute to his Russian heritage. But it wasn't the regular Stoli Elit in its easily recognizable slim, tall bottle. It was the Himalayan Edition, costing three thousand dollars per bottle. Made from pure mountain water taken from underground springs, it was the most expensive vodka on the planet. The freezers of each of Roberto's homes always had a bottle ready for his arrival. And there were a couple more in the pantry in case he got really thirsty.

He carried his martini to the patio table, came back inside and walked to a cigar humidor the size of a dormitory refrigerator. Its motor hummed quietly as it maintained a steady seventy degrees humidity. Roberto opened the door and retrieved a 2001 Cohiba Edicion Limitada cigar, a cutter and wooden matches. Seated at the table, he clipped the cigar, lit it and exhaled a satisfied puff. Each of these wonderful Cubans cost over fifty US dollars. No matter. Roberto Maas had the money, and he had the best. He sat back and took his first sip of the martini. It made him cough – it always happened that way, and he laughed at himself every time it did.

Life is good. Look at me – a twenty-nine-year-old centimillionaire, enjoying a cigar and a martini on the twentieth floor of a condo I own, overlooking Lake Lucerne and the Alps. A new identity thanks to my preparations for just such an event, and a potential threat eliminated.

He would like to have known who the Russians were and how they'd found him. But that wasn't going to happen; he wouldn't risk his new identity in a search for the people trying to kill off his last one. His security precautions and contingency plans, painstakingly prepared years before and constantly updated, were excellent. It was highly unlikely whichever organization had figured out who Juan Carlos Sebastian was could ever link that man to the newly incarnated Roberto Maas. No need to spend time worrying about something that wasn't likely to be a problem. And if someone did figure it all out, which could certainly happen, he would deal with it just as he had in Prague.

CHAPTER EIGHT

Two Years Later
Lucerne, 2009

Roberto Maas ended the call to London then spoke to his colleague across the room. "The closing's set for Friday on the Bridgewater building. Do you want to fly over or should I?"

Philippe Lepescu glanced at the calendar on his phone. "If I go, I'll need to come back that evening. I've got the football match in Geneva on Saturday. If your schedule allows it, I'll pass this time."

"Perfect. I'll stay the weekend."

"Really? I can't believe it!" Lepescu laughed and returned to his work. It was no secret that London was one of Roberto's favorite places. And there was that British Airways flight attendant he'd met a few weeks back. Philippe would have been amazed if Roberto hadn't wanted to go.

From the beginning of their business partnership the men had chosen to office together in one large upstairs room of the mansion Roberto had purchased for his headquarters. The three-story medieval building was located on the old city square facing the lake. Through floor-to-ceiling windows they could see the mountains standing majestically in the distance. The building's ground-floor exterior was adorned with beautiful murals that caught the eye of tourists. As they snapped photos, almost no one noticed the small brass sign that said "Ciprian Investments." A buzzer was nearby but little used. Despite his vast wealth and holdings, Roberto's company had few visitors.

The business name had been chosen by Philippe to honor his deceased father Ciprian Lepescu, a proud Romanian gypsy who had been murdered by police when Philippe was five years old. At the time of his death the elder Lepescu was engaged in his trade – stealing – and made the mistake of setting off a silent alarm in a building he was burglarizing. When he crawled out through a hole he'd cut in the roof, five policemen shot first and asked questions later. For them, another rotten gypsy was out of their hair. For Philippe, his beloved daddy was gone and he would never forget it. The gypsy in him would avenge his father's death somehow, somewhere down the line.

For years Philippe carefully hid his hatred for the authorities as he went through university, graduated and took a position at a major Swiss bank in Zurich. The genes he'd inherited from his gypsy parents accounted for his handsome, dark features and a quick mind. At the bank he'd progressed up the corporate ladder rapidly. By the time he was twenty-five he was second man in the side of the institution that managed the bank's own portfolio of investments.

Three years ago Philippe had been sent to New York for a conference. In a rare stroke of fortune, his first-class seat was next to that of Roberto Maas and they were both staying at the Plaza Athenee in Manhattan. On the plane the men chatted over cocktails and dinner and exchanged business cards. As they spent the week in New York, they met for drinks one night, dinner another, and ended up enjoying each other's company.

Over time Philippe shared secrets with his new friend, considering himself lucky to have someone to talk with about the hatred that lay just beneath his polished veneer. He had been pleased to learn that Roberto, a very wealthy man only two years his senior, had the same disdain for authority. Roberto told how he'd been on his own for several years, having lost both parents in an automobile accident near their home in Luxembourg. After finishing university, so Roberto's story went, he spent his time traveling the world, enjoying the good life and living off investment income.

Except for the part about his wealth, the story Roberto told Philippe was fiction. What was true was that Roberto was opening an office to be the headquarters for the management of his far-flung investments. He offered a second-in-command position to his new friend Philippe. Six months after these two young men met, they were working together. Today, two years later, they were close friends and colleagues with no secrets between them. At least Philippe thought so. Actually Roberto still had plenty of secrets. Philippe just didn't know about them.

CHAPTER NINE

Roberto settled in easily to his new life in Switzerland. Unlike his previous incarnation as a bartender in Prague, he chose to put down roots this time. No longer would he be living in a cheap flat, ready to flee in a heartbeat should things turn against him.

The decision to be more visible – living in one of his owned houses and maintaining an office – came at a price. It meant Roberto had to be much more careful about his past. The night he left Prague, he'd abruptly cut off communications with the United States government people he'd known. That night had been a turning point; somehow he'd been careless enough that he might have been killed. He couldn't be sloppy anymore. Now no one, not even his CIA employers, would know who or where Juan Carlos Sebastian was. His appearance had changed – different hair color and style, a neat mustache and beard, a more formal wardrobe – and his thought process had changed too. There would be no more mistakes.

It was a foregone conclusion Juan Carlos would eventually work again. Roberto thrived on the danger, intrigue and mystery associated with his other life. When he felt sufficient time had passed, he used a foolproof chain of encryptions to send a one-line email to his contact, his former lover at the US Embassy in the Czech Republic. It said, "Juan Carlos lives."

Within two hours a response worked its way back through the same web of addresses. "Wondered what happened to you. Miss you at the bar. Other places too! Looking for work?"

"Always."

As simple as that, the relationship restarted, although it was different this time. His American handler would never hear the name Roberto Maas or know he lived in Switzerland. She knew how to hire Juan Carlos Sebastian, but there would be no more face-to-face meetings as there had been in Prague. He was anonymous now. And his price had gone up. Even the assassination business had been affected by inflation.

Not long afterwards she had contacted him using prearranged signals. He received a one-word text. "Four." That one word told him where to go and how to get his instructions. He responded "*Oui.*" Yes, he would accept the assignment.

Roberto sent Philippe a brief text saying he'd be out of the office the next day to handle some personal business. At six a.m. he boarded the train from Lucerne to Dijon, France, where he rented a car using the papers and identity of one Marcus Hildebrand. He drove the rental car aimlessly around the countryside for an hour. Certain no one was following him, he returned to the train station and dropped off the rental vehicle. He was in Paris ninety minutes later. He spent the afternoon reconnoitering the job he had accepted, and by midnight he was back in Lucerne via Lyon, France, finalizing a plan for the weekend.

Early Saturday he flew to Brussels as Roberto Maas then switched identities. Marcus Hildebrand took an express train to Paris. He ate an early lunch, strolled the neighborhood where his target lived, and confirmed that he had a dinner reservation at the Ritz. From his very predictable habits, Roberto knew dinner would be followed by several hours of drinking at one of the expensive strip clubs near the Arc de Triomphe. Everything seemed fine.

At ten p.m. he picked a lock on an empty apartment he'd found during his visit to Paris a few days ago. From its front windows he could clearly see into a dimly lit flat just across the tree-lined street and one floor down. It was a perfect place for his assignment. Roberto Maas, in Paris as Marcus Hildebrand, transformed back to the assassin Juan Carlos Sebastian for the evening.

He settled in to wait. An expensive rifle lay on the floor next to him, ready for use on a moment's notice. Conditioned by years of practice, he sat quietly. Sometime after midnight a taxi dropped off a heavily intoxicated man in his sixties who unsteadily entered the building across the street. Soon lights came on in his second-story apartment and seconds later the man lay dead on the floor of his flat.

Juan Carlos put the rifle back on the floor, lowered the window he'd cracked and left the empty flat. The latex gloves he'd worn all evening were discarded at the train station. From the train he sent an email. "Done."

On Monday the body of a high-ranking member of the Palestine Liberation Organization was discovered in his Paris flat. The rifle that killed him turned up in the empty apartment across the street. By then Roberto Maas was already working at his desk in Lucerne. He checked a bank account in Montserrat around lunchtime. His half-million-dollar fee had arrived.

There would be no further clues and no solution to the Paris murder. Another job completed successfully.

CHAPTER TEN

The two men proved to be perfect partners. The administrative skills Philippe Lepescu possessed blended perfectly with Roberto's intuitive business sense. Roberto's degree from university had been in languages, but his real talent lay in making deals. He was a natural at sensing when to buy, when to hold and when to sell. He would have made a great fund manager, but with his vast wealth Roberto didn't have to work for others. He used his overt skills – his business acumen – solely for his personal benefit.

His covert skills – his marksmanship, cleverness in dispatching a person needing to be eliminated and the like – were specialties for which he found himself in frequent demand. There was more of that business than he could accept. Ciprian Investments took more and more of his time, but a part of him, the "Juan Carlos" part, loved the wet-ops work and the thrill that accompanied it. More often than not his employers got a "non" response to their coded requests for Juan Carlos's services. At other times he disappeared from the office for a day or a week, handling his "personal business." Philippe never questioned him. *None of my business*, Roberto's partner thought.

As Roberto Maas's fortune grew, Philippe's followed suit. He had started with nothing, but after only a couple of years in partnership with Maas, Philippe had a personal net worth of more than three million dollars. Roberto gave him a small interest in most of the deals the company did. Philippe ran the numbers, did the due diligence, and offered suggestions and ideas. He hired the lawyers and accountants who inevitably were required to close complicated transactions in one of a dozen countries. Roberto always made the final call. But he trusted Philippe Lepescu more every day.

Trust was both a blessing and a curse for Roberto. Humans were social animals. Even the lowest of them had a basic need for socialization, friendship, companionship. Many people found it in marriage, others in lifelong relationships with one or two close friends. Philippe was closer to his partner than anyone else. They shared confidences and he would do anything for Roberto. And he was sure Roberto enjoyed his friendship too, but not in the same way. Roberto *himself* was different – often distant and icy. He could be cold as a serpent, especially with people with whom he dealt in business. Roberto always smiled and joked with Philippe, but he sometimes felt it was forced – it didn't come naturally. His partner was a man who played his cards close to the vest, a man who kept his feelings locked away inside. Or maybe he didn't have any. Cold as ice, they called people like Roberto Maas.

Years ago when his father sold fifteen-year-old Slava Sergenko to the brothel in Moscow, the boy did in fact switch off his emotions. He suppressed the thoughts, feelings and desires that would allow him to be close to another person. Never again would he feel the shock, abandonment and despair that had engulfed him when his own father handed him over to a sex ring for money. No one would ever get close again. No one would ever hurt Roberto Maas that way again. But although the professional killer Juan Carlos Sebastian could perform his art without compunction, somewhere deep inside the feelings remained.

Roberto actually *did* care for Philippe. In no way was this a sexual thing. Roberto Maas had been down that road. He didn't give a damn what other people did in private.

Homosexual or heterosexual – he accepted the old adage "to each his own." At this point in his life, sex was with a woman. Bought and paid for. No love, just lust. No feelings except the feelings that came with a satisfying climax. No commitment, no long-term connection, no nothing. Cold as ice. Always.

As his friendship with Philippe developed, Roberto grew more and more concerned about the strange concept of letting someone else get close. Something inside him wanted, *needed* a friend. Desperately. He enjoyed spending time with Philippe. He appreciated the man's intelligence and his contribution to the company, but even more he was becoming genuinely interested in Philippe as a person … as a *friend.*

But that can't happen, can it, Roberto?

For all those years he had quashed emotion. He never got close to another person. All he remembered about caring was that it hurt. It wrenched your guts and made you scream in pain. But humans were *human.* They laughed, cried, confided, shared jokes and secrets — they developed genuine relationships. Philippe was the first person in Roberto's adult life that could have become his friend. But Roberto wouldn't allow it. He wouldn't accept the pain that came with attachment.

And he didn't want a friend to die because that friend had learned Roberto Maas's secrets.

CHAPTER ELEVEN

London

When you strolled the narrow lanes of the area known as the City of London, literally everything you saw – buildings, houses, sidewalks, streets – hid secrets that lay below. Today the City, a tiny, square-mile part of the sprawling metropolis of London, was the financial hub of England. But its roots were ancient. In the 1500s when Henry VIII's wives were imprisoned in the Tower of London, the City was already very old. When William the Conqueror was crowned King on Christmas day 1066 at Westminster, the City had been occupied for more than a thousand years. When Jesus Christ was born, Romans already lived here.

Today much of the old City had been demolished to make way for modern skyscrapers housing banks and insurance companies, but a simple one-block turn off one main thoroughfare or another would land you squarely back in medieval times. Fifteenth-century buildings lined the mazes of narrow lanes so cramped a modern car couldn't possibly navigate them. Names like Milk Street, Fishmonger Lane and Bakers Hall were the same as they were in the Middle Ages when merchants of all types sold their wares in the twisted avenues.

Most of the secrets that lay hidden below the modern City of London were ancient indeed. Every time a construction crew began demolition of a block of old structures, a team of archaeologists stood ready to respond to the inevitable. One never knew what he would find down there. But it was guaranteed to always be something old and something interesting.

CHAPTER TWELVE

Three Years Earlier
St. Mary Axe Street, London, 2006

The morning Thomas Russell discovered the crypt began uneventfully in his basement. Belinda had told him a hundred times not to go down there when she wasn't around. "You're not as young as you once were, Thomas. If something happened to you, I don't know what I'd do."

He knew her chiding was a labor of love – he didn't consider Belinda a nagging wife. They cared deeply for each other. They'd been married over fifty years, and life wouldn't be the same for old Thomas if she weren't right there every day.

Now, having ignored her stern admonitions, he lay in a heap of rotted flooring, dust everywhere. And she was gone to the hairdresser's for two hours. *Damn the luck. She won't be happy.*

He tested first one arm, then the other. They seemed okay although they were sore as hell. One leg was twisted underneath him; that would be the problem. He tried to straighten it, but a jolt of pain stopped that plan immediately. He couldn't lift himself.

Thomas Russell shifted a bit to be more comfortable and settled in to wait for Belinda's return. He was seventy-five years old and had gone to the basement to find a crate that would hold a few books he was shipping to a customer in Yorkshire. Business slowed a little this time of day, and he doubted anyone who came into the store two stories above would hear his cries for help anyway.

The building that housed The Necromancer's Bookshop had been built in 1620. The two-block-long street named St. Mary Axe had mostly escaped the Great Fire of London in 1666; fortuitously, the thatched-roof wooden row houses that crowded the rest of the City were absent in this primarily commercial area. The ancient building occupied today by Thomas and Belinda's bookshop was built partially of stone – that had helped too when the fire roared through central London. It had withstood the passage of time well.

In Gilbert and Sullivan's operetta *The Sorcerer*, the street of St. Mary Axe was where the sorcerer's shop was located. And today, on the very spot where the ancient Church of St. Mary Axe had stood more than fifteen centuries before, there was Thomas and Belinda Russell's occult bookstore.

The world was a different place in 1950 when they married. With very little money but a great love of books, they decided to open a bookstore. The building in St. Mary Axe Street was in disrepair from years of neglect, and the landlord was pleased to sign a long-term lease. For two years, provided the Russells made improvements and occupied the building, the rent was forgiven. For a time the owner received the benefit of the improvements the couple had made, but before the two years was up, he went bankrupt.

A representative from Lloyds Bank showed up at the shop one morning and offered the couple a proposal – in order to get the foreclosed property off its books, the bank entered into a rent-to-own arrangement with them. Thirty years later, through times of alternating struggle and prosperity, the couple finally paid off the building they'd carefully maintained. Today it was a valuable property in a bustling area of the City. St. Mary Axe itself was still coming into its own; there were empty structures here and there, but things were definitely looking up. Today one of its primary draws was tourism. The appearance of the two-block street had changed very little since the Middle Ages. People found it quaint and interesting. Guides led groups of tourists along its narrow sidewalks every day.

Competition from major chain retailers made it harder and harder for independent booksellers to survive, so Thomas and Belinda opted to specialize. Situated in a street straight out of a Harry Potter film, the store became a haven for those seeking to learn about the dark arts – witchcraft, communication with the dead, potions, spells and the like. The Russells weren't that interested themselves – this niche was purely a business decision – but it made them a good living. The store sold not only books but an extensive array of supplies used by those who were followers of black magic. It was unique in London and therefore had a steady, albeit unusual, base of customers.

As Thomas Russell lay sprawled on the floor of the dank room, he wondered where he was. It was common knowledge that every building in central London had secrets below it. Sometimes it was the foundation of a building centuries older – maybe one from medieval times or even the Dark Ages. Other times it was the wall or casement from the days of Roman occupation. Often a construction project was put on hold for weeks or months while the people charged with archaeological preservation conducted excavations on whatever had been found.

In the fifty years they'd occupied this building, the Russells had never known there was a room below their basement. As far as they knew, the entire floor of the basement was made of stones with the earth underneath. No one ever thought there could be a chamber down here.

The building was erected in 1620; logically the basement was too. But this place he now lay, this dark room two stories below the bookstore, looked far older than that.

In the basement they had found old fruit jars, ancient tools and a few seventeenth-century coins from time to time but nothing that interesting. This place wasn't like that at all. This place looked exactly like a crypt.

Today Thomas had been down in the basement, puttering around in a dark corner, looking for something to put books in, when unfortunately he learned that a small area of the floor was made of wood, not stone. He made that discovery when he took a step to one side and fell through rotten planks. Fortunately the wood crashed to the floor in a pile, helping ease his six-foot fall into the chamber. If he'd hit the stone floor outright, he'd have been in far worse shape.

Right now the heavy stones that made up the floor of the basement were six feet above him. They weren't just a basement floor – they also formed the ceiling of this place. That room's single overhead bulb provided a tiny shaft of light, the only illumination in the subterranean chamber where he lay. Once his eyes adjusted, he could see that the room was around fifteen feet square. There were heavy wooden poles spaced throughout. They supported large wooden beams that held up this room's stone ceiling. He ran his hand along the floor where he lay – like the basement above it, this too was made of stone. So were the walls. There were several dark-colored boxes sitting on the floor across the room. Maybe they were made of wood. Thomas wondered if wood would rot after centuries in this dampness. There was also a heavy door with a large keyhole in the opposite wall. That door absolutely was wood; it had strips of metal like one would see in a dungeon, and it was closed. He wondered where it led.

Seeing a sudden movement to his left, he jumped and cried out in pain as he jerked the leg that lay useless under his body. The eyes of a huge rat glinted in the dim light. Curious about this intruder, he came to check Thomas out. Within seconds he saw another set of eyes, then more. The rats were everywhere and some were as large as a small dog.

He'd have to stay alert – no need to have one of those nasty creatures gnawing on a finger or an ear.

A piece of the rotten flooring lay next to him and he closed his hand around it, sat up slightly and banged it on the floor. The sound made the rats scurry off; he watched them slide under the wooden door.

Thomas couldn't remember if he'd closed the door leading from the shop to the basement. If it were open, Belinda would come looking faster, although his absence in the shop would alert her that something was wrong regardless. He glanced at his watch frequently and listened every time he thought he heard a sound from above.

"Help! Help me!" he yelled loudly now and then. "I'm down here!" Each attempt shot arrows of pain through his injured leg, but no one heard.

Finally he thought he heard a noise; then someone started down the wooden stairs that led from the shop into the basement above him.

"Help! Help!"

"Grandfather? Are you all right?"

Thomas's relief was palpable. "Edward! Thank God! I've fallen through the floor. Be careful, son. It all looks like stone, but I just found out it isn't! It's rotten in places."

Edward Russell, the only living direct descendant of Thomas and Belinda, peered down through the hole where Thomas had fallen. "Where are you? I can't see anything in the dark."

"There's a torch in the drawer under the cash register. Grab it and let's see how I can get out of here. I think I've broken my leg, so this could take a while."

Within a minute Edward was back, shining the flashlight into the subbasement. Without a ladder and ropes, there was no way he could descend, rescue his grandfather and get back up.

"I'm going to call 999. We'll need help to get you out." He carefully tossed the flashlight down to Thomas so he could have illumination in the dark room. The younger man went up into the shop, dialed the emergency number, and shortly the shrill sound of sirens permeated the narrow street of St. Mary Axe.

Firemen and an EMT were hard at work in the chamber when Belinda returned from her appointment at the hairdresser's. She had been terrified when she turned into St. Mary Axe Street and saw the Fire Brigade and an ambulance outside the bookshop, but her grandson quickly gave her an assessment of the situation. Thomas's leg was severely sprained, but he was otherwise fine. The EMT gave him a sedative, splinted his leg and secured him on a stretcher. They raised him up to the basement level, then up again into the bookshop and finally carted him to the waiting ambulance.

While he had waited for help to arrive, Thomas shined the torch all around the room. Half hidden in shadows there was a large stone box covered in grit and dust. He thought he could make out a symbol on the side and a raised area on its top. It was about six feet long – he couldn't see how wide it was – and two feet tall. As he squinted his eyes to see better, he thought he made out a cross on the side. And those raised things on the top – were they – could this be – an ornately carved coffin bearing the likeness of the occupant on its ancient lid? Was he in a crypt?

CHAPTER THIRTEEN

It was fortunate Edward Russell had stopped by to see his grandparents that morning. A perpetual university student, the lanky man was in his mid-thirties but looked older. With his long, prematurely gray beard, he fit perfectly in the black magic bookstore. If he'd worn a robe and held a wand in his hand (several types of each were for sale at The Necromancer's Bookshop), Central Casting could have used him as a magician. His visit had a dual purpose – he wanted to see if the store had an ancient book he needed in his thesis research, and he wanted to visit the only relatives he had.

A tragic event when Edward was sixteen left him both effectively orphaned and well off financially. In a rage his psychotic father had savagely murdered Edward's mother, Ellen, the only child of Thomas and Belinda Russell. The man had hurt her many times before; this time he went too far. Convicted of first-degree murder, he was sent off to a prison in Scotland for the rest of his life. Edward's mother was dead and his father removed from society permanently. With the exception of Thomas and Belinda Russell, the teen was on his own. As he grew more and more reclusive and eccentric, he also became very close to his grandparents, the only family he had.

When Edward was born, the Russells took out a life insurance policy on their daughter as a precaution against her untimely demise in an accident. The baby was the beneficiary and they were trustees until his majority. God forbid, if they ended up as guardians of their grandchild, they would require funds to provide for his well-being and upbringing. Oddly their fears were realized, although not in the accidental way they envisioned. At sixteen Edward Russell ended up with three million dollars in trust from the insurance proceeds. Five years later it was his, lock, stock and barrel. He had spent the next thirteen years engaging in two passions – ancient history and continuing his education. As he matriculated, he spent little money. The financial markets did well, and now, although you'd never know it by his appearance or his habits, Edward was wealthy.

Edward had two bachelor's degrees, a master's, and two PhDs so far, one in archaeology and the other in medieval literature. Studying now at the University of Central London, he was hard at work on his thesis for doctorate number three in early British history. He'd chosen his subject because of his grandparents' occupations. His thesis was entitled "Dark Arts, Magic and Sorcery in the Middle Ages," and he was savoring every minute of the extensive research such a project required.

That day Thomas Russell fell into the subbasement, Edward came into the bookstore and called out to his grandparents. Hearing no response, he stepped behind the counter and looked in the small sitting room-cum-kitchen where they usually ate lunch. No one was there, but the door to the basement stood wide open, lights on at the bottom of the wooden staircase. When Edward descended, he heard his grandfather's cry for help.

His grandfather was never the same after that accident. It turned out he had torn ligaments in his leg, and at seventy-five, he mended slowly. Always a private man, he confided only to Belinda and Edward what he thought about the room down below The Necromancer's Bookshop.

The firemen who rescued Thomas had wondered out loud what the room was. One of them said Thomas should call the authorities so an archaeological crew could be dispatched. But Thomas didn't do that. It was no one else's business and he didn't want anybody poking around in his basement. Whatever was down there, it was extremely old. The past was past and the things in the basement belonged to them.

"I have to get down there," he told Belinda repeatedly as his leg mended in a cast. "I looked online and I think that's the crypt from the Church of St. Mary Axe. There's nothing else it could be. No telling what we'll find down there. I want you to help me go down there."

"Everything in its time, dear. Don't push the healing process. It may be a long time before you're climbing down a ladder into a musty old crypt. How about asking Edward to go down and look around? He's been anxious to see what's there and you've kept him at bay."

"No. I want to see what's there first. Indulge an old man, dear. This may be the most excitement I get for the rest of my life. Of course Edward will be part of our discoveries down below. I just want us to be the first."

Thomas spent the next two months studying everything he could read about the ancient Church of St. Mary Axe. The church was originally called St. Mary, St. Ursula and her 11,000 Virgins, a reference to an entourage including St. Ursula and her handmaidens, who were beheaded with axes in 451 AD. Some thought the church itself was that old; others thought it was built a few hundred years later.

A document from the reign of King Henry VIII described one of the two actual axes used for the beheadings. The story was that the relic was displayed in the church; it gave both the church and the street their odd names. In the early 1560s, refugees from Spain used it as a place of worship, but by then it was in a state of disrepair. It was demolished shortly thereafter, taken down to the foundation. Another building, the one which Thomas and Belinda Russell owned today, was built in 1620 on the ruins of the ancient church.

Finally came the Sunday morning when Thomas and Belinda lowered a ladder down the hole he'd fallen through. She descended first with the idea she'd help him down. Neither of them was young anymore nor in great physical condition. It was an ordeal, but they both made it to the dank chamber, flashlights in hand and a camera around his neck.

Thomas wanted to examine the stone box first. It was clearly ancient and almost certainly a sarcophagus. There was a cross on its long side and the carved figure of a person on the lid. It was impossible to tell much about the carving due to its age and the encrustation of grime and dirt from centuries underground. The person appeared to be wearing a kind of hat and its right hand was wrapped around a long sword. He snapped several pictures of the coffin and the carving.

He muttered, "I'll have to figure out how to clean this lid. We need to know more about who this person is."

Suddenly Belinda let out a bloodcurdling scream and ran across the musty room. Thomas was startled and dropped his flashlight. As he bent to pick it up, he saw the source of her alarm – a rat over a foot long was partially illuminated by the beam of the torch. Thomas attempted a kick with his foot and picked up his light as the animal moved slowly away, undaunted by the presence of humans.

"I hate rats! I have to get out of here!" Belinda ran to the ladder, shining her light here and there to ensure no more nasty creatures lurked nearby.

"Give me another minute. I have to see if we can open that door." He walked to the wooden door with the iron struts crisscrossing its surface.

"I can't, Thomas! I have to go upstairs and you can't stay here alone!"

"Climb the ladder and sit on one of the rungs. Rats can't go there. You can help by shining some light over here."

Like the stone coffin, the door also looked very old. It was about six feet tall and four wide, curved at the top, with a large keyhole opposite three enormous iron hinges.

Thomas hoped after all this time the door might open without a key. That had probably disappeared centuries ago. There was no knob – opening the door required inserting and turning a key, then pulling it open. At least that was how it appeared.

As Belinda sat on the ladder, Thomas put his fingers into the keyhole and gave the door a tug. It held firmly, not even a tremor as he pulled as hard as he could. *The damn thing could be a foot thick,* he thought grimly. *There's no way to break through this or knock it down. Somehow I'm going to have to find a key that'll work.*

He shot several pictures of the door and the keyhole. Then he pulled out a tape measure, pad and pencil. He measured the door and the lock area, drew a picture of the keyhole and noted its dimensions.

Further efforts proved futile, so he went over to the last thing he'd seen while lying down there – several dark-colored boxes on the floor. He saw that they were made of some type of metal and were perfect cubes about two feet on each side. The top of each was hinged and a hasp with a tiny lock kept each lid tightly closed. He tried to pick one up; it was heavy and obviously had something inside. In his weakened state he couldn't lift it.

"What is that?" Belinda asked from across the room, the beam of her light picking up the box he was examining.

"It's some kind of metal box and there's something in it. It's got a tiny lock." He looked at the others. "They all do. I'm going to see if I can break this one."

Pulling a screwdriver from his pants pocket, he inserted it in the hasp of the small padlock. It easily snapped when he applied pressure, and he eagerly removed the lock and stuck it in his pocket. He opened the metal lid.

"What's in there?"

"Books. It's full of books. Maybe seven or eight of them. They look really old."

"I have to get out of here, Thomas. This place is really giving me the willies. Take the box upstairs and let's look at the books there."

"I can't lift it," he responded, walking over to her with one of the books in his hand. "You take this one up and I'll take another. Maybe tomorrow I'll rig a pulley system from upstairs and we'll raise the boxes that way."

Back in the bookshop, they sat at the table, each with a book, sandwiches and tea laid out for lunch. As they ate, they looked at the books. The one he held was large and its covers were made of wood. It reminded him of an old family Bible, maybe four inches thick and filled with heavy pages probably of vellum. Hers was similar in size and with the same type of pages, but it was bound in rich leather. Their conditions were remarkable given they'd sat in a metal box for centuries. Fortunately they'd stayed dry and secure.

The Russells were familiar with ancient books. After all, they'd owned a witchcraft bookstore for fifty years. Their primary stock in trade was musty old volumes – works of magic, sorcery and necromancy. Many of the books for sale in their shop were centuries old, just like the ones they held now.

They also knew how to approximate the age of the old tomes. Books had become much more lightweight with the introduction of paper pages around the fifth century. The ones Thomas had found today were older, their pages folded into sections and bound by being sewn together. It was a process they had seen countless times.

Thomas ran his fingers over the wooden cover. "Sixth century or earlier, wouldn't you agree? This title's in a foreign language. It's not Latin, but I can't say for sure what it is. Maybe Welsh? It's hard to make out after all these years."

She was thumbing through the first few pages of the volume she held. "Mine's in old English, as far as I can tell. I recognize one word in the title. *Angleland*. The Anglo-Saxon word from which the name 'England' is derived."

"Remind me how long ago the Anglo-Saxons arrived, dear. My schoolboy English history isn't coming to mind as quickly as it used to."

She smiled at him and said, "I can look it up, but from memory I'm thinking around 400 AD. Given how it's made, this book may be from that period, but it could also be a history of those times that was written several centuries later. But if it's much past 500 or so, I'd think it'd have paper pages."

CHAPTER FOURTEEN

They didn't get back into the ancient chamber that day or for the next week. Once Monday came, the shop got busy and there wasn't time for the two of them to close the store, rig up a pulley system, climb down the ladder and move the metal boxes full of old books. Things could wait; whatever was down there had sat undisturbed for centuries. A few more days wouldn't matter.

On Friday Thomas suggested they try the chamber again on Saturday afternoon. Belinda agreed but only if he'd string a set of proper lights to keep the creatures at bay and allow them to see well.

Late Friday afternoon it was almost closing time when the bell tinkled on the front door. A stranger entered, a man perhaps in his late forties, dressed impeccably in a three-piece suit and a beautiful silk tie. Gold cuff links glistened on his starched white sleeves. *He's a banker, I'll bet,* Thomas thought to himself as he asked how he could help the gentleman.

"I'm hoping actually that I can help *you*," the man replied cordially. "May I presume you're Thomas Russell, the owner of this establishment?"

"At your service. And whom may you be?"

"I'm Gordon Peterson. I have a client who's looking for real estate in the City and, to cut to the chase, I'm here to ask if you'd consider selling your property."

Belinda had come from the back room by this time. "You're American, I'd guess from your accent and your abruptness. Where are you from, and why are you interested in this particular building?"

"You're absolutely correct – I am originally from the States, but I've been living in London for over a year. My client's looking to acquire properties that have historical value, put several million pounds into renovation and restoration, and generate greater value and returns. These two blocks along St. Mary Axe are perfect for his plans to create a medieval-themed shopping experience that puts tourists straight back into the Middle Ages."

"We're not interested–"

"One moment, Thomas. At least let's give this nice gentleman the courtesy of listening to his proposal."

"But, dear, with what …" He gave her a sideways glance and glanced down at the floor.

She shushed Thomas with a fierce glare. "Mr. Peterson – is that correct? May we excuse ourselves? Feel free to look around. Won't be a moment." She tugged at Thomas's arm.

In the back room they spoke in whispers. "What if he's offering us millions in profit, Thomas? What does it hurt to listen to him?"

"I suppose nothing, but now we have the crypt. I want to know more about what it is before–"

"Don't say another word about that. That's no one's business. If we had to, we could take care of the things down there before the building was sold. I'm not saying do it. I'm saying we can listen."

"And we've talked about passing the shop and the building along to Edward …"

"That's true, and certainly that's still my thinking. We're set to live comfortably the rest of our lives already, and Edward, bless his heart, needs to stop studying and get into the real world at some point. But what if this is too good to pass up? We have to hear him out."

"All right, all right. Let's hear what he has to say."

The man stepped from behind the counter seconds before they pulled the curtain and emerged from the back room. He had heard everything. The fireman who had contacted him was telling the truth! The subterranean chamber truly did exist. Excellent.

"See anything you can't live without?" Thomas joked as he saw the man browsing the strange assortment of wares.

"You have some very unusual things here, that's for sure. If I ever want to put a hex on someone, I'll know where to come!"

"All right. We're willing to listen. At least my wife is."

They invited the American to the back room and sat around the table. He described his client, the former CEO of a major British company, now retired and wealthy. The man believed that London real estate was currently an excellent investment.

"He's prepared to make you a cash offer for both your business and the building, and I think you will find it better than going market rates."

Belinda was surprised. "You want the *store* too? Why in Heaven's name would you want it?"

"It's part of the charm of St. Mary Axe. He'd be happy to leave you with it as tenants if you're willing to sign a long-term lease." He paused and smiled at the couple. "Frankly, at your ages, I wondered if you might not like to take a break from the grind of running a store and relax. With the money you'd get, you could spend your retirement years in the south of France."

Thomas asked, "Who would run our store if we sold it to your client? It's our own creation. We built it from scratch and it's been part of our lives for decades."

"I assure you our goal is to make St. Mary Axe an attractive street for shopping, having a coffee or a pint and absorbing its charm. From what I'm privy to, his initial thought would be to turn your store into a museum. You have so many old things here – a museum of antiquities would be perfect. It could look almost exactly as it does today. You must admit that Harry Potter could step inside at this very moment and no one would raise an eyebrow. It's that kind of shop."

Tired of the banter, Thomas said, "All right. Let's get down to brass tacks. How much money are you talking about?"

"I'll need a few days to present a formal proposal, but I'm authorized to offer you six million dollars."

Belinda's eyebrows rose as they both sat silently. Finally she said, "Why would any sane person pay six million for this building? We're not stupid people, Mr. Peterson. We keep up with property values in this area. You know and we know that's twice what the building is worth, maybe more. And the store? You surely can't place much of a valuation on a bookshop catering to the black arts. What exactly do you and this anonymous 'client' really want?"

Peterson smiled. "The man has deep pockets and a keen sense of the future value of this part of the City. You needn't worry about his valuation methods – think more about the cash offer I've set in front of you. It'll make you safe and secure for the rest of your lives, free from the worry of running a business and financially able to do anything you want. And frankly, you're the first people I've approached in this area. My client's willing to pay more for the first parcel of land than the second or third. The first one gives him a presence, a foothold in this quaint street. The others would be mere additions, properties he can do without if need be. He likes your ancient building and thinks it's an ideal place to start our project."

"Has this person ever been inside our store?"

"No, but he's seen it from the outside. It'll work perfectly for him, he tells me."

Thomas responded curtly, certain now that things weren't right with this sudden offer. "This is all too strange for me. You have a client willing to give us millions more than this place is worth and he hasn't even seen the inside of it? I don't think so. I don't know what you think you're doing, but I'm having no part of it. I listen to your talk of being interested in our welfare, but that's really none of your business. There are a lot more things to consider than money, and you can't just breeze in here one Friday afternoon, throw down a lot of cash and expect us to give up something we've spent a lifetime building. Yep, there's more than money. So why don't you just run along? We need to close up now." He pushed his chair back and stood, the meeting over.

"We'll think about it, and thank you for talking with us." Belinda diplomatically lightened the conversation. One never knew if things in their life might change overnight. They might want to accept the offer someday. It never hurt to leave people in good spirits.

Gordon Peterson said, "If you don't mind, I'll go ahead and send over a formal offer just so you'll have it. Take a few days to think it over. We don't need an answer tomorrow. But I must caution you that our offer will carry an expiration date. If we can't make a deal with you, I promise you we will find others who are more amenable to our concepts. Please consider this opportunity carefully."

CHAPTER FIFTEEN

At home that Friday evening the Russells discussed the stranger's visit. Out of the clear blue, a man walked in their shop and offered them millions of pounds more than the building and business were worth. What was really going on? Who were this man and his client? What did they really want? Thomas and Belinda had all the questions but none of the answers. They went to bed confused and more than a little concerned.

Saturday morning in the store was a busy time for Belinda. There were more customers than usual, and she hardly stopped once the entire time. Thomas worked in the basement, stretching out the lights he'd brought from home and hooking up an extension cord. He laid out a toolbox and nails, everything ready for their descent into the crypt at noon when the store closed for the weekend.

After a quick lunch the elderly couple carefully crept down the ladder. Thomas put nails into ancient timbers that supported the ceiling of the dank room. He strung a set of lights and plugged them in. Suddenly the room was flooded and bright. A solitary rat, watching from a corner, jumped a foot when the lights came on and scurried through a hole at the base of the ancient stone wall.

Belinda went up and down the ladder with the rest of the books in the metal box Thomas had opened earlier.

Thomas used his screwdriver to pry off the little padlocks from the other metal boxes. He opened each lid and saw each box was full of more old volumes. There were dozens – he thought the ones on top looked to be in pretty decent shape. He closed the lids. They'd take the other books up later on.

He'd put the first little padlock in his pocket the other day when he pried it off. He'd searched the Internet in a futile attempt to find something similar in order to see how old it might be. He found nothing remotely resembling it. The lock itself was very simple and not designed to keep anyone from breaking it. It was more for keeping the lid tightly shut and protecting its contents.

Today his efforts were aimed at unlocking the heavy wooden door. There was a box full of old keys that had sat on a shelf in the basement for many years. He had no idea where most of them belonged, but every time a key turned up he threw it in the box. Some were quite large, others very small. Some were skeleton keys, others perhaps used to wind a clock, and some looked very unusual. Belinda brought the box of keys to the crypt, and Thomas rummaged through them. He tried first one, then another. None of them was large enough.

He carefully inserted a long screwdriver into the keyhole and moved it up and down, side to side. He could feel an ancient tumbler mechanism move slightly, but the screwdriver wouldn't open the door. He finally gave up and turned to the stone sarcophagus.

The lid was four inches thick. He gave it a halfhearted push but wasn't surprised when nothing happened. It would take a winch to move it.

He'd taken pictures of the coffin the last time he was here. After having the photos developed, he researched those too. One thing was clear. Just like others he'd seen, the cross on the side of the sarcophagus was definitely Norman. That alone wasn't enough to date the coffin or whoever lay inside, but if they found other evidence, this could help narrow the time frame.

One of the old books for sale in the store gave Thomas exactly what he needed. *Burial Practices in Medieval Britain* had lithographs and descriptions of stone caskets. They were in cemeteries and crypts in England, Scotland and Wales. He found a picture that showed one very similar to the coffin here in the chamber. Thomas was excited. The one in the book was truly ancient. Maybe theirs was too!

They had to clean the stone lid to see its carvings. Belinda brought down a pail of warm water, a scrub brush and some rags. Starting at the carved head, she daubed water on the stone lid. Thomas came along behind her with the brush, carefully removing centuries of caked dirt and grime. Within thirty minutes nearly half of the carving was much more distinct, and now they could see faint writing on the lid.

"Do you still think this looks like one in your book?" Belinda asked when she'd finished.

"It does! It absolutely does! I'm going upstairs to fetch that book."

"No sir. I won't have you go climbing that ladder and stairway again. I'll get it."

Shortly he was comparing the lithograph to the coffin.

"See? Doesn't it look very similar to you?"

She agreed that it did. "Whose coffin is that?"

"They don't know his name. The picture's from Somersaete, what today is called the county of Somerset in western England not far from Wales."

He read the entry in the book. "The coffin is that of a knight, a Briton, buried in Somersaete, a region first mentioned in a Saxon law code around 675 AD by Ine, the king of Wessex.

"The carving on the lid depicts a helmeted man holding a six-foot staff in his right hand. When the lid was removed, they discovered a shield lying on the knight's chest. One of only two known to exist, today the shield is displayed in the British Museum."

He finished and said, "My God, Belinda. The coffin in the book dates to the Middle Ages, maybe even earlier. We apparently have another British knight right here. We have to figure out how to get this lid off without letting anyone know what we've found. We have to get that door opened too. This could be something really incredible."

"There's no way you and I can move this lid. Let's be realistic. I agree we shouldn't get outsiders involved, but don't you think Edward can help figure it out?"

They turned to the faint inscription on the lid, writing down each letter they could read and leaving a space where a mark was illegible. Thomas would ask Edward about this; given his education, he was their expert in all things medieval.

Before leaving for the day, Thomas and Belinda moved a circular rug to the basement, covered the hole that led into the chamber below and set a couple of boxes on its fringes to keep anyone from stepping there. Although not secured, the hole to the crypt was at least well hidden.

At home that evening they talked things over and agreed they required Edward's help. They'd call him tomorrow.

At two a.m., a man wearing a headlamp flashlight stood in the crypt below The Necromancer's Bookshop in St. Mary Axe. His hands covered by latex gloves, he opened one of the metal boxes and looked at its contents. He snapped photos of several book covers, then closed the lid without taking anything.

Finally he ascended the ladder and the staircase into the shop and left through the same small side window he'd easily jimmied to climb inside.

Belinda called Edward first thing Sunday morning. His answering machine message advised he was out of town. Remembering he had gone to Oxford to research his thesis, she asked him to call when he returned.

Thomas spent most of Sunday and Monday studying the seven ancient books he and Belinda had carried up the stairs. There were several varieties – some had covers of wood, others appeared to be leather, and two were encrusted with dull stones. None was in modern English although when he flipped through pages some words resembled the old English in *The Canterbury Tales* Thomas had studied in school. The script in most was totally foreign to him. All were equally old and in remarkably decent condition for having lain for centuries in metal boxes in an underground room. In-depth examination would take time and probably require outside resources such as those available at the university Edward attended, he thought.

FedEx delivered an envelope to the bookshop on Tuesday morning. It was a formal offer on the letterhead of a company called City Properties Limited Partnership IV with an address in North Carolina. The Russells had five days to accept the offer and return the document. Gordon Peterson's business card was clipped to the offer letter with the words "call me, please" written on it. His cell number was highlighted.

Less than a mile from The Necromancer's Bookshop, Gordon Peterson looked closely at the photographs of the things that lay in the room below the bookshop in St. Mary Axe Street. Regardless of the couple's decision, he was ready to implement his plan.

Thomas and Belinda gave the American's offer serious consideration despite the fact that it seemed too good to be true. Three days after they received the FedEx packet, Thomas called Gordon Peterson and declined.

Peterson's response surprised him. The man's previous cordiality was gone. A hard voice said, "That's a mistake, Mr. Russell. You'll be sorry you turned me down."

Thomas angrily fired back, "Sorry? What are you planning to do – kill me?"

Ten feet away, Belinda heard only his side of the conversation. She stifled a scream and said, "Thomas, hang up now. Hang up the phone."

Before that could happen, Peterson responded. This time his attitude and voice were that of the man who'd visited their store.

"Of course I'm not planning to *kill* you, Mr. Russell. What a thing to say! It's just that you're missing the chance of a lifetime. Are you certain of your decision? You still have a couple of days."

"We're absolutely certain. Don't call us again." Thomas slammed down the receiver, still surprised and angry at the man's hostility.

St. Mary Axe Street lay dark and deserted two nights later when someone lobbed a concrete block through one of the large front windows of The Necromancer's Bookshop. The next morning the police cordoned off the area as Thomas and Belinda took a rough inventory. From what they could see, nothing had been taken in the showroom itself, and the cash register still held the same fifty pounds sterling they always left in the till overnight. While Belinda talked with a detective, Thomas went down the basement stairs, spent a few minutes then returned.

"What's down there?" one of the investigators asked.

"Just a storeroom. I took a look around. Nothing's been disturbed."

As the policemen compared notes and began wrapping things up, Belinda pulled Thomas aside. She whispered, "I think we need to tell them about that American, Gordon Peterson. I'm sure he threw the block through our window because we turned down his offer."

Thomas leaned in and responded, "Don't say anything. Nothing. Trust me. I'll explain when they're gone."

The lead investigator, a man named Dalton, closed his notebook. "Unless you find something missing later, this one will go down as an act of vandalism. Looks like maybe some kids got their kicks destroying the front of your shop." He suggested the Russells consider installing video surveillance cameras inside and on the street. Thomas thanked him for his advice.

As soon as the officers were gone, Belinda lit into Thomas. "What in the world did you shush me up for? Why shouldn't I have told that policeman about that man and his threat that you'd be sorry?"

Thomas's face was grim. "I went down into the basement while you were talking to the policemen. The rug that covered the hole was thrown aside. Whoever broke our front window went straight to the hidden chamber. We need to go see what he took."

They hurried to the basement. He'd hastily dragged the carpet over the hole and now he removed it again. Slowly maneuvering the ladder, they went into the crypt and turned on the lights.

The stone sarcophagus appeared untouched. Thomas wasn't surprised. It would take more than one or two intruders to find out what was under the massive stone lid.

There were pry marks on the wooden door next to the keyhole. Belinda ran her hand over them. "Looks like he worked on the door but didn't succeed."

Thomas wasn't listening. She saw him staring at the metal boxes on the floor, deep in thought.

"Have you found something?"

"I guess it's what I *haven't* found that matters. There were seven of these metal boxes originally. We took one upstairs. That left six. But now there are five. He took one of the metal boxes and the books inside it."

Their immediate chore was to ensure the books were safe from now on. They spent an hour carrying the rest of the books upstairs into the shop. There were many ways to hide these particular old tomes among thousands of ancient volumes lining dusty shelves throughout the store. They chose one particular shelf that was situated safely behind the sales counter and away from browsing customers. The fifty-odd books from the crypt blended perfectly with hundreds of others scattered everywhere throughout the crowded store. They were in a perfect hiding place, right in plain sight.

CHAPTER SIXTEEN

Because of the unusual nature of The Necromancer's Bookshop and the strange assortment of wares it sold, one of the London television networks picked up the vandalism report from the police blotter. It sounded like a great human-interest story. A reporter called Belinda for an interview. The couple decided to do it because the publicity would help increase both sales and visibility of their odd shop. The crypt would remain their secret alone – there would be no mention of it.

When the story aired on the nightly news, spooky music and scenes from a Halloween haunted house merged into a shot of St. Mary Axe Street and the newly repaired front of the store. The place really did look straight out of the Middle Ages and the reporter capitalized on the strange things that were sold at the store by the wizened old couple who had owned it for years. Belinda pointed out wands, books of sorcery and amulets as the reporter asked question after question. The piece wrapped up with news that someone had vandalized the place a couple of nights before. "Beware. Beware," the reporter said in an ominous, deep voice. "The forces of darkness will seek out those who attacked this shop. Betsy Conklin, ITV News, reporting from St. Mary Axe Street in sixteenth-century London. Back to you in the studio."

Disturbed by the news story, a man at home on his couch, watching TV, made a phone call. The next morning he gave his statement at the police station in Leadenhall Street, six blocks from The Necromancer's Bookshop.

CHAPTER SEVENTEEN

Two days after the news story on television, things were crazy at the shop. The number of curious browsers had skyrocketed and sales were higher too. Today a dozen customers were shopping – two more were in line to pay. The phone rang – neither could break away to answer it, so they let it go to the answering machine. Belinda heard the caller's message as she took a customer's money.

"This is Inspector Dalton of the Metropolitan Police. We have important information about the crime at your shop the other night. Please call me urgently." He left a number.

Around one there was a break when no customers were in the store. In the back room Thomas heated soup in the microwave while Belinda returned the officer's call. She listened for several minutes, nodding her head now and then. Thomas strained to hear her side of the conversation but didn't get much of it. At the end he heard, "Thank you so much for working on our case. Of course we want to cooperate. I'll see you at five."

Belinda said, "Well, this is interesting."

"I'm all ears."

"Our news story on television apparently created more than sales for our bookshop. One person felt guilty after seeing it and called the police."

"Really? Who in the world would that have been?"

"It was one of the firemen who helped pull you out of the chamber. Remember how they looked around at everything and told you that we should call the antiquities people? Apparently he told people about it that night at his pub and–"

The tinkle of the bell on the front door signaled the arrival of another customer.

"Hold that thought," Edward said as he walked into the showroom. As anxious as she was to tell him, it would have to wait.

One shopper after another traipsed through the bookshop that afternoon, and it was four before they had a moment to themselves. As they handled customers, several phone calls went unanswered, including one from Edward. Belinda recognized his voice when he left a message.

"Tell me the rest of what the inspector said," Thomas said eagerly when they were finally alone.

"Let me listen to Edward's message first. We need him to help us with the things in the crypt as soon as he returns from Oxford, and I want to know when that'll be."

Edward's voice was cheery. "Well, if it isn't my famous grandparents! On the national news, no less! And proprietors of one of the strangest shops in London. Congratulations on all the free publicity. And condolences on having a rock thrown through your front window, although in this case prosperity may follow adversity! I'm home soon and can't wait to hear all about it!"

He advised his train would arrive Saturday around ten. He'd drop off his things at home then come straight to the shop. They couldn't reach him this week – he hadn't left a contact number in Oxford – but Saturday would work fine. The store closed at twelve, and they could work on the crypt all weekend.

Thomas said impatiently, "Now may I please hear the rest of the story?"

"All right, where was I? Oh yes, at his pub the fireman apparently regaled a few people around the fireplace with a story of what lay in our basement. Four people, to be exact. Four good friends of his whom he's known for years. He'd trust them implicitly, he told the policeman."

"Then why the guilt? He told a few close friends about the secrets in our basement. That doesn't seem too nefarious."

"There was something else. The pub was crowded. He apparently made no attempt to lower his voice – he was excited about the things he'd seen in our store and it made a good story. A man was having a pint at a table two feet away. An American, the fireman assumed from the blue jeans and tennis shoes he wore. That Yank heard everything he said. And he came over and introduced himself."

"Gordon Peterson."

"Brilliant deduction, Sherlock Holmes! Peterson handed the fireman a fifty-pound note and asked for information. He said he was an archaeology professor from the States. He told the fireman he wanted to visit us and maybe see the subterranean chamber. Having had enough ale to dull his caution, he did something he regrets now. He believed the American. He gave him our names and said our shop was in St. Mary Axe. He called the police after he saw our story on the television and realized that man could have been the perpetrator."

"So the police are looking for Gordon Peterson, I presume? Do they think he threw the rock through our window? He didn't seem the type for vandalism to me. And did I hear you tell the inspector you'd see him at five today?"

"Yes. He asked me why we hadn't told him about the crypt. He thinks that's the entire reason for the window breakage, and of course, we do too, now that a box of books is missing. He wants to see the chamber and I said he could. I hope you agree with that. I think now he has to see it.

"I also told him about the man's business card and the offer agreement he sent over, and he wants to borrow those. He needs to find Gordon Peterson and these things might help. They don't know what Peterson's involvement might have been, but they want to talk to him. The inspector said it sounds suspicious. I agree!"

Inspector Dalton arrived right on time. They spent a half hour showing him the underground chamber and the volumes of ancient books they'd found. He took pictures and notes. He concentrated on the metal boxes that had held the books, since the perpetrator had stolen one of them.

Finally he was finished. Back upstairs he said, "I've no idea what you have down there, but it's imperative you contact the antiquities authorities. I've no doubt it'll create a firestorm of interest and publicity because whatever's there is both ancient and interesting. You may end up with more traffic than you can handle. It's your decision whether to involve them. Who knows if that stone coffin might impact the history of our very nation! The archaeologists should be examining all this. I can't force you to do anything, but I strongly urge you to make that call."

Inspector Dalton took Peterson's offer letter and his business card. He promised to keep them informed of developments. They agreed to do the same.

Over the next couple of days when he had a free moment, Thomas pulled down one after another of the dusty volumes. He wrote each title on a notepad. He had no idea what language most of them were written in. Some might be Welsh, but he wasn't sure. Languages weren't his thing. Edward's background in medieval literature and history was what they required.

As usual these days, there were lots of customers Saturday morning at The Necromancer's Bookshop. Inspector Dalton came by around ten to give the Russells some good news. The man who called himself Gordon Peterson had been located, interrogated, charged with burglary, surrendered his US passport and was now in jail. The policeman requested the Russells attend his arraignment in a couple of weeks.

Peterson's real name turned out to be Gordon Foxworth. He was from Raleigh, North Carolina, and was engaged in two occupations. Primarily he was a tomb robber who masqueraded as an antiquities dealer. He'd spent two decades in one exotic locale or another, entering sites after dark to take what he found. He'd arranged the disposition of some very nice and quite rare objects, none of which was legally his to sell. His ultra-wealthy customers turned a blind eye in order to acquire unique pieces that unfortunately would never be examined by archaeologists.

Gordon also had been a financial advisor. Since his advice to clients consisted solely of his selling them stolen artifacts, the authorities eventually shut him down. One time he'd been charged with fraud but never convicted. By the time his trial date came around, he had disappeared. The alleged fraud was perpetrated against a wealthy, greedy individual who knew better than to trust Gordon. Once Foxworth skipped town, the police closed the case for lack of interest. Gordon changed his last name to Peterson and assumed the social security number of a long-deceased individual. Voila! He was back in business.

During the interrogation, Inspector Dalton learned that the break-in at the shop was just what it appeared to be. An antiquities huckster from America was now plying his trade in London. In a stroke of luck he'd overheard the fireman's tale of ancient things hidden beneath a sorcerer's bookstore. Foxworth decided to see for himself if there was something worth stealing.

The first time he visited the crypt he had gone in through an unlocked side window and looked around. His second visit was after they turned down his offer, and this time he was intent on burglary. He used that same side window again to gain entry and went downstairs.

Once inside the crypt, Gordon had no more success than the Russells had. He couldn't figure out how to jimmy the door lock and couldn't move the heavy stone sarcophagus lid. So he stole the only thing he could carry – one heavy box full of books. That box and seven old volumes had been found in Foxworth's hotel room, the policeman said. The metal box was exactly the same as the others Inspector Dalton had seen in the basement, and the ancient books were similar to those Thomas Russell had shown him.

"They're held as evidence for now. Once we wrap up our case, you'll get them back," he explained.

Inspector Dalton finished the story. Once the thief had the box safely in his car, he noticed a large block lying near the abandoned building next door. He tossed it through the front window to make it look like vandalism. Then he drove away.

Dalton asked if they were going to call the antiquities people now.

Belinda said they weren't inclined to do so now, but they'd talk it over with their grandson, Edward, to see what he thought.

Saturday morning was hectic at the store. The usual noon closing time passed with customers still lined up at the checkout counter. Edward arrived around 12:30, hugged his grandparents, and helped them handle the last sales. Finally he locked the front door and said, "So what's new with the hidden room? I've been dying all week to know more about it. I can't think about anything else!"

There was much to tell him. They talked about the steady increase in customers as a result of the newscast, the offer by Mr. "Peterson" to buy the building and the store itself, and the burglary and the man's arrest.

"He's sitting in the City of London jail at this moment," Thomas said with satisfaction. "The inspector says he hasn't been able to make bail thus far."

"Really? Well, it's obvious he didn't intend to buy the building. He wanted whatever you've found in the basement!"

Belinda nodded. "Without a doubt. Whatever's there is really old and possibly very significant. So we've been patiently waiting for your young, strong arms to get back to London to help us figure out what actually *is* there! Your grandfather thinks he's got a dead British knight in the basement. My word, what if that were true! It boggles one's mind, doesn't it?"

Edward was as enthused as they were. "It does, in fact, but you know, it might make sense. I've had precious little time to do any research while I'm finishing my thesis, but the other afternoon I took a break. I rummaged around in the library at Oxford and found a book with a great description of this area prior to the Great Fire of 1666. You know, of course, that everything in the square mile around you sits on top of things far, far older. Back to the Roman occupation, in fact."

Thomas nodded. "And we also know that this particular building sits on the exact site of the ancient Church of St. Mary Axe. I'm thinking that room below our basement is part of the crypt of the old church."

"I agree. The old book I found said the church was probably built in the mid-fifth century, around 450 AD or so. That's the same time the Saxons were battling the Britons. We know for sure St. Mary Axe church was torn down about 1565, sixty years before this current building was erected. I think the church floor was much lower than the street today. It's possible that in the 1500s what is now your basement was the ground floor of the church. Here's what I think – the people who built today's building kept the existing stone floor of the ancient church nave because it happened to still be there and was very solid. By then it was much lower than the street level, so it became the floor of the basement. No one remembered that a room – maybe even a series of rooms – lay beneath it."

Edward watched his grandmother's excitement grow. "A series of rooms! Wouldn't that be something? And if what you just said is true … well, the room underneath must be the crypt. And it could date as far back as the fifth century? My word, how amazing! It all makes perfect sense!" She clapped her hands. "I can't wait any longer. Let's get to it!"

Before they went downstairs, Thomas showed Edward the shelves of ancient books in foreign languages that they'd removed from the chamber. "Your grandmother and I looked at a couple of these the other day – I think those could be from the fifth century or so, given their binding and vellum pages. One's in old English and mentions Angleland.

Sounds Anglo-Saxon to me. When you have time, I'd like you to find out more about them."

They descended the basement stairs and pulled aside the rug. Thomas went down the ladder first and turned on the string of lights. Belinda and Edward eagerly climbed down after him.

CHAPTER EIGHTEEN

Gordon Foxworth was actually pretty good at his trade. A damned fireman who went to the cops shouldn't have tripped him up this easily. If that one unfortunate thing hadn't happened – if the fireman hadn't remembered him from the pub – he would have at least relieved the Russells of those ancient books in their basement. And maybe the other stuff too. All he wanted was a signed purchase contract. The words in that document would allow him to examine the building. Given time alone in the chamber, he would have figured out how to open that coffin.

There was no doubt in Foxworth's mind that the sarcophagus and the heavy locked door hid important information from maybe as far back as the Middle Ages. Gordon was highly educated, one of those people who could have made a decent, honest living. But he was drawn to the sometimes lucrative, always exciting world of flimflam. He loved ancient things and he was a confidence man – smooth, glib and easy to like. He had made a lot of money over the years; it was a shame that Foxworth's one weakness – gambling – had perpetually left him one step from poverty. He was always working on the next deal, always promising himself after this one he'd quit going to the casinos. He'd avoided jail time before. But now he sat incarcerated in the City of London, awaiting arraignment in a few days. Gordon

Foxworth needed two things quickly – a good lawyer and ten thousand pounds for bail.

Gordon had a fallback position. As soon as he saw what was in the crypt, he knew who to call – a shadowy European from Prague who had bought hot artifacts from him twice before. That man had money. That man was his exit strategy.

The guard handed Gordon Foxworth his mobile phone and waited while the prisoner memorized a number he looked up. He handed the phone back and was escorted to the jail's pay phone. The guard looked at the screen, hoping to see the number Gordon had looked up, but the phone was locked.

As the jailer stood a few feet away, Foxworth called the man he believed would want to know about the crypt and its ancient contents. He had faith this individual would bail him out. After all, someone had to do the dirty work. Someone had to get those things out of that dank, dark chamber and into the hands of Juan Carlos Sebastian. The wealthy young collector Gordon had never met was his ticket.

———

After only one afternoon in the crypt with his grandparents, Edward was hooked.

There had been two goals that day – opening the stout wooden door and sliding the stone casket lid sufficiently to see if anything was inside. They'd tackled the lid first. Thomas and Belinda weren't in shape to help physically. And there turned out to be an insurmountable logistical problem. The sarcophagus had been placed in a recess of the stone walls exactly large enough for it to fit. When the lid had originally been put on, it was merely slid on top of the box from the front. Taking it off would be an entirely different matter. The rear and both sides of the stone box were tight against the wall. As easy as it had been to install, it was impossible to remove without equipment. A person couldn't get behind or beside the sarcophagus in order to push the lid. And no one, not even five strong men, could have pulled the thick stone slab forward and off the box. It would take a pulley system with a winch to lift it. The sarcophagus would have to wait.

His grandparents showed Edward the faint inscription on the coffin and the copy of it they'd made. He touched each letter with his fingers. "It's medieval Welsh. It says something like 'the eternal guardian of my King.'"

That was exciting – it sounded more and more like a fearless knight, maybe one who'd died in battle. There were many skirmishes between Angles, Saxons and Britons in those days. Edward promised more research on the inscription soon.

Next they moved to the massive old door. Edward knelt and examined the lock closely. He directed his flashlight into the massive keyhole and peered inside. Finally he stood.

"This isn't going to be any simpler than the coffin lid. The door's at least eighteen inches thick. And look at the size of the keyhole. The key that fit this lock must have weighed ten pounds and been a foot long. It won't be hard to spot if we ever come across it. Usually the way these medieval doors work is that there is a sliding iron bar on the other side of the door that moves left and right when the key is turned. In this particular case, the door is locked when the metal bar is all the way to the right, which is how it is now. In my opinion there are two ways to get in here. Find the key or work for days with saws to cut through the door."

All three were bitterly disappointed. They were inches from something that could be incredible, but they might as well have been miles away. They were totally unable to proceed without involving others, something that Thomas and Belinda wouldn't consider. They had found what was at the very least a historically relevant site. And if their speculations were correct, this place was fifteen hundred years old and contained the body of a knight. Bringing in outsiders would inevitably lead to governmental intervention, which would mean the project wouldn't be theirs to control anymore. Not acceptable. Wouldn't happen.

Edward took a cab home to his flat. He had two of the metal boxes full of books. One heavy box at a time, he hauled them up the stairs and into his living room. He couldn't deal with them tonight – he had to work on his thesis. He poured himself a glass of wine and settled in at the kitchen table, where research papers were strewn everywhere. For an hour he struggled to accomplish something. He tried to read. He tried to take notes. He tried a lot of things, but all his mind could do was wander back to the stack of ancient books sitting in the next room. Finally he gave up. *I'll get back on the research tomorrow,* he promised himself. *Tonight I'll see if I can find out what these books are all about.*

Since tomorrow was Sunday, the bookshop would be closed. Edward called his grandparents that morning and asked if they wanted to join him for lunch. "I stayed up half the night going through the books, and I can shed some light on what we have here."

Two hours later everyone was having a pint and lunch in the garden outside the Horse and Harness pub in Lower Thames Street. The river flowed lazily thirty feet in front of them, and off to the left the magnificent buttresses of the ancient Tower of London reached to the sky.

Belinda laughed as Edward explained how he'd gotten off track yesterday evening. The carefully laid plans to work on his thesis went by the wayside as the ancient volumes beckoned.

He pulled a notepad from his jacket pocket and consulted it. "I took fourteen books home with me. Eight of them were bound with leather covers and had vellum pages, three had wood covers and paper pages, and two had wood covers, vellum pages and some sort of dirty-looking colored glass stones affixed to the covers with tiny metal clips of some kind. I didn't look closely at the stones, but later we can dig one out if you want."

He paused and took a drink of ale. "All of the books except one are in Welsh. Not modern Welsh – Welsh the way it was written in the Middle Ages from, say, 400 to 600 AD.

I can't read ancient Welsh, but I'm getting some reference materials that'll help me translate. So I can't tell you what they're about, but they're in excellent condition for their age. They're handwritten with some beautiful illustrations, mostly of people. I'll finish my thesis as quickly as I can, and then I'll translate them."

"And?" Belinda asked as he stopped talking and took a bite of lunch.

"And what?"

"That accounts for all of the books except one. What about the fourteenth one?"

Edward grinned at her. "Good job paying attention, Grandmother! I saved the best for last. That one's something else for sure. It has a beautiful dark leather cover and is maybe two hundred pages long. It's handwritten on pages of vellum with broad, flowing script. It also probably was written in the fifth century and has a few colored illustrations like some of the others. Since it's in Latin, I spent more time on it than the others. Latin's easier; I can read it fluently. The big problem is interpreting the handwritten Latin of someone who wrote it so long ago. It's like trying to read a letter Henry VIII wrote in the 1500s. Bad penmanship, poor vocabulary and lousy spelling. Know what I mean?"

He stopped, took another swig of beer and sat back with a sly smirk.

Belinda scolded him. "Edward, what are you doing? You're teasing us! Now you tell us right now what this book's all about. You're hiding something. Don't tell me any more about what kind of cover it has or what kind of pictures are in it. Tell me why this one's so special."

"The title is …" He glanced at his notes. "*Bellum in Monte Badonis*."

"Thank you very much for that enlightening information. What does that mean?"

"In English it's called *The Battle of Badon*."

"Do I have to pull this out of you? I'm tired of waiting." She laughingly wagged a finger in his face. "Why is that book significant?"

"According to everything I can find, this could be the first book ever discovered that was written at the same time as the Battle of Badon. Any books I've seen were written hundreds of years after it supposedly happened. This one may be an account of the battle by an eyewitness. Think how significant *that* would be!"

Thomas said sarcastically, "You know, I'm fascinated watching you lead your grandmother on like this. But don't you think it's cruel? Isn't it time to confess what you're talking about, Edward? What in hell is the Battle of Badon and who cares if an eyewitness wrote about it?"

Edward leaned forward, excitement in his eyes.

"The Battle of Badon has long been thought to be a myth. The story goes that it was fought between the Britons and the Saxons around 500 AD. It was the battle that heralded the Saxon downfall and established the Britons in England and Wales."

Weary of Edward's answer-dodging, Thomas said, "My word. That *is* important. Come on. Is that all there is to it? A book that establishes a war was actually fought that up to now everyone thought was a fable? Big deal, if you ask me."

"Oh, there may be one more thing I neglected to mention. In that mythical battle, the Battle of Badon, do you know who led the Britons to decisive victory over the Saxons?"

"Who, pray tell?"

"None other than King Arthur and his legendary Knights of the Round Table. Men who until now have been considered by most historians to be fictitious. Now do you see why this book may be so important? It could be the first book ever found that dates from the actual time of Arthur's reign and mentions him by name. An eyewitness account about a king who really existed, if my initial thoughts are correct. A *really* big deal, I think. Right, Grandfather?"

CHAPTER NINETEEN

The call went straight to an answering machine. Its one-word response was, "Speak."

"Juan Carlos. Gordon Foxworth here. I'm in the City of London jail. I have information about what may be a priceless treasure hidden right here in the City, and I immediately thought of you. I need an attorney to bail me out. Here's how to contact me." Foxworth recited the information pasted on the wall above the pay phone. Maybe Juan Carlos would call him. Then again, maybe this number wasn't even his anymore – it had been years, after all. Maybe Gordon would never hear a word. It was worth a try. All he could do now was wait.

The answering machine sat on a table in a mostly empty flat in Eastern Europe. The rent and utilities were paid a year in advance, but no one ever visited the premises. Like others he maintained, that answering machine had one purpose – to allow people to contact Juan Carlos Sebastian. Sometimes it was for wet-ops assignments, but he also gave the number to others. From his office in Lucerne, Roberto Maas listened to the message Gordon Foxworth had left.

Four hours later a guard came to Gordon's cell. "You have company. Come with me."

The officer led him to a small room with a table and two chairs. A man with a dark complexion who was maybe forty sat at the table. "Sit down, Mr. Foxworth. I'm Curtis Pemberly – I'm here to help you." The guard remained standing in one corner of the room, arms crossed.

The man's appearance surprised Gordon. Foxworth had made a lot of money selling the things to Juan Carlos. He'd expected an expensive barrister. This man looked seedy. His suit and shirt were rumpled and he needed a shave.

"Did Juan Carlos send you?"

"Who else?" The man laughed and opened a briefcase. He brought out a document and a pen. "Sign this. You're appointing me as your legal representative. Let's get you out of here quickly. We can talk afterwards."

It took half an hour to process paperwork. Finally Gordon was taken to a room where he changed from an orange jumpsuit to his street clothes. A door clanged open and he was again a free man, standing in the lobby where the lawyer was waiting.

"Now let's go talk," Pemberly said. A half hour later they were alone in a dingy East London flat in what appeared to be an empty building. The elevator had smelled faintly of urine and the walls needed a coat of paint. Gordon was wary; this didn't seem right. However, the guy was obviously legit. He'd shown up after Gordon's call to the mystery man. And he'd put up ten thousand dollars to spring him from jail. That was what Gordon had asked for. *Don't look a gift horse in the mouth, and all that.*

"Thanks for paying bail. I guess I owe your boss–"

Pemberly interrupted him. "We'll deal with all that later. First things first. Let's hear about that priceless treasure you mentioned in the phone call."

That's strange. Is that all he cares about?

Cautiously Gordon replied, "First I've got some questions. Where are we? Pardon my frankness, but this rat hole looks like a tenement. Why aren't we at your office? Juan Carlos obviously hired you. I want to know what's going on here. Who are you, exactly?

"Mr. Foxworth, may I call you Gordon? We're going to get to know each other better, that's for certain. Might as well be on a first-name basis. Call me Curtis. I was told to get you out of jail and find out what was going on. You have me to thank for your release, and of course Juan Carlos. He paid your bail and he's trying to protect you by arranging a safe meeting place. My office is in London but far from here. This place was available, simple and close. I don't question Juan Carlos. Neither should you. Now I want information. Talk to me."

So Gordon Foxworth talked. He told about the ancient sarcophagus, the heavy locked wooden door and the boxes filled with books. "I took one of those boxes. I'm sure the cops have the books now since the box was in my hotel room."

After Foxworth had told about the bookshop, its elderly owners, the items in the subterranean crypt and how valuable they might be, Curtis Pemberly said, "One last question. Who's Juan Carlos?"

Gordon was stunned. "You know who …" Suddenly he realized something was terribly wrong. He stood, tried to appear nonchalant while sweat began to pour from his forehead, and stuck out his hand.

"Well then. I guess I should be going. I should get out of town before they come looking for me. Thanks for bailing me out!"

Curtis drew a small pistol from under his jacket.

"What the hell … What's going on? What do you want from me?"

"Sit down. It's not time to go yet. Tell me about Juan Carlos."

Initially Gordon Foxworth tried to take the high road, refusing to say a word unless this man told him exactly what was going on. That didn't work. An hour later Pemberly had what he wanted. A bullet in his leg, Gordon lay semiconscious on the floor and begged for his life. That didn't work either.

Curtis Pemberly finished and calmly walked out the door. That evening he placed a call to Juan Carlos's number. When he heard the word "Speak," his response was short and sweet.

"I got this number from Gordon Foxworth. He's been in a bit of an accident, you might say. Before his untimely demise, he told me everything. Call me." He left his mobile number.

CHAPTER TWENTY

A Year Later

For months the dank chamber below the basement of The Necromancer's Bookshop had lain undisturbed. There was much that had to be done but even more that couldn't be done.

Inspector Dalton told them a man who said he was a barrister signed the jail register as Curtis Pemberly and paid ten thousand dollars cash for the con artist's release. He'd bailed Gordon Foxworth out of jail. Foxworth missed a court date a week later and a warrant had been issued for his arrest. An anonymous tip, probably from a homeless man looking for a place to sleep, led the police to a badly decomposed body in an abandoned East London flat. An autopsy was impossible at this late stage, but it appeared there had been a gunshot to his leg. That wouldn't have killed him – Foxworth's death was ruled inconclusive and the case was closed.

It was fortuitous indeed that Edward was alone in the bookshop the morning Curtis Pemberly walked in. Thomas and Belinda had taken the train to Brighton to spend a week sightseeing at the beach. As things turned out, it was far better for Edward to have met Pemberly than for either of his grandparents to do so. He didn't need them involved in this.

Pemberly introduced himself and asked to speak with Thomas Russell. Edward explained his grandfather wasn't there and asked the nature of the man's business.

"I presume you know who Gordon Foxworth is."

Edward tried to mask his surprise. "Certainly. And it's *was*, not *is,* from what I hear. What's this all about?"

"You have some very interesting things here in your store," Pemberly said, gesturing at the crowded shelves around the walls. "And even more interesting things down there, I hear." He pointed at the floor.

"I have no idea…"

"Oh come now, Edward. I may call you Edward, right? Of course I may. You know precisely what I'm talking about. Gordon saw some interesting things that night. He told me all about them. They sound fascinating – something the news broadcasters would love to have as their lead story one evening. But you know the thing that surprises me? Even though your grandfather literally fell into this discovery, and even though Gordon Foxworth was arrested for being here, nothing's been made public. Someone's keeping all this very quiet. Very quiet indeed. And that, my good man, is why I'm here. I'm here to help your family keep it that way."

At that point two customers entered the store. Since he was running the place alone, Edward asked Pemberly to come back at five p.m. The man leaned over the counter and whispered, "I'll be back promptly at five. Keep this to yourself. Tell no one about my visit. Lives could be at stake here." He turned and walked out the door.

Yes indeed, you smarmy bastard, Edward thought to himself.

Promptly at five Pemberly returned. Without a word of acknowledgment Edward closed and locked the door behind him. He walked to the table in the back room and Curtis followed.

"We can talk here." Edward waved to a chair. "Have a seat."

"I want to see the chamber."

Edward spoke harshly. “That’s not going to happen. Sit down and tell me what you want.”

“Have it your way,” the man said smugly as he sat. “You *will* show me. I promise you that.” He told Edward he had information to trade, what he wanted in return for it, and said that he personally had sent Gordon off to eternity.

Two hours later Curtis Pemberly was at home, a satisfied man. Things had gone extraordinarily well the past few days. A jailer who listened to Gordon’s call owed Curtis a favor. So he’d passed along a tip that Gordon Foxworth was talking about treasure hidden in London. Curtis acted quickly, bailing Foxworth out of jail before whomever he’d called could arrive. With proper persuasion Gordon had revealed everything – what and where the items were, who to contact, and what little he knew about Juan Carlos Sebastian – just a name and a phone number.

Tomorrow Curtis would be a hundred thousand euros richer. He couldn’t have cared less about the artifacts, simply some ancient stuff in the crypt of an old church. Extortion was his game and this had gone well. He had played masterfully against a surprisingly weak opponent, Edward Russell. Once Curtis revealed that he’d killed Gordon, Edward had caved in and trembled in fear. In exchange for learning what Gordon had told Curtis, Edward was willing to pay the money. *Of course he was, the puny weakling!* All this was satisfying indeed. And Curtis downplayed one important part – the information about Juan Carlos Sebastian. Curtis had plans of his own for the mystery man – another extortion! This Juan Carlos person would pay up too before this was over.

That trembling, pitiful bookshop owner tried to stand up to me at first, but he was no match. He’s weak – he’s actually scared of me. That made Curtis smile. *Tomorrow when I go back to give him my information, I’ll make him show me the chamber even though I don’t give a flip about what’s there. It’s a matter of principle. And maybe I’ll stop back by in a few months to get more money from this spineless little shit. This could go on for a while!*

When Curtis's mobile phone rang at ten p.m., he saw the blocked caller ID, answered and had a ten-minute conversation with Juan Carlos Sebastian. He revealed very little – there was an ancient sarcophagus and a locked door beneath an occult bookstore, but Juan Carlos wouldn't have a clue how to find the exact location. There were dozens of necromancy shops in London, after all.

Exciting thoughts raced through his head as Curtis lay in bed. *This is incredible. I'm certain I'm going to be able to sell the same information to this man Juan Carlos, whoever he is. How about that! Two scores in one!*

Curtis Pemberly slept well that night, the slumber of a man on top of his game, who was playing to win the jackpot.

CHAPTER TWENTY-ONE

At eleven the next morning Curtis Pemberly confirmed a hundred thousand euros was safely tucked into his bank account. *Thank you, Edward! This was working very satisfactorily.*

He went to the bookstore around twelve and found the bookseller finishing up with a lone customer. Just as yesterday, he walked to the front door, locked it and hung a sign that said, "Back at one p.m."

Today Edward's demeanor was submissive. "We can go to the back again if that's all right with you."

Curtis loved the dominator's role. "It's fine. And by the way, you *will* show me the chamber today."

"Of course, sir. I'll show it to you once we're done here. Did the wire transfer arrive?"

"It did. Lucky for you to have moved quickly. I have another party who could use my information. He's a mysterious man named Juan Carlos. But you'd better be careful. He could be more fearsome than I am!" Curtis was having a ball, positively ecstatic playing the master-servant game with this puny man.

For half an hour Edward took notes as Curtis told him everything. When he mentioned Juan Carlos's name, Edward asked about him. Curtis smugly replied that he was a shadowy collector. That was all he'd say.

Edward wanted to know more, but it couldn't be helped. *Don't worry about what-ifs*, he thought to himself. With Gordon Foxworth out of the picture, one loose end had been tied up. One less person alive knew about the crypt. Thinking last night on the whole Curtis Pemberly thing, Edward knew a hundred thousand euros was a small price to pay. He had to find out what Curtis knew. Then he could wrap up another loose end that was still untied – the one sitting right in front of him.

Playing role of weak fool masterfully, Edward assumed a meek countenance when Curtis finished talking. He bent his head slightly, subserviently.

"Tea?"

Curtis glanced at his watch to impress upon Edward how busy he was. "Yes," he snapped. "Make it fast; then we're going to see the crypt. I've things to do."

"Sounds as if you're dying to see it," Edward murmured, smiling as he turned away and put the kettle on the burner. "And I'll make it fast."

Ten minutes later Edward puttered around the kitchen, humming a tune as he cleaned up the mess on the floor. He glanced at the table. "Curtis, would you care for another cup of tea?"

But Curtis didn't answer. His head lay on the table, the shattered teacup and saucer on the floor where it had landed following the first long drink of Edward's excellent brew.

Edward smiled. "You think you're such a smart man. You shouldn't drink tea with the proprietor of a sorcerer's shop. Even if they found your body, they'd never figure out how you died. Okay. It's time. *Now* you get to see the chamber."

He hauled the body downstairs, stuck it in a heavy plastic construction bag he'd bought just for this purpose, and made a mental note. This Juan Carlos might appear one day to steal the things in the crypt. That was unlikely, but Edward would be ready just in case. He'd have a plan.

Killing that man was fun, his bad side said over and over inside his head.

Any further work on the sarcophagus and the heavy wooden door would require the help of others. The Russells – Edward, Thomas and Belinda – unanimously agreed that was not an option. The crypt would remain their secret. More vexing was the fact that his aging grandparents were of no help whatsoever. A true outsider, a third party, would eventually have to be enlisted. For now things were on hold, unexplained and unfinished.

Whatever moral responsibility the trio should have felt to contact the antiquities people was easily outweighed by the excitement of a once-in-a-lifetime discovery. We're good, law-abiding citizens, Thomas and Belinda said to themselves whenever this subject arose. This find is *ours* – in *our* basement – and we want this for ourselves.

Now that Edward had used the chamber to dispose of a body, he didn't want anyone nosing around down there, especially his grandparents. Over two nights during the Russells' vacation, Edward had dug up floor stones, removed soil underneath and buried that asshole Curtis Pemberly in the chamber he had wanted to see so badly. The dirt went out the back door and into a dumpster one bucketful at a time. He bought lime to eliminate the odor, spreading the white powder liberally over the body inside its sturdy plastic bag. He replaced the floor stones and swept them clean. Even with careful examination, it'd be hard to tell they'd ever been moved.

In the coming weeks Edward focused on finishing his thesis. He earned that third PhD in record time. When he began work on it, Edward had promised himself a prize when it was done – a trip to Ephesus to visit the place where the apostle Paul had lived two thousand years ago. But the tantalizing anticipation of what they'd found in St. Mary Axe Street put that trip on hold. He had more exciting things to work on. Now he could concentrate on the crypt.

While wrapping up his thesis, Edward had snatched an hour here, an hour there to examine the ancient books that had been in the chamber. He'd already looked through fourteen of them, the ones he took to his flat and then returned. Now he tackled the rest, cataloged every one on a notepad, and listed what scant information he could glean from casual observation. He had no formal education in the medieval Welsh most of them were written in, so he gave a couple to his professors at the University of Central London for study. A couple in Latin he tackled himself. Still others were in French and old English. Those he put aside for now since they were likely more recent. There were around fifty volumes total, of various sizes and thicknesses, tucked safely into the shelf behind the counter.

The one book that Edward treated differently was the one he'd examined more closely at his flat – the one in Latin that was about the Battle of Badon. This one could be unique – a critically important manuscript any major museum would pay big money to own. If this book confirmed the existence of King Arthur and his band of knights, it could be a rare prize.

The Russells agreed to keep the Badon book in a safety deposit box at the bank just around the corner. The plan was that Edward could pick the volume up whenever he had a free moment, study it, then take it back for safekeeping. Eventually they might turn it over to experts at Oxford University, where scholars could translate, study and authenticate it. But that couldn't happen right now. Revealing the existence of a fifteen-hundred-year-old book would raise all sorts of questions as to its provenance. Thomas, Belinda and Edward weren't telling anyone about the crypt. So into the bank vault it went. And there it would stay for years, ignored and eventually forgotten.

CHAPTER TWENTY-TWO

By mid-2008 Edward had moved in with his grandparents and was running the bookshop. He was a huge help – he fixed every meal, prepared afternoon tea, ensured they had their cocktails every evening promptly at seven and provided much-needed company for the elderly couple. Edward was their succession plan and they were thrilled at his willingness to assume that responsibility.

Eagerly learning about the many strange things they offered for sale, Edward soon was assisting the unusual customers who traipsed through The Necromancer's Bookshop, buying ingredients for potions, spells and charms. He was eccentric and strange, and he fit in perfectly. He sold capes, wands and ancient books of magic. He used the Russells' extensive Rolodex of connections to locate anything and everything customers needed for their often-bizarre rituals and ceremonies. It was amazing to him that there were so many of these people – witches and warlocks, magicians and conjurers – in a civilized, twenty-first-century metropolis like London. As he visited with customers, he learned more and more about the dark arts these individuals practiced.

Edward couldn't have come at a better time – shortly after he arrived, the Russells' health began to rapidly deteriorate. Belinda often told Edward how fortunate they were that he had come to live with them; within just a few weeks after he left university, they just didn't have the stamina to get out and do the things they'd done before. Thomas knew his decline began the day he fell into the chamber, but now Belinda wasn't feeling well either. They were lethargic much of the time. They struggled to get to the shop with Edward, and many mornings, too weary to get out of bed, they sent him off alone.

Edward got their assent to hire an assistant – a man his age with whom he'd become friends at the university. That allowed Edward more freedom to run home during the day and take care of his grandparents. He was a caring, giving man. He fluffed pillows, opened drapes to allow sunlight into their room, cleaned house and brought their meals in bed. What a blessing, they said often to each other. And they thanked him too. He pooh-poohed their gratitude. "You'd do the same for me," he'd respond.

At home one day Thomas and Belinda had the conversation they'd put off for a long time. At dinner that evening they told their grandson they were considering moving to the coast of Portugal, to a place where some expatriate friends were living out their golden years. It would be a good climate and perhaps would give their failing health a boost. They closed the shop for a week and the three of them made a trip to see the facility. The place was idyllic – the weather and scenery were beautiful, and the Russells had accumulated sufficient funds to buy a home and live comfortably. That trip was very difficult for the older Russells, but Edward had been a prince to help in every way possible. They were hoping Portugal might be the ticket to recovery.

A month after their return, they made Edward an offer he enthusiastically accepted. A deal was struck, giving their grandson the store and the building for a million dollars – a fraction of its value. With his significant assets Edward could have paid cash, but his grandparents wanted a monthly income for their retirement. Edward's payments would cover their needs and provide a cushion for extras they might want.

Their own wealth would remain available in case of a crisis. They made an initial deposit on the Portuguese property and began packing.

Two months later the move to Portugal was ten days away. But by now Thomas and Belinda were not well at all. They could hardly walk and both had spent the last week in bed.

"I don't think it's wise for you to go," Edward said gently one evening as he helped his grandmother drink her tea. Most days her hands shook uncontrollably, and right now it was worse than usual. "The facility in Portugal isn't set up for assisted living and you're better off here with me."

"You're a wonderful grandson," Thomas responded, tears flowing down his face. "I don't understand what's happening to us, but we're blessed to have you in our lives. This is a hell of a way to live, but I agree with you. I don't think I'm up to going, Belinda. I think we'd better stay put."

The thing that kept the old couple's spirits high was talking about the crypt each evening. Thomas and Belinda loved to hear Edward spin tales of Arthur, Guinevere and the Knights of the Round Table. He enthralled them with vivid theories of what they might find behind the ancient wooden door and just who might lie in the sarcophagus. This time the three of them spent together kept the old couple going. But the day came when that wasn't enough.

Edward was at the store one afternoon when he got a call from a sobbing Belinda. "He's gone, Edward. Please come. Now."

Thomas had died peacefully. Edward had left them both in bed after serving them breakfast. They'd been watching the news, she told him, when she noticed Thomas's head was lolling forward. She'd tried to fluff his pillow, but when she touched his clammy skin, she knew it was over. This man she'd known and loved for decades was gone.

Just two weeks later Belinda died. With Thomas gone, her health, will to live and strength just faded away.

They were buried together without fanfare. There was no autopsy, no eulogy, no funeral, no weeping. Two elderly people succumbed to old age. It happened every day.

That was fun.

Stop saying that.

Edward became the sole heir and executor of the estates of both his grandparents. There was no need now for a buy-sell agreement on the bookshop. It belonged to him lock, stock and barrel – the building, the assortment of bizarre books, magician's supplies, chants for raising the dead, potions, and a thousand other mysterious things stuck on one shelf or another, in this drawer or that. And, of course, those things down below were now his too.

CHAPTER TWENTY-THREE

Twelve months after the deaths of his grandparents, things were much different in the life of Edward Russell. Everything was going very, very well.

First, there was the incredible spike in sales at The Necromancer's Bookshop. Although there were more walk-in customers than before, that wasn't where the real activity was. Today thousands dealt with the occult bookstore via the Internet or by mail. Early on, Edward and his assistant Alexander Whitwell had created a website and begun advertising; the immediate surge in sales was surprising. Obviously a lot of people around the world had a burning interest in the dark arts, and there weren't many stores online that catered to their bizarre needs. But The Necromancer's Bookshop did. Within months there were three employees. His assistant Alex, the friend from university who was also a computer whiz, was handling a million dollars a month in Internet sales. A young man spent the day packing and shipping orders. Edward and a female college student who worked part time handled over-the-counter sales with help from the others when things got busy.

He'd learned a great deal from the books they'd found in the chamber. The eccentric bookseller's nonexistent social life meant plenty of extra time to work on the ancient volumes. Most appeared to have been written between the fourth and sixth centuries AD. So far he didn't know who wrote them, but the books could be extremely rare examples of writings from Roman Britain.

Edward turned some of the Welsh volumes over to his university professors for examination. He told them he'd bought a collection and these were part of it. The books were a hodgepodge of poetry, novellas, plays – the kind of thing Elizabethan Britons had turned out in droves, only these were written a thousand years earlier. They were valuable not for content but because of their age, the educators said. They estimated each book would sell for several thousand dollars.

All that was interesting, but he didn't have the answers he really wanted. He still had no idea how or why the books had ended up in the crypt of St. Mary Axe.

The sarcophagus and the massive wooden door remained the enigmas they'd been for two years. Edward couldn't risk the public finding out the secret of the subterranean room. He kept the basement door locked; he alone went downstairs, where the ladder was still stuck through the hole in the floor. He frequently spent hours in the crypt, going over every surface to see if there was anything else to be discovered. So far he'd come up empty-handed.

Edward decided to tackle one puzzle at a time. The heavy wooden door would have to wait – he didn't have a plan to open it. The sarcophagus would be first. Online he learned how to construct a system strong enough to raise an automobile engine. He hoped it would lift the lid. One Saturday morning he went to a do-it-yourself hardware store and bought all the parts he'd need – lumber, pulleys, a winch, nylon rope and chain. After the shop closed at noon and everyone went home, he dragged his purchases into the crypt. There everything sat for months until he found someone to help him.

At last he couldn't wait any longer to find out what was inside the coffin. He began to develop a plan involving neither publicity nor the authorities. This wouldn't be easy to figure out, but he had to do it.

Fortified by a couple pints of ale one Saturday afternoon, he sat alone as usual at his pub and finalized his plan. He needed one more person. The most trustworthy, logical choice was Alex – his friend from university who'd become his first employee. But Edward relied on Alex for so much at the shop – the computer guru was virtually indispensable – that he couldn't be the one to help find out what was in the chamber. Edward couldn't do without him. Whoever helped Edward would have to be dispensable. That was the simple fact and that was part of the plan.

So Edward called his young shipping boy. He was strong and smart – Edward would need that – and they agreed to meet at the shop Sunday morning for a special project.

"Don't say anything to anyone about where you're going or what you're doing," he admonished his young employee. "You'll find out why this needs to be secret when we meet. Trust me – you're not going to believe what you see!"

At ten a.m. they sat at the table in the back room of the bookstore, the locked basement door five feet across the room. Edward explained that he must swear his employee to secrecy.

"Did you tell anyone you were coming here this morning?"

The young man answered excitedly, "No! I did exactly as you asked! What are we going to do?"

There could never be a disclosure to anyone about the things he would see or hear today, Edward explained. The man eagerly agreed, his mind racing in anticipation. Edward revealed that there were some very unusual things he'd discovered in a crypt downstairs. They descended the ladder and ended up in the ancient room.

Edward's employee was fascinated with the sarcophagus. "My God, this is absolutely incredible! What do you think this is? Norman? Saxon? And how old can it be? This is crazy!"

"It is incredible, the coffin of a Briton, I think. It probably dates from the Middle Ages. But as I said, this is a secret. Do you understand?"

"Oh yeah, I understand!" Positively exuberant, the young man turned to look at the old wooden door. "This looks like the entrance of an old castle! What's behind it?"

"I have no idea. That's not what we're working on today." Edward's voice was quiet and calm. He was strangely saddened at how excited the boy was. Mystery, intrigue, the thrill of the unknown – all those things worked against this man whose help Edward needed. There was no way he could keep this information quiet. All along Edward planned to deal with the young man once he no longer needed his help. But part of him hoped it might be avoided. The boy was a great clerk in the store and he'd be missed. But it couldn't be helped, especially now.

Using the extensive collection of tools that Edward's grandfather, Thomas, had kept in the basement, the men built the winch system within two hours. The boy crawled up on top of the sarcophagus and found only an inch of clearance at the back of the stone lid. It might be enough to insert a hook. If they could, the lid could be slowly winched up and slid away from the back wall. Then it could be hoisted up and off.

Around one Edward asked the boy if he wanted to stop for lunch.

"No way! Let's get this lid off!"

That was the enthusiastic answer Edward had expected. Within thirty minutes everything was ready. Edward stood next to the sarcophagus to keep an eye on the back side where the hook was affixed to a chain running to the pulley overhead. As the young man turned a wheel, the chain became taut, then groaned against the weight of the lid.

"Is it moving?" he asked Edward.

"Not yet. Be very careful but give it a little more pressure."

An additional half-turn was enough to raise a few puffs of dust from the coffin. Now the back side of the lid was slightly elevated so that the entire slab was tilted up in the back and downward on the front side where Edward stood.

"It moved a little!" Edward cried.

The eager boy mistook Edward's excited comment as tacit approval for another turn of the winch. A second later Edward yelled as the raised lid slid off the coffin toward him. He jumped back just in time to avoid being crushed as it hit the floor.

"What the hell!" Edward tripped and fell sideways as the heavy lid broke into a dozen pieces six inches from his legs.

The boy rushed over to where Edward lay. "Oh God, Mr. Russell! I'm sorry! Are you all right?"

"I'm fine. What in hell caused you to keep moving the lid?"

"I thought you wanted it raised. I thought you were telling me to winch it up. I'm so sorry! My God, I've broken it. Look what I've done!"

Thick clouds of dust from the shattered stone lid filled the room. It was getting difficult to see or breathe.

"Let's get out of here until things settle down!" Edward groped his way to the ladder and the boy followed. Reaching the basement, he pulled the rug over the hole so dust wouldn't permeate the room above. They went upstairs and sat at the same table in the back of his bookshop.

The boy was equally apologetic and exuberant. "This is so exciting! I'm so sorry I broke the lid, but now I can't wait to see what we find inside that coffin!"

Edward brewed tea at the counter. He brought it to the table and said, "It is amazing, isn't it? I couldn't have done it without you and breaking the lid was most likely the only way we could have accomplished it. Don't give it a thought. It won't be long before I ... before *we* ... see what's there."

"Shall we run out and grab a bite of lunch while we wait for the dust to settle?" the boy suggested.

"Let's have our tea and calm down," Edward replied quietly. "First things first."

That was fun!

Thirty minutes later Edward again went to the basement, pulled back the rug and saw that the dust had settled. Tugging and shoving, he maneuvered the young clerk's body to the crypt and into another of the construction bags he'd bought. Soon the bag rested under the floor stones next to Curtis Pemberly.

That task complete, Edward stepped over and around the broken lid littering the floor and looked into the ancient coffin. Although he didn't know it then, his were the first eyes to see its contents in a thousand years.

On Monday morning the members of his team at The Necromancer's Bookshop would ask what happened to their young shipping clerk. He didn't seem like the flighty type, but he hadn't called and hadn't shown up for work. None of them knew much about his personal life, so they wrote his abrupt departure off as the stupid actions of a kid who must not have cared much about his job.

Edward's employees worked every day in the bookshop totally unaware that the boy was nearby – just below them, in fact.

CHAPTER TWENTY-FOUR

Edward stood speechless in the crypt, transfixed at what lay in the sarcophagus. He had been half expecting a body covered with a funeral shroud, perhaps holding a cross or other memento from his past. But this took his breath away.

Lying in the coffin was the body of a man maybe six feet tall, dressed head to toe in battle gear. Not an inch of skin was visible. His face was shielded by what looked like a bronze helmet and faceplate. One of his arms was tucked underneath a heavy shield that reached from his neck to his knees; the other, sheathed in a thick glove, grasped a massive sword with a golden handle. It was two feet long, its inscribed blade slightly rusted but not as much as Edward would have expected after all these years. The tightly fitting stone lid had done a good job keeping out the elements.

The figure had impressive, well-preserved leather boots that reached halfway up his calves. Extending from underneath the shield down to his knees was a garment made of interlocking metal rings. It was a coat of mail, used defensively to protect a soldier in battle. He would wear it like an overcoat. Edward had seen some displayed at the British Museum. In fact, there had been a life-sized, fully battle-ready medieval knight. The body before him could have been its twin.

This all was amazing, unbelievable, and of such significance it would make news worldwide. Part of his brain told him to report it to the authorities. That part wanted the fame and publicity that would inevitably accompany the things in the crypt. But the realistic, pragmatic part of his psyche said no. Anyone examining things in detail would scour the entire room to see what else might turn up. An examination of the floor might reveal the other bodies.

Someday he'd contact the archaeologists. There would have to be some housecleaning before that would happen.

So for now the entire thing – the chamber, the knight, the books, the still-locked door – everything would remain a secret.

Edward went out and bought a large sheet of Visqueen. He stretched it tightly over the sarcophagus as best he could. Hopefully it'd keep the body from further decay in the damp air of the basement. He needed time to figure out what he'd do next with this amazing find. Just before sealing up the warrior with the plastic sheet, he'd done one thing to satisfy his immediate curiosity. He reached inside the coffin and used a cloth to wipe down the blade of the man's sword. He wanted to see if he could make out the inscription. It was faint and the puny string of lights hardly helped. He snapped several pictures so he could examine the writing later. All done, he turned away, then jerked his head back again. There was something else – something etched into the handle he'd almost missed. One discernible word.

Lamorak.

Is that a name?

Is that your name, Sir Knight? Lamorak? It would be incredible to have a medieval knight in the basement, holding a sword that bears his name.

Will your sword tell me who you are?

Edward had spent years preparing for degrees in medieval history and literature. Somewhere in the past he'd come across that odd word, but he couldn't recall where. One web search later, it all came back to him. According to

Arthurian legend, Lamorak was a Knight of the Round Table. A lesser-known one, his name was among twenty-five that appear on a huge round table that today hangs in Winchester Castle. Those who believed Arthur lived said the table dated to the legendary king's reign in the fifth century. Most modern scholars disagreed – they thought it was made in the 1300s. Medieval festivities called *Round Tables* were frequently held to imitate the feasts and jousts of the famous knights of yore. Many historians thought this table was created for one of those.

Lamorak was a prince, the son of a medieval king named Pellinore and brother of Sir Percival, both of whom also were Knights of the Round Table. According to legend, Lamorak was one of the bravest and strongest of Arthur's band and the best at jousting. He had a notable weakness – he enjoyed beautiful women who were married to someone else.

That evening Edward stood in front of the sarcophagus. The yellow lights overhead cast an eerie shadow across the body. For over an hour he neither spoke nor moved. He contemplated what had happened. This discovery was one of the most historically significant events in Britain in two thousand years. If it were truly Lamorak. And if he chose to ever reveal it to the public.

CHAPTER TWENTY-FIVE

Edward glanced up as a smartly dressed man in his thirties snaked through a throng of customers, walked to the counter and said, "Good morning. May I speak with Edward Russell, please?" The man spoke excellent English with a hint of an accent.

"That would be me. How may I help you?" This wasn't his typical customer. With his three-piece suit and fancy silk tie, this man looked more like a businessman than a magician. What was he doing here?

He offered a business card. "My name is Philippe Lepescu. My firm represents a client who is interested in the possible purchase of your building."

Edward looked at the business card and saw the name Ciprian Investments with an address in Lucerne, Switzerland. Philippe Lepescu was the company's president. Recalling Gordon Foxworth's futile attempt to scam his grandparents by offering to purchase the place, he wondered if this visit was connected. He smiled.

"Did I say something amusing?"

"Sorry. Yours isn't the first offer I've had and I was just recalling the last one. The building isn't for sale." Even if he were interested, Edward couldn't sell. He'd be asking for a prison cell since he knew where the bodies were buried, literally.

"I appreciate your interest, but I'm afraid if this was the sole purpose of your trip to London, you've made a journey for nothing."

"My late father once said everything has a price. Everything."

Edward wondered what this was all about.

"I'm sure your father was a wise man, but I really have no interest in selling. I have a thriving business here and the charm of this ancient street adds a lot to my particular niche of retailing. I've been told a real estate transaction requires a motivated buyer and a motivated seller. Sadly, I'm not the least bit motivated. All that said, I'd be curious to know why your client's interested in this particular property and why he'd send a representative all the way from Switzerland to approach me about it."

"I'd be happy to explain everything. I can see how busy you are at the moment. Perhaps I could buy you a drink later?"

They agreed to meet at Philippe Lepescu's hotel, The Stafford, in a fashionable area of west London near Piccadilly. At seven they were comfortably settled into a booth at the hotel's American Bar, a small, interesting place with knickknacks and memorabilia hanging from the walls and ceiling. The waiter brought a gin and tonic for Edward and a dry martini for Philippe. After a toast and a drink, Lepescu began talking.

"Our firm is solely owned by my partner. One of his trusts is the client who's interested in your building. My partner's a wealthy man with investments around the world. He owns a few corporations whose names the public would recognize, but most of his assets are in real estate, oil and gas, and the mining of precious metals. He also has a passion for ancient things. He has a very extensive private collection of artifacts from around the world."

Lepescu paused to take a sip and then continued.

"You mentioned the charm and medieval nature of the two blocks that comprise St. Mary Axe Street. Those very things are what interests my partner as well. We see a tremendous opportunity for the real estate in your area. We envision a boutique hotel, a pub, more shops like yours – in short, we want to develop St. Mary Axe into a mini-destination within the City of London. It could become a step back in time to the Middle Ages, right here in the hustle and bustle of one of the world's great cities. Our company currently holds an option on the vacant building next to yours, and I'm hoping I can convince you to consider an offer."

Edward listened closely, satisfied this new offer had nothing to do with the shady Gordon Foxworth. What Lepescu was saying made sense on the surface, but they didn't have a clue what *really* ancient things lay beneath his particular parcel of real estate. The crypt and its sarcophagus would put this period theme idea over the top. It would be incredibly interesting to a developer. Despite the problems inherent in ever selling the property, Edward wanted to hear more.

"Why would you divulge your plan to me? Don't you think that would make me raise my price, especially when you've told me you want to buy up the entire two blocks? Why wouldn't I hold out until the end, presuming I was ever willing to sell. Which I've already said I'm not."

"An excellent question. The particular trust that's interested in the St. Mary Axe properties is one of the wealthiest private institutions in Europe. I hesitate to use the cliché 'money's no object,' but in this case, I'm authorized to pay far more than what the property would otherwise be worth in order to achieve its goals."

"What's the name of this partner of yours? Have I heard of him?"

"His name is Roberto Maas and he's the chairman. I seriously doubt you've heard of him – he maintains a low profile, as do many people in his position. He's originally from Luxembourg and now lives part of the time in Lucerne." Edward had never heard the name.

Edward was an intelligent individual – he was a PhD times three, after all. He took a moment to think. With a little advance notice, the bodies could be dealt with. Moving them would be difficult but not impossible. What was wrong with hearing this man's offer?

"What's your price?"

"May I assume then that you're interested?"

"No," Edward responded with a slight smile as he stroked his scraggly beard. "But you may assume I'm listening."

CHAPTER TWENTY-SIX

Roberto listened with interest as Philippe explained what had happened in London. The quirky Edward Russell apparently wasn't motivated to sell, but Philippe's initial offer of five million dollars had gotten his attention. It might ultimately require even more money, Philippe surmised.

One thing had to happen next. Before anything else, Roberto had to be certain this was the right bookstore. If it were, he'd pay whatever it took to buy the property.

Over the years Roberto had spent tens of millions acquiring ancient things, the more unique and rare, the better. He'd learned about the bookstore in St. Mary Axe from Curtis Pemberly, a man he'd never met who vaguely described the location, but that had been enough. Cleverly attempting to conceal its location, Curtis bragged that he knew about an occult bookstore. It was on an ancient street in London, and down below were a medieval sarcophagus and a heavy, locked wooden door from the Middle Ages. He wouldn't say how he'd gotten Juan Carlos's number, but Roberto assumed it came from the recently deceased Gordon Foxworth.

He tried to call Curtis Pemberly back, but there was no answer. After a few days Roberto gave up. It was strange the man who'd seemed so interested in speaking further suddenly was unavailable.

Thanks to the Internet, Roberto quickly learned there were only a few occult shops in London. Most were in the posh West End on major avenues; another catered to tourists and was smack in the middle of one of London's busiest places – Trafalgar Square. The Necromancer's Bookshop was the only one in a quaint sixteenth-century street called St. Mary Axe in the old City of London. Bingo.

Sight unseen, Roberto paid two thousand dollars for a six-month option on the empty building next to the bookshop. The absentee owner jumped at the chance for income from the decrepit structure that hadn't had a tenant in ten years. He hoped against hope this Swiss real estate person, whoever he was, would come through after the option period ended and buy the damned thing. When he'd spoken with Roberto Maas by phone, it seemed all the man wanted to know was how large the building was – how many floors, did it have a basement, all that. When Roberto learned it was about four thousand square feet total, three floors aboveground and an old basement that was musty and damp, for some reason he was still interested.

"The building … uh, well, it would be fair to say it needs a lot of work." The owner tried to be honest without scaring off the prospect. And Roberto Maas apparently wasn't scared. He offered an option – two thousand dollars to tie up the property for six months – sufficient time for Maas, a busy real estate investor, to send his people over to evaluate the site. That was Maas's story, and the owner accepted it without question, thanking his lucky stars there was a glimmer of interest from someone. The building had been for sale for years; taking it off the market for six months was no problem. Papers were signed, money transferred, and a key mailed to Lucerne.

Roberto's first move was hiring a locksmith to rekey the doors. It would have been a problem if the owner casually dropped by one day to check the premises. There would be questions about all the activity in the basement that would begin soon. The six-month option period gave

Roberto plenty of time to finish his work and put things back like they were today. Or to buy the building if he hit pay dirt.

In the meantime we'll see how things go with my new next-door neighbor, one Edward Russell. Hopefully he'll be reasonable. If not, maybe Juan Carlos will have to pay him a visit.

CHAPTER TWENTY-SEVEN

"Good morning, Mr. Russell."

As he turned to see who was behind him, Edward shuddered involuntarily.

Inspector Dalton laughed. "I usually don't have that effect on good people! Only the bad ones tremble when they see me coming!"

Edward tried to appear nonchalant. "Oh. Oh, I'm sorry. You startled me, that's all. What are you doing here? I mean … why did you come to the store?" He stumbled on his words.

The policeman's demeanor changed from frivolity to concern. "Are you all right? I really didn't mean to alarm you. I just thought I'd come by and see how things are going. I was wondering what you've decided about the secrets in the basement."

"The secrets?" Edward blanched and stuttered.

"My God, man. You look like you've seen a ghost! Do you need to sit down?"

"Perhaps a glass of water. Give me a moment." Edward walked behind the counter, through the curtain into the back room and composed himself. He knew what the officer was referring to and had jumped to the wrong conclusion. *That was a mistake, acting like that right in front of the policeman.*

"My apologies, Inspector. My mind was a million miles away and I was surprised, that's all. The things in the basement. I really haven't done anything. There's been no time for much research …"

"So you're following your grandparents' decision not to inform the antiquities people?"

"Yes, at least for now. You can see how busy we are." Edward waved a hand around the store. "Between walk-in customers and the Internet, we're up to our eyeballs in work. I won't disrupt the business with a lot of interference from outsiders right now. Perhaps later."

"Understandable. Well, I'll leave that to you, then. It's not my call to make although I do think the things in the crypt would make interesting research, don't you? Speaking of which, if you have a moment, would you mind if I took another look down there? That old sarcophagus fascinates me."

Edward's Adam's apple bobbed up and down as he swallowed. "Well, I appreciate your interest …"

The front doorbell tinkled and another three people walked in. His female assistant waved at him from across the room where she was assisting two men. "Can you help those customers?" she mouthed.

Saved by the bell.

"I'm afraid I don't have the time, Inspector. I do appreciate your interest. At some point we'll try to make it happen."

"If it would help, I could just pop down myself …"

Edward answered more quickly than he'd wished. "No! That won't help. Not today!"

"I see. No problem at all. Thanks for your time and good luck with your shop, although it doesn't look as though you need luck!" The inspector turned and left. Edward breathed a sigh of relief as he approached the customers who needed assistance.

Amazing how jittery Edward was. I suppose he's got a lot on his plate now that nice old couple has passed on and left the store to him. But it feels like he's hiding something.

All three of them certainly were protective of that crypt. I wonder. I just wonder if they found something.

At his desk in Scotland Yard the policeman soon forgot about Edward Russell. There were cases to investigate, people to interview. He had more to do than wonder about what was going on at the bookshop. But there was still that little something in the back of his mind.

CHAPTER TWENTY-EIGHT

Ten days after his visit, Philippe called Edward Russell.

"I'm just following up on the offer I made when you and I met. I wondered if you'd had time to make a decision."

Edward had enjoyed Philippe's company, but this time he didn't mince words. "I'm not interested in selling. Your offer was generous, but as I told you when we met, I'm not motivated to sell. Quite the opposite, in fact. For my business, this old building in this particular street is absolutely perfect. To be frank, your group might come in, buy the two blocks, and spiff the place up with new façades, hotels, pubs and the like, but selfishly I'd like my occult bookshop to look exactly as it does today – like part of a film set. And it does, I think you'd agree."

Lepescu responded cordially. "It certainly does, and I understand your thinking. Regardless, we're going to continue working on a plan to revitalize St. Mary Axe. I hope you'll allow me to stay in touch."

"Certainly. I just don't want to lead you on. If you buy the entire area, you may find The Necromancer's Bookshop the last thorn in your flesh."

"Understood. Thanks for your time."

When the call was finished, Philippe looked across the office, where Roberto had listened in on the conversation.

"I'd say he truly isn't interested. And for a valid reason."

"I'm not so sure. Even someone with valid reasons wouldn't summarily dismiss a ridiculously high offer. It might not come along again. I wonder …" Roberto stopped short. He hadn't told Philippe anything about the phone calls from Gordon Foxworth or Curtis Pemberly. Lepescu incorrectly believed his partner truly was planning a redevelopment project for the St. Mary Axe area, a real estate plan that could generate a massive profit once it was finished. He had no idea this entire exercise was a personal matter. He didn't know his partner was chasing a rumor of ancient things in a crypt that might not even exist.

Like every other man, Edward Russell had both a price and a place one could apply pressure. Roberto first had to find out if Curtis Pemberly's information was accurate. If there really was an old crypt below Edward's store, Roberto Maas wanted to see it. Then he'd decide how to handle the bookstore's owner. Edward would eventually give in. It might take money; then again it might take pressure. Every man had something to hide. Roberto was very good at finding out secrets.

A few days later Roberto told his partner he was taking a couple of weeks off, heading to the Greek Isles for a cruise on a private yacht he'd chartered. Lepescu was highly capable of managing things and Roberto was a mere phone call or text message away should something come up.

The day of his departure Roberto flew west, not east. Instead of Swissair to Athens, he flew British Airways to London, eagerly anticipating the work ahead of him. He'd spent much of his life as a paid operative for shadow groups within or without governments. More recently he'd been a businessman and investor. But this trip held the first tangible excitement he'd felt in years. It was an expedition, a treasure hunt. Roberto was looking forward to this exercise more than anything he could remember.

He checked in at The Liverpool, a new five-star hotel less than a quarter mile from St. Mary Axe. That afternoon he strolled down Bishopsgate, pulling a rolling suitcase, and turned into a narrow block-long lane called St. Helens. He looked at a map then kept walking. The street dead-ended at an old church, devoid of people but with doors wide open. He exited out a back door, walked through its graveyard and a rusty iron gate that led into St. Mary Axe Street.

The Necromancer's Bookshop was the busiest of maybe a dozen shops situated there. He joined strolling tourists who were experiencing a brief trip back in time to the Middle Ages along this charming, slightly shabby street. Roberto passed the bookstore and glanced inside. The shop was full of customers. He didn't see Edward; although he hadn't met him, Philippe had described the forty-something man with an odd stringy gray beard. Like Gandalf the Great, he'd said.

Pausing in front of the abandoned, dirty building that was his for the next six months, Roberto looked first one way, then the other. No one paid him the slightest attention. He unlocked the door, quickly stepped inside and closed it. Rays of sunlight here and there pierced dirty, cracked windows. Dust an inch thick covered everything. Broken pieces of discarded furniture – old desks and chairs left by the last tenant – lay in disarray here and there.

In the back he took rickety stairs to the dark basement. He opened the suitcase and pulled out a bright lantern. He donned a jumpsuit over his street clothes and put on a headlamp. Next came an entrenching tool – a handy combination shovel and pickaxe. Roberto began to examine the floor stones at the south end of the basement. Finding one that was somewhat smaller than the others and therefore lighter in weight, he dug around it. It loosened easily and soon the stone was ready to remove. Roberto took out a contraption consisting of four hooks connected to one strong wire. He worked his hands down around the stone, inserted a hook beneath each of its four sides and began to pull the wire straight up.

Although it was heavy, the stone moved almost immediately. Several strong tugs later it was out. Only a hole full of dirt remained.

Now came the reason Roberto had paid two thousand pounds for an option on the building. If he were correct, his gamble would pay off. If he wasn't, he'd have wasted a little money and time.

He pulled a hammer and a two-foot piece of rebar a half inch in diameter out of the bag. He put the bar in the hole where the stone had been, held it upright and hit it hard with the hammer. The dirt was compact but gave way an inch or so as the rod went into it. Roberto gave it another solid whack, then one more. Suddenly it slid through the dirt and disappeared. He heard a muffled clang somewhere below.

Roberto smiled. There was a hollow place below the basement floor.

Late in the day, his phone dinged an alarm. He'd set it for five p.m., and the hours had flown by. It was time to go; it would be dark soon and he didn't want to call attention to himself or the building by leaving in the night like a burglar.

A lot had been accomplished. He had removed five stones total; it was difficult, laborious work, but he loved it. He could literally feel anticipation in the air. The damp old basement, the ancient rock floor – he was close to the exciting next step.

Roberto left the suitcase and its contents in the basement with his jumpsuit and walked to the front door. He opened it, glanced both ways and saw no one. He stepped out to the sidewalk and locked the door. As he walked in front of the bookshop, its door suddenly opened and a thin man with a gray beard emerged, ready to lock up. They were the only two people on this block, and there was no avoiding contact.

"Good evening," Roberto said casually.

"And to you. Were you coming to the store? I could stay open …"

"Oh no, thanks. I'm just taking a walk and looking at the neighborhood. I'm staying in a hotel nearby and I've heard about this old part of London. It's fascinating. So's your store, for that matter."

Edward tugged at his beard as he talked. "There's a lot of strange stuff in there and just as many odd customers to go with it! Stop by sometime if you're back in the area. You might find a potion or two that you could use."

Roberto laughed and began walking away. "Have a good evening."

He couldn't go back the way he came because he figured the little church would be closed by now. He walked up St. Mary Axe to the busy Houndsditch Street, turned left and then right onto Bishopsgate. A block from his hotel, his senses went on alert. Something wasn't right. He walked right past The Liverpool Hotel and went another block, turning at the corner into a shadowed alley. He stepped into the darkness and watched.

In a moment he saw someone stop and look down the alley. Seeing nothing, the person walked away.

The man's profile was silhouetted against daylight from the street. Roberto knew who'd been following him – there was no mistaking that scraggly beard.

CHAPTER TWENTY-NINE

Edward's initial annoyance at seeing Inspector Dalton come into the shop disappeared as quickly as it had arisen. The officer was pulling one of those portable sets of wheels with a square box on it. Edward knew immediately what it was – the last of the seven metal boxes from the basement – the one Gordon Foxworth had stolen when he broke into the shop. Things had gotten so hectic he'd forgotten about it.

Dalton had obviously forgotten too. "Sorry to be so long returning this. Forgive me, but it completely slipped my mind. I should have gotten it back once Foxworth's body turned up, but instead it's just been sitting in our evidence room."

"No harm done. Is this one full of books like the others were?"

"It is. I glanced inside this morning when the custodian brought it to my office. More of the same thing, I'd guess. Have you learned anything interesting from the other books?"

Edward shook his head. "There are over forty, as you know. I've cataloged them by name, language and anything else I could easily ascertain, but I haven't really gotten into any of them. It's been a little crazy around here. I just haven't had the time."

"Good thing you have help," the inspector replied, gesturing to the young woman who was arranging items on a shelf. "Speaking of which, this looks like a rare slow moment for you. How about that quick look at the chamber?"

This time Edward was ready for him.

"The floor in the basement's beginning to give way in several places. It's not safe in the crypt anymore – or the basement either, for that matter. I've closed it all off until I can get repairs done. Once it's fixed, I'll give you a ring."

The inspector wasn't surprised at again being denied access. "I understand. I'll look forward to your call when it's all worked out."

Once the shop closed, Edward removed eight books from the old metal box. This one held more volumes than the others because three of these books were very small, only slightly larger than a current paperback novel. Each had less than a hundred vellum pages and was bound in leather as most of the others had been. Etched into the leather cover on each were the initials G.P.

He flipped through one of them. It was obvious what it was, even though the words were in Welsh, a language with which he wasn't terribly familiar.

Its entries were clearly laid out in the form of a diary. It was a daily journal written by someone whose initials likely were G.P.

And it was very, very old. The date on the first page was easy to decipher.

14 Ebrill 497.

April 14th in the year of our Lord 497.

CHAPTER THIRTY

The diaries turned out to be the most important things of all.

Edward hadn't planned to spend much time on those three little books. He doubted they were any more significant than the other ones they'd found. Less, most likely. The others could be valuable – they merited further attention. The daily ramblings of G.P., whoever that was, could wait.

Edward was becoming overwhelmed. He had a locked door to open. He had the book he'd examined earlier – the one about Arthur and the Battle of Badon that might help prove the mythical king's existence. There were fifty other ancient books that needed attention. He had a body in a sarcophagus. He had more mysteries to solve than one man could handle.

He could use some help, but the crypt held too many secrets. What he did have plenty of was time, as long as he could keep Inspector Dalton and the antiquities authorities at bay. And he could. His bookshop was private property. Maybe in medieval times the police could have forced their way in. But not today. In modern England the law respected a man's right to privacy and ownership.

He prioritized his tasks. First he should deal with the body.

But something in his head kept steering him back to the diaries. A thought kept popping up. What if the diaries belonged to someone significant? What would it hurt to take an hour and find out? That night he settled in at his flat and opened each of the three small books, looking at the first date entry until he found the earliest. The first book was the one he'd looked at a few days back, the one that began in 497.

The moment he began laboriously translating the first journal, he became captivated. As he learned its incredible significance, he could think of nothing else all day long. He rushed home every evening and spent hours with the book. Soon he knew this trio of journals was the epitome of everything that they'd found in the crypt.

The diary was the secret journal of a girl whose name was Gwenhwyfar. Although it wasn't mentioned, he immediately knew her last name too. He knew what the "P" in the initials "G.P." etched into the cover stood for. The realization of whose diary he held made the hair on his arms stand up. It made him shudder as he considered whose hand had written these entries.

Her last name was Pendragon. Gwenhwyfar Pendragon.

Her name in English was more recognizable.

Guinevere.

Guinevere, the wife of Arthur Pendragon, a mythical figure whom legend said was King of the Britons fifteen hundred years ago, a man whose existence had never been proven.

Edward was holding Queen Guinevere's handwritten diary. Suddenly the other book he'd seen, the one that was a supposed eyewitness account of Arthur's battle, became very important. It spoke of the legendary King as well. Could it be that everything in this crypt, everything from the ancient Church of St. Mary Axe, was related to King Arthur in some way?

He could barely contain his excitement as he worked his way through the diary, spending hours translating page after page. Guinevere was faithful at keeping her journal, but the same couldn't be said for her marriage. Mundane events of the day were recorded along with the thoughts and deeds of a devious, sneaky, crafty, beautiful and powerful twenty-three-year-old girl who loved sex and danger. She loved King Arthur too – that was evident throughout the book. But she strayed from the marriage bed as often as she thought she could get away with it.

"Either she didn't get enough at home or she needed way more than a normal woman." Edward chuckled as he read.

One evening he came to an entry dated the twelfth of October 498. The Queen wrote that she was traveling by convoy to London from her home in Glestingaburg. Edward stopped, astonished at yet another validation of legend. From medieval history classes he knew well that ancient city in western England, which today was called Glastonbury. He also knew the mystery associated with Glestingaburg.

According to legend, Glestingaburg was the mythical island of Avalon. On that island stood Camelot, the castle and home of Arthur and Guinevere and the seat of power for the King of Briton. If it could be proven authentic, the diary Edward Russell held in his hands confirmed that the ancient tale wasn't a legend. Arthur, Merlin, the Round Table knights – they had all existed. This would change history. People had searched in vain for proof for hundreds of years. Edward believed the confirmation lay before him.

He continued the translation.

On October 12 Guinevere had written two pages of thoughts and plans for her upcoming sexual interlude with a dashing knight whose name was … Lamorak.

Lamorak.

Edward began to hyperventilate. The man buried in the sarcophagus below the bookshop held a sword bearing that name. Up to this point Edward had thought Lamorak *might* be the occupant of the stone coffin, but there was no proof. Now the name appeared again – would this diary confirm that one of Arthur's knights was buried downstairs? Would the burial itself be described in Guinevere's diaries?

This information could authenticate a story that had been purely speculation for over a thousand years!

He turned back to the diary, eager to learn more about Lamorak but also pruriently interested in Guinevere's sexual ramblings. Despite their vast age, her words were very erotic. She was extremely detailed about the positions she wanted to try with her new lover, and Edward found himself looking forward very much to the next day's entry. He wanted to hear the rest of the story – to find out how things went. He also saw that he was getting aroused.

It's interesting how stimulating it is to read someone else's secrets, even if they were penned fifteen hundred years ago.

Guinevere had been highly educated and was good at telling a story. Although it took Edward time to translate from Welsh to English, every minute was worth it. Her saucy journal could have made the best-seller list today, a Middle Ages *Lady Chatterly's Lover*. A pornographic look at the life of a monarch in the fifth century. Who'd have thought that would be sensual? But it was.

He turned the page and began to translate the next day's entry. He was ready to undo his pants, release his erection and take care of things while he read the Queen's next steamy words. But he came back down to earth in moments. What he read was the polar opposite of the queen's naughty thoughts yesterday. In places ink had run on the page, blurring a word here and there. He surmised those were the author's tears. Once he finished the second day's entry, Edward knew what Queen Guinevere faced. He knew she had likely sealed both her own fate and that of the monarchy itself. At the bottom of the page, her last three words said it all.

I am afraid.

CHAPTER THIRTY-ONE

Edward read the Queen's account of her trip to London.

On a gorgeous October morning in the year 498, Gwenhwyfar was on her way by carriage from the West Country to London. The hundred-mile journey from Glestingaburg was into its second day, but the young queen's retinues and handmaidens made the trip comfortable. Four brave knights who served as bodyguards, twelve mounted horsemen, servants of various types on horseback, and a wagon filled with provisions and tents accompanied the Queen's carriage. The entourage moved briskly through the countryside.

Last evening and again tonight the men would set up the tents for sleeping and cooking while her ladies-in-waiting bathed her in a stream they invariably camped nearby. Last night after dinner, a perimeter had been established, guards were assigned and people sat by the fire, conversing and enjoying the cool evening breeze.

A troubadour was along to provide entertainment. After dinner he would present elaborate, fantastical stories of magic and mystery, complete with costumes and props. Other nights his bow flew across the strings of a vielle, an instrument similar to a viola, and the group joined in songs. One of the lady's handmaidens sometimes played the lute –

the soft sounds as she plucked its strings were soothing and beautiful. Every day around dusk she entered events and her thoughts in a small, secret book she kept constantly by her side. It was a leather-bound diary with her initials on its cover, a gift from her husband over a year ago.

Wouldn't he be surprised if he read what I've written in this little book he's given me! That was why she kept it secret. Everything … absolutely everything was in there.

The knight Lamorak pulled up alongside her open conveyance and said, "My lady, we are but a few miles from where we will camp this evening. We should be stopping soon, God willing, and be in London late tomorrow."

She smiled and thanked the handsome young man. He gave his horse a flick with the whip and joined his companions bringing up the rear of the caravan. She felt safe and secure with these brave soldiers who had faced battle after battle in service to her husband. They would gladly lay down their own lives to protect her; Arthur knew which of his men were the most trustworthy and had chosen those to make this long trip. At the last minute she had asked him to add Lamorak, mentioning his bravery and her trust in his strength and sense of duty. "I'll sleep better at night knowing he's along," she had told her husband.

Oh yes, I'll sleep better, that's for certain. Or perhaps I won't sleep at all!

She had plans for that one. She smiled as exciting, naughty little thoughts danced through her head. She'd have to be careful. She always was – her husband was no idiot, but so far he hadn't found out. If she were caught, his retribution could cause a faithful knight – a handsome well-endowed young stud – to lose his head. And possibly she'd lose hers too.

The only minor inconvenience was that other knight, the fearless one leading their caravan, steadfastly guiding them toward London. She'd led him to believe he might be the chosen one to share her bed tonight. But she'd had that one already. She wanted something new. She wanted the young knight Lamorak. The lead knight would be furious if he found out. But he wouldn't. She'd be sneaky. She smiled mischievously, imagining the ecstasy she'd experience later this evening. She always loved the first time. Everything was so new, so exciting. She felt herself becoming aroused as she played out scenes in her head. Before dinner tonight, she'd tell her diary the plans she had for Lamorak.

The dashing young man had no idea he was the subject of her next adventure. He'd find out when they stopped for the night. He certainly wasn't her first knight, and so far none had declined Gwenhwyfar's advances. As dangerous as it was, none of the men she had selected in the past ever resisted the beckoning arms of this beautiful young temptress.

After all, would a knight deny the demands of the Queen of Britain?

CHAPTER THIRTY-TWO

Precisely at one a.m. the flap of Gwenhwyfar's tent slipped aside. Her trusted handmaiden Lydia ushered the knight Lamorak into the Queen's makeshift boudoir. As she had done before, the girl would stand guard outside until Gwenhwyfar was finished with her new plaything. Lydia knew what she was doing was wrong, but it was exciting too, being a part of the intrigue – the secret late-night frolics of her lady the Queen.

For half an hour Lydia listened to whispers, laughs, coughs, grunts and groans of ecstasy as the pair jostled around inside the tent. Most of the entourage was asleep; a sentry came around every ten minutes. Each time he passed, he gave her a wink. The Queen's misbehavior was a poorly kept secret, but no one would tell. Her husband would be furious. He'd likely also be heartbroken, the sentry mused. Everyone loved the King, and in turn he loved Gwenhwyfar dearly, or so it appeared to all who served the royals. Mum, therefore, was the word. No one wanted to hurt the King or lose his job – or his life – because of what he had seen late at night.

Lydia stood to stretch her legs. From the muffled sounds, the activity inside was nearing its peak and it wouldn't be much longer now before she could at last go to bed. Suddenly a strong arm wrapped around her neck and a hand clamped over her mouth, stifling her startled scream. She looked into the eyes of the King's most trusted knight and knew things would never be the same again. Not for the King, his Queen, even this knight, who undoubtedly would tell his master what had happened tonight.

The man pushed her away with a whispered admonition to be silent. Fearful for her own life, she crept off to her tent.

The knight threw open the flap roughly. Candles provided dim flickers and outlined the naked bodies of Lamorak and Gwenhwyfar, both of whom were groaning as they simultaneously reached the climactic end of their lovemaking.

Lying on her back, legs spread wide open and Lamorak still inside her, the Queen glanced at the intruder. She finished the heaves of her climax and broke into a naughty smile.

"Well, well," she breathed heavily. "Are you here to join us, Lancelot, my love?"

CHAPTER THIRTY-THREE

13th October in the year of our Lord 498

I have deceived my husband, a man who loves me with all his heart. I am an adulteress, unworthy of the love he has for me.

I have betrayed him over and over again. So many times and with so many men that I cannot even recall them. I have excused my actions by saying that my husband is older. His interest in the physical aspect of marriage is far less than mine. I love him, I say to myself, but I demonstrate that love by having intercourse with the men my husband trusts the most. Men who would die – men who have *died, giving their very lives for their King, my husband. I tell myself it means nothing. But of course it does. It means everything.*

Lancelot has said nothing since he burst into my tent in the night. To my knowledge he and Lamorak have not spoken, because nothing seems changed. I fully expected Lancelot to expel Lamorak and send him home to confront the King and confess his misdeed. But both of them are honorable men. Lancelot fully understands the reason for Lamorak's indiscretion. He knows it was my doing, not the knight's. I know, however, that he will tell Arthur everything when we return to Camelot. Nay, not everything. Even the brave Lancelot has no desire to put his own life on the line.

My dalliances with him *shall remain a secret. I have no doubt of that. So we continue our trip to London. And I will be anxious until I return to face my husband.*

Arthur will be furious. How could he not? What loving, caring husband would not be angry, embarrassed, ashamed at the blatant, public betrayal of his love and trust by his young passionate wife? Because of his steadfast refusal to stop loving me, Arthur's anger will likely be manifest against Lamorak, his loyal servant who would give his very life if my husband required it. Lamorak is not at fault in this matter. It is I who enticed him to my bed, promised him a night of incredible pleasure, and opened my passion and my body to his for nothing more than a moment of climax and yet another conquest. But Lamorak will pay. I fear he will pay with his life for a crime he did not commit. He will pay for giving in to me, his Queen, who demanded his sexual prowess in her bedroom last night. This time Arthur will demand the life of the man who slept with his wife. But in truth if he took the lives of all my lovers, his beloved Round Table would have many empty seats.

My life feels unfulfilled, yet I have everything a woman could want. I am the most powerful woman in Britain, the wife of its monarch, Arthur Pendragon. Why, dear God, why do I want that which I cannot, nay, that which I should *not have? Because I can have it. I should not, but I can. Men bow to me. Even the mighty Lancelot, the man who caught me last night in my tent with Lamorak. He saw me with Lamorak's penis still inside of me. Did he harken back to when his own was there, not long ago? Was he furious with me? Enough to risk his own life? I have kept that one on my string for longer than any of the others. Now he knows he is not the only one.*

He will tell my husband about my infidelity because he wants to hurt Lamorak, not me.

Merlin warned me. That meddling old sorcerer knows things no man could possibly know – I fear he can see inside my mind – he warned me to be careful of my thoughts and desires. His words burn in my head. Gwenhwyfar, you are the property of your husband the King. You belong to him and him alone. Your body, your very life are his, not your own. Betray him only at great risk.

I did not heed Merlin's words. I laughed at the strange old man who mutters things as he walks the halls of Camelot. He is harmless, I told myself. He would not betray his Queen. But even as I assured myself I was safe, even as I continued to lure brave servants of my husband to my bed, I knew better. I knew Merlin was watching. But I ignored what I knew. Now he will testify against me.

It would grieve me if Lancelot were to tell the entire truth to my husband, the men I've had, my indiscretion with Lancelot himself, my expressions of undying love to Arthur that meant little outside the throes of passion. It is not my desire to strike the soul, the very heart of my beloved husband.

Of all the knights, my husband loves Lancelot most. And that is why I wanted Lancelot most. Oh God. Why am I like this? Why have I done this? And why, if my husband should spare me, will I keep doing it? What is wrong with me?

I have sinned. Over and over I have sinned.

And as much as my husband loves me, now I fear I too must pay.

I am afraid.

CHAPTER THIRTY-FOUR

At six a.m. Roberto left the hotel in jogging clothes. He ran for blocks, keeping an eye out for company. Just before dawn he turned into dark, quiet St. Mary Axe, jogged its entire length then doubled back. No one else was in the area. He ran past the dark bookstore and stopped at the vacant building. Glancing both ways to be sure he was alone, he pulled out a key and stepped inside.

He thought about what happened last evening. Was Edward simply curious and decided to follow him? Had he seen Roberto enter or exit the building next door? Had he heard noise from the adjoining basement as Roberto moved the heavy stones? It could even be simpler – Edward may have merely been walking the same direction as Roberto. He may have been heading towards Liverpool Street Station to catch a homebound train and not following Roberto at all. He might have noticed Roberto slip into the alley, stopped and looked to see what was up, then continued on.

In Roberto's business one considered worst-case scenarios first. This morning he'd left early enough that, all things being equal, he'd arrive in St. Mary Axe Street before Edward Russell. And he'd leave mid-afternoon when things were busy at the bookstore next door.

Before donning the jumpsuit, he unhooked a water bottle from his belt and took lunch, a sandwich he'd ordered last night from room service, from the pocket of his shorts. He set them aside for later.

Roberto had a single goal today. Using the entrenching tool, he removed one small shovelful of dirt at a time in the two-foot-square area where the floor stones had been. When he'd dug down three feet, he put his foot down in the hole, hung on to the sides of the existing floor and stomped down hard on the soil that remained. The dirt gave way slightly, but there was resistance. That was encouraging. *If my theory's correct, I'm right on top of a support beam.* He moved to the left and stomped again. This time more dirt fell and a small hole opened up.

He patiently removed more stones and cleared more dirt with the shovel. After several hours he stopped for lunch, then resumed the dig. Rather than stamping down with his foot and risking a fall into what he hoped was a chamber below, he used one of the floor stones he'd removed. He lifted it over his head and slammed it down into the dirt as hard as he could. After a few tries, he got the hang of it; finally he created a series of holes between which were straight narrow rows running the length of the room. Those would be the ceiling beams in the chamber below.

He took a rope from his suitcase, tied the lantern securely and lowered it. In the dim light he saw a room like the one he knew was under Edward's store next door. From the description he'd been given by Curtis Pemberly, this one seemed identical, yet another room in the crypt of the ancient church. As the light swung back and forth on the end of the rope, he noticed that the room was large – he could see a couple of walls, but the other two were hidden in the darkness. He glimpsed a wooden door – from its location it had to be the opposite side of the one Gordon Foxworth saw next door. As his eyes grew accustomed to the half-light, he could see faces grinning up at him. Skulls, actually. This was a burial chamber.

Three p.m. came quickly – he needed more time, but he stuck to the plan. He stopped for the day. He glanced through the dirty front window at the sidewalk. There were a half dozen tourists taking in the sights and several odd people who were likely going to The Necromancer's Bookshop to pick up a spell or two. It was a good time to move. He took one more look, stepped outside and locked the door.

As he turned, he was startled to see Edward Russell standing on the sidewalk ten feet away. *How the hell did he do that? He wasn't here ten seconds ago.*

"Fancy meeting you here. Some sightseeing in the area you didn't get done yesterday?"

This man's going into territory where he doesn't belong. He's certainly brimming with self-assurance – I'll give him that.

Roberto didn't know if Edward had seen him leave the building. "I'm out for a run. I enjoyed this area yesterday and my hotel's in the neighborhood."

"Which hotel would that be, Mr. …?"

Roberto's words were terse. "With all respect, I don't think that's any of your business."

"If I were a gambling man, I'd wager I could guess your name."

This guy's brash. Strange as hell too.

"And what would that be?"

"I'd guess your name is Juan Carlos Sebastian."

Roberto blanched. *What the hell – how did this guy know that name?*

"You'd be wrong, then." He turned and started to walk away.

"I know what you're up to," Edward called out. "And I've got my eye on you."

You have no idea who you're up against, you bastard.

At precisely the same time, Edward Russell was thinking precisely the same thing.

CHAPTER THIRTY-FIVE

There's a simple answer to all this. There was only one logical way Edward Russell could have heard the name Juan Carlos Sebastian – from Curtis Pemberly. Gordon Foxworth, who knew nothing about him, in turn would have told Curtis.

Roberto faced a dilemma. There were consequences in introducing himself as Roberto Maas. For the first time, someone who had called him Juan Carlos would know he was Roberto – the two names would be linked to one person. That was dangerous.

But he *had* to be Roberto Maas. Philippe had told Edward his wealthy partner, Roberto Maas, held an option on the vacant building next door. If Edward had seen Roberto entering or exiting the building, the reasonable explanation was that he was the option-holder, doing fieldwork on the building's suitability for ownership. At some point, now or in the future, Edward Russell actually *would* meet Roberto Maas, presuming he agreed to sell his building. He had to be Roberto, as risky as that might be.

The next morning at six, Roberto did exactly the same thing as the day before. He jogged around the neighborhood, then into St. Mary Axe Street. He ran from one end to the other then back, looking closely at the sides and tops of the buildings that were on either side of the vacant one. He examined The Necromancer's Bookshop particularly closely.

Before entering his building, he took a close look at its decrepit front doors. Last evening after his second sidewalk encounter with Edward Russell, he had thought this all through. He was missing something. How did this guy always know exactly when I left the building? Roberto was a trained operative, skilled in surveillance and counterespionage. But after years with no danger, he was getting sloppy. Once again he'd let down his guard. He hadn't expected anyone to be watching. That was a bad call and he knew it. He had to always be on alert. And he had to pick up his game.

He ran his fingers up and down the place where the front doors fit into the frame. He felt years of caked dirt and finally found what he was looking for. A tiny motion sensor had been tucked in a corner and daubed with mud. It was virtually invisible, but it activated every time the door opened or closed.

He'd already caught the other half of Edward's spy equipment. On the awning above the bookstore's entrance was a tiny camera that would be unnoticed by anyone not looking for it. It was aimed directly at the place where Roberto now stood.

He'd lingered here only a minute. He resumed jogging and gathered his thoughts. The camera would have caught him turning into the doorway of the vacant building, but from its angle Edward couldn't see that he'd searched the doorframe for a motion device. All Edward would know about this morning was that Roberto paused for a moment at the doorway to the empty building next door.

It was time to stop the charade. Edward was aware of his comings and goings. Edward knew when to step outside because of the motion detector and the camera.

Roberto decided to change his plan for today. He jogged back along Bishopsgate to his hotel and went inside. It was 6:45 a.m.

After a leisurely shower, he ate breakfast in the lobby café, read a newspaper and responded to a couple of emails from the office. Around 8:30 he walked to a hardware store nearby and bought a lightweight collapsible ladder.

He carried the bag and ladder the few blocks to St. Mary Axe Street. He noticed lights inside the bookshop as he passed. Someone was already there. When he reached the door of his building, he made no attempt at subterfuge. He reached up, ripped off the motion sensor and stuck it in his pocket. Inside, he went straight to the basement.

He widened one of the holes he'd made in the basement floor. Soon it was large enough to accommodate both him and the ladder, which he extended to full length and lowered through the hole to the stone floor six feet below. Headlamp on and lantern in hand, Roberto descended. He needed more light down here – later today he'd arrange for electricity to be turned on so he could use high-powered lights. For now this would suffice.

The room was actually a long hallway ten feet wide. To the north there was a large wooden door with iron hasps, exactly as Gordon described Edward's to Curtis Pemberly. Edward's building was also directly north of Roberto's. This door was definitely the same one Gordon had seen.

On the south side there was no wall. Instead there was a tunnel extending into the darkness. He shined his light but couldn't see its end.

He started with the large wooden door that would open into Edward's crypt. A heavy bar slid into a metal loop that kept the door shut. It would take a key to open the door unless he could somehow remove the loop that was anchored solidly into stone. The door would have to wait.

Roberto walked down the corridor nearly a hundred feet, his light barely penetrating the murky blackness. The walls and floor were made of the same large stones he'd seen in the first room but with vaulted ceilings. It was very similar to a crypt he'd seen below the Sistine Chapel in the Vatican. It was Roman.

Ledges were randomly cut into the walls on both sides in no apparent sense of order. There were words etched into the stone below some, presumably names or dates. Words on the first one he saw were too faded to read. Rotting wooden caskets lay in pieces on a few ledges, simple piles of bones on most. Sometimes skulls were there, other times they'd rolled onto the floor. He could see maybe thirty feet down the hallway; there were four ledges within his scope of vision.

After fifty feet he stopped and aimed the beam of light down the corridor. It went on much further than the light's beam. He was going roughly south; if this passage continued, he'd get to the Thames River eventually because St. Mary Axe was less than a half mile away from it.

As he walked, his light reflected dimly off something to his side. In one of the cutouts on the wall he saw a body with a detached arm lying beside its torso. The hand gripped a metal staff about five feet long. Below the ledge were the first legible words he'd come across.

AVILIUS CASTOR
CIVIS ROMANUS A LONDINIUM
MORTUUS
CCCLXXXVI

Latin was easy for Roberto. It took ten seconds to find out who was lying in front of him.

Avilius Castor. A Roman citizen of Londinium. Died 386.

Interesting!

He kept walking south, passing several faded inscriptions. He paused at the next clear one. He was beginning to figure out what this place was. He hoped this inscription would confirm his thinking.

Lucius Accius. Orator and husband of Aemilia. Died 384.

This was exactly what Roberto thought. Here was confirmation of another Roman burial. He wasn't in the crypt of the Church of St. Mary Axe; this passage was centuries older. These weren't Christian burials. These were citizens of Rome who lived in Londinium, the settlement that had been abandoned around 450 AD and thereafter became the Anglo-Saxon City of London.

From his history classes Roberto knew Constantine had been Emperor of Rome during the fourth century AD. He died maybe a half century before these two Roman citizens of London. Constantine was widely believed to have been the first Christian Emperor, but as Roberto recalled, his legacy was more due to his toleration of Christianity than his personal acceptance of the religion. In the decades after his death, the religion of Jesus became more and more accepted by Romans. But the people buried on the ledges in this passageway showed no evidence of being Christians. No crosses, no religious symbols etched into the walls, nothing that would indicate they had embraced the new religion.

He spent hours exploring the tunnel. He saw a few more inscriptions with legible dates. He'd bring paper and pencil tomorrow to try rubbing the illegible first etchings closest to the heavy wooden door where he'd dropped through the ceiling. Most of those ledges still contained decayed wood – remnants of caskets – so they might be later burials. The further he walked down the dark hallway, the earlier the dates, and all were Roman. It was a fact that St. Mary Axe Church was built on this site. But the church was constructed on top of a far older Roman burial chamber. That had long since been forgotten.

That afternoon Roberto wrapped up early. He'd made great progress and he had to call the electric company. He wanted power restored to the building. He also wanted to do some research on Londinium. He locked the front door and looked around, expecting to see Edward on the sidewalk. But he wasn't there. Roberto went into the bookstore and up to the counter, where a female assistant greeted him.

Roberto asked if Edward was around.

"He's due back in an hour or so. Is there something I can do for you?"

He pulled the small motion detector from his pocket and handed it to her. "Tell him I'm the man who has the building next door. I found this and I'm sure he'd like it back."

"What is it?" she asked, turning it over in her hand.

"It doesn't matter; it's his, so please tell him Roberto brought it back."

Two hours later Edward Russell sat alone in his back room, staring at the small device on the table.

You arrogant son of a bitch. Roberto, eh? Roberto Maas, the partner of the guy who wanted to buy the building? I'll bet that's not your name. I'd wager you're Juan Carlos Sebastian and you're after the things in my chamber. Get ready, whatever your name is. You have no idea what you're in for.

CHAPTER THIRTY-SIX

Philippe was finishing up the fifty-page report that was emailed to Roberto every Friday. Even in Greece on vacation, his partner would dig through the numbers closely, getting a snapshot update of his far-flung investments and holdings. It was the same every week; this was how Roberto stayed involved.

His assistant rang. "There are two men downstairs in the lobby who'd like to see you. They're from Russia and want to discuss a proposal."

She told him the men had originally wanted Roberto. Learning he was away, they asked to meet with his partner. Philippe clicked on his computer and saw images from the security cameras in the lobby. There were two men in suits, fifty years old or so. One held a briefcase in his lap.

Why not? "Bring them up, please. Put them in the conference room and offer coffee."

The men introduced themselves as owners of a privately held oil company headquartered in St. Petersburg with major drilling operations in the North Sea off the coast of Norway.

Philippe offered a business card and noticed they had none to give him in return. That was odd.

"What can I do for you, gentlemen?"

In reasonable English one of the men replied, "We'd like to know more about Roberto Maas. He's the chairman of your firm, correct?"

Confirming, he gave the Russians the same story everyone who inquired about Ciprian Investments received. Yes, the company was an investment management firm, but by far its largest customer was one wealthy individual and the various trusts and corporations he controlled.

"And that man is Mr. Maas?"

Philippe fielded the man's blunt questions smoothly. "Our firm is privately held and headquartered here in Switzerland for a reason. As you undoubtedly know, this country is noted for discretion and confidentiality. Although some of our clients might be household names in the financial world, we maintain the strictest confidentiality as to the identities of those persons. I'm sure, should you become clients yourselves, you'd be pleased that your information was held in trust."

Intent on determining the reason for their interest in Roberto without giving anything away, Philippe countered every pointed question with a vague answer. After several wasted minutes, one of the visitors said, "Perhaps these will move our conversation along."

He opened his briefcase, pulled out ten grainy black-and-white photos and tossed them across the table. Philippe picked one up and looked at it, amazed and disgusted. It showed a thin, naked boy on a bed with his legs spread wide open, smiling. He couldn't have been more than fifteen.

Without looking at the rest, he said angrily, "What the hell is this about? You don't own an oil company. Who are you, and what do you want?"

The Russian waved his hand at the photos. "Take a look at the other pictures. You know that boy well."

"I know him?" Philippe sputtered his response, confused and beginning to be slightly worried. "You've … I think you've made a big mistake. Are you trying to blackmail me? I have no idea …"

"Relax. No, we aren't oil tycoons. But we do represent one or two. We're looking for someone. None of this is about you. It's about your partner. Roberto Maas. The first photos are of a child prostitute named Slava Sergenko, fifteen years ago in Moscow. The others are of a man named Andrey Bodrov. He appears to be sleeping, but he's not. He's dead, thanks to young Slava there."

"And you're saying Roberto was involved with this child prostitute? I find that hard to–"

"Oh no. We're not saying that at all. Much worse, in fact. Roberto Maas *is* that boy. He was Slava Sergenko. We've been looking for him for more than fifteen years."

CHAPTER THIRTY-SEVEN

The pictures of the naked boy and the dead Russian lay untouched on Philippe's desk as the visitor explained why they were looking for the child prostitute. For forty-five minutes he told Philippe a story which, if true, was almost beyond belief.

Slava Sergenko, the name with which Roberto had been born, was a cunning teenager who watched and listened while he was a virtual slave at the Moscow bordello owned by Andrey Bodrov, a very wealthy businessman. Slava and ten other boys and girls ages thirteen to sixteen were transported by van to a private tutor every morning and received an excellent education. The tutor, of course, had no idea what was going on; he was paid a lot of rubles to keep his questions to himself.

Philippe interrupted, asking why Bodrov wasted time and money educating the children, since they were nothing more than sex toys for wealthy Russians. The answer made sense. As these children became young adults, Bodrov intended to keep them engaged in the same occupation. The fabulously wealthy Russian oligarchs who frequented lavish, expensive brothels in the new Russia wanted educated companions. Once these kids grew up, they would fill that need. These men wanted to show off their "dates" – they wanted intelligent, beautiful, young and sexy girls and boys to accompany them to nightclubs and fine restaurants. No matter that these men were married – their wives were old-style Russian women. They knew which side their bread was buttered on. Silence about things like this kept them in the opulent lifestyles they enjoyed. They simply pretended nothing was going on. So long as their husbands' activities didn't embarrass their families, everything was fine.

The workers in restaurants and clubs who saw these men sporting twenty-year-old girls, or a girl-and-boy couple, laughed behind their backs. Fat old men with limp penises and plenty of rubles! But in a society where the have-nots were subservient, nobody made waves. The men got away with their activities because those who witnessed their dalliances were afraid of their money and power.

As teenagers, their bodies were sold in the sex trade, and later they'd mature into twentysomething adult prostitutes. The men who owned them would profit at their expense for years so long as everything went well.

The Russian continued. Sixteen-year-old Slava had sneaked around sufficiently to learn where the brothel's records were kept. After he killed Andrey Bodrov with a darning needle to the heart, he calmly put on his clothes and took Bodrov's money and ATM card. Then Slava went into a next-door office and made off with client records. He charged credit cards, withdrew cash and made life slightly uncomfortable for these men. But it was a minor inconvenience – they had plenty more rubles and didn't want any publicity about their little indiscretions with children – boys, in fact.

"If that had been all Slava Sergenko had done, our employers would have let things go," the Russian said. But the boy went a bit further. He instituted a systematic program of blackmail. If they didn't pay, he promised to ruin their careers, their personal lives, their very existence. Lots of Russians hired whores – it was hardly even considered a sin and would certainly have been forgiven. But not at Andrey Bodrov's whorehouse. If it became known that these rich men crossed the line – they were having sex with teenage boys – they would be ruined. Instantly.

So the johns paid. Probably more than a hundred of them were involved at first, the Russian told Philippe. Some were still paying today; two of those victims of the decades-long blackmail had hired these men to find Slava.

It had taken years, but using Slava's fingerprints, they tracked him to Prague. They first heard the name Juan Carlos Sebastian and learned about the bar at the Princi Palace Hotel. In 2007 two operatives were sent to finish the matter. They cornered Juan Carlos in a dead-end alley. But somehow he'd executed them instead. Then he vanished once again.

Blind luck was often what allowed a cold case to break wide open. Those who sought Slava Sergenko spread money liberally around Europe and waited for something to happen. He would make an error someday. Finally, five years later, it happened. Juan Carlos Sebastian had made a small but critical mistake.

The Russian stopped talking and sat back in the chair. He folded his arms over his chest and said, "What do you think?"

Philippe paused a moment then replied evenly, "I have no idea why you're telling me this or even if it's true. My partner is a respected businessman. There's no way he could be this child from Russia. I think you have no proof whatsoever that he actually is. Maybe fingerprints tied Slava to Juan Carlos, but you've mentioned nothing that ties Juan Carlos to Roberto. I'm sure you haven't told me the end of the story, but I'm finished with all this. It doesn't involve me. Or Roberto. If you want to know what I think, I believe you're going down the wrong path and you're making a huge mistake. There's no way Roberto Maas could be the man you're looking for, and if you attempt to malign his reputation, I can assure you he'll retaliate in the courts. Now if we're finished, I have work to do ..." Philippe stood and pushed the black-and-white photos towards the men who sat on the other side of his desk.

The Russian said coldly, "We're not finished, Mr. Lepescu. Sit down and shut your mouth. I'll decide when our meeting is over."

A shiver of fear went down Philippe's spine as he sank back into his chair. He'd never dealt with organized crime figures before, but he had an idea this was what sat in front of him. These men looked like they'd kill anyone who stood between them and their quarry. Fortunately it was Roberto they wanted. Hopefully. This had nothing to do with him. Hopefully.

The man pulled one more photo from his pocket and tossed it to Philippe. "Does this man look familiar? Does he look like anyone you know?"

Philippe had to admit the person resembled Roberto although he was far younger and his hair was darker and much longer. If he'd been casually shown the picture, he would never have identified the man as his partner.

"You're grasping at straws …"

"Juan Carlos Sebastian was a bartender in Prague. But he was more than that. He was a major collector of artifacts. I wonder how, on a bartender's salary, he managed to purchase hundreds of thousands of dollars of antiques and relics, some of which were one of a kind, priceless. Do you know how he did that, Mr. Lepescu? Has your business partner told you he's a cold-blooded killer for hire? An assassin for the American CIA, among others?"

Philippe blanched, swallowed hard and said nothing.

"After Juan Carlos disappeared from Prague that night in 2007, someone else picked up where he left off. Another man began buying the same pieces from the same dealers. Roberto Maas, your partner, somehow stepped right into the buying routine of the vanished Juan Carlos. His taste in antiquities, his knowledge of the markets, and his list of contacts were identical. An amazing coincidence, you might think. Not really. Your partner couldn't resist continuing to feed his passion, his pastime. And that was a fatal mistake."

"With all respect, Mr. … I don't believe I got your name."

"I believe you're right!" The Russian expelled a hearty, cruel laugh and slapped his compatriot on the arm. "I don't believe we told Mr. Lepescu our names!"

He stood, put both fists on Philippe's desk and leaned over. His face was so close Philippe could smell the stale odor of cigarettes that seemed to be a part of every Russian's makeup. The man's demeanor changed. Suddenly he was malevolent, brutish.

"After Juan Carlos Sebastian left Prague, our men searched his flat. We took pictures of his precious collection but touched nothing. Beautiful things – gold masks from Greece. Ancient amphorae from Roman times. A dagger from an Egyptian tomb. Three weeks later a firm of attorneys removed his artifacts and shipped them away. Do you know where they went? The boxes were sent to a bank in Geneva. A few months later they ended up right here in Lucerne. Amazing, correct? Yesterday, Mr. Lepescu, I saw the artifacts with my own eyes. You're an intelligent man. By now I'm sure you know where this is leading. Where in the world do you think Juan Carlos's artifacts are today?"

Philippe averted his eyes, now aware of the truth. "They're in Roberto's apartment. I've seen them too."

"Of course you have. And now we come to the crux of our conversation. You are going to help us finish our odyssey. You are going to help us capture your partner, Slava Sergenko."

The conversation continued as the men explained what would happen next, what his part would be and how he'd be expected to perform. When Philippe Lepescu showed the men out of the building, his assistant noticed that he was pale and shaking. He went into his office, closed the door and soon left for the day.

Philippe had been told exactly what the men were looking for. He knew they would do anything to accomplish their goal. He was guaranteed a handsome payment for his cooperation, but he also had no choice. It wasn't hard to figure out what would happen to those who impeded this search for Slava Sergenko. These men were killers. Philippe was afraid for his life.

Regardless of his fear, he felt obligated to tell Roberto about the visitors. But how much should he tell? Would Roberto protect him? How could he?

He spent a sleepless night but awoke with an answer. He knew what he had to do.

CHAPTER THIRTY-EIGHT

Philippe arrived to work the next morning prepared to tell his partner everything about the Russians. He owed Roberto at least that.

Around ten Philippe took a call from London. Edward Russell's voice was full of venom.

"Your partner's hard at work in the vacant building next to my bookshop."

"I'm afraid you're mistaken. That's impossible – Mr. Maas is on holiday in Greece. He's been there several days."

"I'm afraid *you're* mistaken, Mr. Lepescu. Roberto's here in London, doing something clandestine in a dilapidated old building that hasn't had a tenant in years. Obviously he hasn't broken the news to you, so now we can both wonder what he's up to!" Edward Russell's smug voice was irritating.

"If you don't mind my asking, what's the purpose of this call? To tattle on Mr. Maas?"

The response was cold, almost frightening. "The purpose of my call is to give you a warning. I'll give it to him too, once I see him. Stay out of my affairs. Both of you. Or you'll regret it."

———

"How goes the holiday? Any Greek goddesses on those islands?"

Philippe forced his comments to sound upbeat. He trusted Roberto, his friend and his boss, not that strange man he'd met in the bookstore in London. If Roberto said he was in Greece on a cruise, then that was where he was. Edward Russell was obviously wrong. Mistaken identity, stolen identity, something. Philippe would discuss it with Roberto and he'd explain everything.

"Change of plans, actually. I'm in London."

Philippe couldn't conceal his frustration, the feeling of betrayal. His voice broke. "Were you going to let me know? Is there a reason you told me you were going to Greece?"

"Slow down!" Roberto laughed. "I'm on a secret mission!"

"So I hear." Philippe's voice was frosty.

"Really? From whom? Oh, I see now. That crazy Edward Russell called you, right? I'll explain everything–"

Angrily Philippe interrupted. "You lied to me! You sent me to London on the pretext that you wanted to develop St. Mary Axe Street. That's not true, is it? You wanted only the one building. We haven't done any work on development plans since I approached Edward Russell. That's not even the plan, is it? But I, your so-called 'partner' – I'm operating totally unaware of your real motive. You used me, withheld information and sent me out to spin your lies and buy a building. Now you have a 'secret mission' in the abandoned building next door to his. What's going on? How about the truth for a change?"

The man was obviously upset and Roberto chose words he hoped would ease Philippe's frustration. "I owe you an apology. I *have* kept you in the dark, and I used your persuasive talents for what I hoped would be an easy real estate purchase. A couple of stories below Edward's bookstore there's an ancient room – a crypt. It contains a sarcophagus and a locked wooden door. There were also some metal boxes filled with books. I have no idea what all this is, but I think it dates back to the fifth century when the

Church of St. Mary Axe was built on this site shortly after the Romans abandoned Londinium.

"You know my interest in antiquities. I want to find out about the things in Edward's basement. They've been there for years; apparently his grandfather found the crypt when he fell through the basement floor. And, Philippe, listen to this. Today I found something absolutely fascinating! Something even older that's underneath my abandoned building!"

"In the derelict building next door? The one you locked up with a six-month option? Thanks for finally letting me in on your little secret only after I confronted you. I thought we were partners. So much for that idea!" Philippe's voice was shaky, emotional.

Roberto answered calmly, "We *are* partners. But this isn't a business deal. It's personal – a search for some relics I'm interested in as a collector. I made it sound like a business deal when I explained the St. Mary Axe development project and sent you to buy Edward's building. But it wasn't. It never has been. I kept you out of the loop on that and I apologize. But there's no big secret and I wasn't trying to mislead you."

But you did. You lied to me.

Philippe was hurt. He'd been deceived by a man whom he considered his closest friend, if it were possible to get close to Roberto Maas. From the Russians and now from Edward he'd learned there were secrets. Huge secrets, if yesterday's visitors could be believed. He wasn't going to tell Roberto anything now. Who knew where he stood with his so-called "partner," a man who apparently had a murderous hidden past and even today held secrets from his associate. Obviously he'd been mistaken all along. He wasn't Roberto's friend. He was Roberto's errand boy.

There was nothing more to be gained from dwelling on this. Philippe changed the subject, describing the phone call from Edward Russell and his threat at the end.

"So now that I know you really are in London, can you tell me what you found? I'd like to know."

Roberto told him everything he'd learned up to now. He explained how Edward was maintaining surveillance on the building and described the Roman burials. He laughed when he told how he'd dropped off the monitoring device at Edward's store that afternoon. "I'm sure I pissed him off! That's why he made that threatening call to you. He's a really different individual, as I'm sure you noticed when you met him. Very strange. Probably psychotic, delusional too. Lots of bluster, but I'd bet that's all."

Philippe tried to sound upbeat even though he felt his world falling apart. "Just be careful. You don't know this guy – there's no telling how crazy he actually is. How long are you going to be there?"

"Long enough to find out what this is all about. If anything earth-shattering comes up, I'm not that far away. Call me if you need something and I promise to let you know everything from now on."

You expect me to believe that?

When the call ended, Philippe held his head in his hands, overwhelmed with sadness. He felt betrayed and deceived, but even more he felt disappointed. Things between them would never be the way they had been before. Roberto obviously didn't trust him enough to share his most exciting adventures. The man undoubtedly had even more secrets, ones Philippe would never know. And others he didn't know Philippe had already learned.

So Roberto had secrets. Now Philippe did too, thanks to the Russians. Philippe had called specifically to let Roberto know about the men who were here yesterday, what they wanted and about the pictures. He'd decided to tell his partner the entire story. Even now, with betrayal overpowering his senses, he didn't believe Roberto Maas was the person they were seeking. But deceit flowed both ways. So Philippe told Roberto nothing about two Russians who were looking for the former child prostitute they believed was now Roberto Maas.

Two can play this game, he thought bitterly.

Suddenly an interesting thought popped into Philippe's head. *Why not make the best of it? Turn that anger of mine into revenge!*

His new idea made him both frightened and grippingly intrigued. A part of Philippe yearned for excitement – he knew it was genetic, flowing through the bloodline of his Romanian gypsy ancestors. Philippe's mother had told him stories about his father's passion for the cause of his people, and he grew up with a stylized concept of the fierce, dark rogue he envisioned his dead father would have been.

Philippe dismissed his own flaws, his own human failures, his own little secrets, as part of his gypsy heritage. Everyone did something wrong now and then, and he was a gypsy, after all. It was easy to shrug off the occasional problem with a call girl who ended up beaten a bit more than he intended, or a shoplift here and there even when he had plenty of money in his pocket. He kept his passions, desires and needs well hidden, especially now that he was running a major private company.

So now he devised a plan. He knew everything about Roberto Maas's operations. He routinely directed the movement of millions of dollars at a time for his partner, the man whom he'd previously considered his friend. He knew exactly how to work things at Ciprian Investments.

With great risk comes great opportunity.

CHAPTER THIRTY-NINE

Roberto sat outdoors at the Bird in Hand, a pub in Covent Garden. A sandwich and a glass of wine before him, he thought about Edward Russell. The strange man was unpredictable. Instead of the bookish, studious, frail individual he looked to be, he had suddenly become a threatening bully.

The man was unstable at the least, dangerous at worst. Given Roberto's years of wet-ops experience, the bookseller would be no match for him, and he also was certain the man was more bark than bite.

Roberto intended to find out what Edward was hiding in the crypt. By now one would have expected the British antiquities authority to be hard at work combing over every square inch of it. But that hadn't happened. Edward hadn't brought them in. Why? That was a question that needed answering.

Unable to buy Edward's building, Roberto had amended his plan. He'd acquired an option on the building next door so he could see if the crypt of St. Mary Axe extended under there too.

By doing that he'd gotten far more than he'd expected. He found an ancient Roman burial passageway dating at least to the fourth century, maybe even earlier. So far he hadn't explored it all the way, but it likely ran more than a thousand feet, all the way to the Thames itself. His big problem with the passageway was lighting it. The old building had been vacant for so many years that an inspection was required before the power company would restore electricity. He couldn't get lights until sometime next week.

What he'd found was exciting, but he was determined to learn what the man was hiding. And he would find out despite his threats. Roberto would be careful; he'd let himself slide a couple of times lately, but he was on heightened watch now. Juan Carlos could help, but Roberto didn't really think that was necessary. Juan Carlos's targets always met a fatal ending. This was different. The others were contract jobs for someone else, strictly business. The situation with Edward Russell was personal. Roberto's emotions were involved. Surely Juan Carlos wouldn't have to handle this. It was a simple archaeological project, for God's sake. Why was Edward so defensive, so threatening, so secretive? What was going on in the crypt?

CHAPTER FORTY

"What the hell do you think you're doing?"

"This lens is filthy. It can't be of much use to you with all this dirt on it. I'm just being a good neighbor and cleaning it for you."

Roberto was on a ladder with a cloth, polishing the lens of the small video camera Edward had installed on the side of his building to keep an eye on Roberto's comings and goings. Knowing how Edward would react, he'd done it anyway to bring things to a head.

"Get away from there before I call the police."

Roberto casually climbed down the ladder and moved it to the front of his building. He turned to Edward with a grim smile and said, "You know, I believe the one thing you absolutely will *not* do is call the police. We need to talk. There are things I want to know and things you need to know."

"Stay away from my premises, Mr. Sebastian."

"It's Maas, actually." Roberto smiled cordially, taunting the man. "Roberto Maas."

That infuriated Edward. He turned in a huff, went back to his bookshop and slammed the front door so hard the windows rattled.

Roberto walked back to his own building and down into the chamber. Even though electricity was a week away, there was plenty he could do so he wouldn't lose time later.

He spent the morning preparing high-powered LED lights FedEx had delivered to his hotel yesterday. These were the same flood lamps used in underground mining operations. He'd purchased six lights and ten one-hundred-foot extension cords. His lighting project extended nearly a thousand feet down the tunnel.

It wasn't easy running the cords and lights in the darkness. He needed both hands to work so he depended on his little headlamp for illumination. Given the tunnel's size, he could see nothing except whatever was directly in front of him.

As he worked along the side walls, Roberto glanced at the bodies lying in wall niches. He wanted time here, to learn who these people had been. The lack of light made examination almost impossible. He had to wait until the power was on. Today he'd prepare the lights. A close study of the corpses would have to wait.

He sat in the crypt, having lunch and a beer, then picked up a set of tools that he'd ordered with the lights. There were a number of long slender picks. He took the tools to the ancient door, knelt and began to work.

Juan Carlos was an accomplished lock-picker; it came in handy now and then. But this huge, clumsy medieval keyhole was a challenge. Its sheer magnitude made it difficult. Modern padlocks were complex but much more easily conquered. He peered into the keyhole. Earlier he'd run a long pick through it and learned it went about eighteen inches through the door then out the other side. Roberto shined a flashlight through the keyhole – the room beyond was pitch black, but now he knew all that separated him from Edward's chamber was this eighteen-inch-thick door.

He spent fifteen minutes moving the picks around inside the keyhole without success. Finally he stood, his knees and back tired from the strain of kneeling. He put the picks into their case and decided to call it quits for today.

Turning, he saw something out of the corner of his eye. Words, lightly carved into the stone next to the door. He'd rubbed away centuries of dust with his palm. Now four words were clearly visible.

Dux ipse habet clavem.

His tired knees were quickly forgotten in a thrill of exhilaration. This gave him a renewed sense of expectation and hope. He had a clue!

Dux ipse habet clavem.

The leader holds the key.

CHAPTER FORTY-ONE

In total darkness Edward Russell sat in a chair in the crypt below his bookshop. He'd been waiting there nearly two hours. Finally he saw it. A tiny shaft of light appeared through the keyhole. Now he heard tiny scraping noises. A pick. Someone on the other side was trying to pick the lock.

After his encounter with Juan Carlos, or Roberto, or whatever his name was, Edward went straight down into the crypt. He figured his adversary had found something below his own building and he was correct. His patient waiting had paid off.

This door clearly opened into whatever was below Roberto's building. Now Edward knew there was a room on the other side too. Roberto had undoubtedly found the extension to the St. Mary Axe crypt. Actually Juan Carlos had found it. He preferred the name of the collector of ancient things over the pseudonym of the Swiss businessman. The bookseller knew who he was. He wouldn't be tricked. This man was after his things, but Edward wouldn't let him take them.

Edward went home, ate dinner, set his alarm and went to bed early.

At three a.m. he was in the attic of his shop. He squeezed up a narrow set of stairs and opened a cover to the roof. He hauled up a lightweight ladder, walked to the edge, dropped down a mere two feet and was on top of Juan Carlos's building next door.

Within five minutes he had found a broken skylight. He carefully removed shards of glass and used a flashlight to look down inside. The drop to the floor below was eight feet. He returned to his own roof, brought the ladder over, stuck it through the skylight and went down.

Moonbeams poked through the grimy, cracked windows as he switched on his torch just long enough to find the stairway. The ground floor was two stories down and he went straight to the back of the building. An open door led to the basement, where he found the hole Roberto had dug. The top of a ladder extended out of it.

Thanks, Juan Carlos, for making this so easy!

He scampered down the ladder into a chamber, which in some ways was similar to his. He turned on his flashlight, saw the other side of the locked wooden door and bodies lying on ledges. This was very different from the single sarcophagus on his side. These bodies were very, very old. Long ago there must have been wood coffins – there were pieces scattered among the bones – but those had been destroyed by the elements. He shined his light down the passageway and saw that it stretched off into the darkness.

Edward had seen enough for tonight. He started up the ladder. Suddenly a light shone in his face, momentarily blinding him. He saw Roberto walk from the dark hallway into the room.

"Fancy meeting you here. Something in my basement that you needed?"

———

The men sat at the table in Edward's back room. It was nearly four a.m.

Edward prepared cups as the kettle boiled on the stove. He went back and forth between the counter and the table, bringing milk and sugar for the tea he was brewing. After the confrontation in the chamber next door, they'd declared a truce.

It was time for show-and-tell. Each knew the other had found a chamber. It was time to join forces and work together. They didn't have to like each other, but they had to work together. It was the smart thing to do in order to figure all this out.

Edward agreed to tell his side first. To Roberto's surprise, he was suddenly friendly and open about what he had found so far.

"I'm glad we've come to this point and I apologize for my earlier caution. It appears we've both found ancient things. Ever since I saw the sarcophagus and the wooden door in the chamber, I knew I was on to something really big. Have you heard the name Lamorak?"

Roberto thought a moment. "Maybe. Although I can't recall where."

"Lamorak was a knight. One of Arthur's Knights of the Round Table."

"That doesn't ring a bell. He's certainly less well known than others in the stories of the knights."

Edward took the kettle off the stove. "But he's the most important one. And they're not myths."

"Really? Why do you say that?"

"Because he's down there in the crypt."

That was a surprise. He had the Romans on his side and Edward had a Knight of the Round Table on his. *Unbelievable.*

Edward held nothing back. He said he'd found several things, each of which was corroboration that King Arthur wasn't just a story. He had lived, been king of Britain, died and was buried.

The bookseller described the fifty-odd books his grandparents had found in the chamber. He'd noted the names and summary information on each but had spent time on only a few. He told Roberto about the eyewitness account of the Battle of Badon between the Britons and Saxons. "In my limited investigation so far, I can tell you it describes in great detail the role of Arthur and his knights as they led the Britons to victory."

They talked about the significance of the sword inscribed with Lamorak's name and how it alone might be enough to prove the Arthurian legend was true.

"But the piece de resistance, the icing on the cake if you will, is a set of diaries. King Arthur *was* real. I have conclusive proof, irrefutable evidence. But we'll get to all that in due time. First let's have our tea, and then we'll see my crypt."

Edward hummed softly as he took the kettle off the stove. He'd told Roberto everything. He'd enjoyed revealing his discoveries. Ever since his grandparents died, he'd wished there were someone to share the exciting information with. It was exhilarating to see Roberto's interest as he heard of the amazing things the Russells had found.

And it didn't matter one bit how much of the story Juan Carlos knew.

His back to Roberto, Edward prepared the tea, pouring it into two cups. He turned, set one in front of Roberto and the other on his side of the table. He put the kettle in the sink then sat down across from Roberto.

"Even though it's only tea we're having, I think a toast is in order, don't you? To the discoveries that lie beneath us and to many exciting hours ahead, learning about what we've found." He raised his cup of tea. So did Roberto.

Just as Edward's cup touched his lips, Roberto said softly, "I switched the cups."

Edward's hand shook and he spilled a little tea on the floor. Holding the cup unsteadily, he said, "I beg your pardon?"

Roberto laughed. The man's response was exactly what he'd expected.

"You heard me correctly. I said I switched the teacups. And I'm ready to join you in that toast you offered." He raised his cup again.

"Goddamn you, Juan Carlos!" Edward screamed, throwing his cup against the wall, where it shattered into a dozen pieces. "What in hell do you think you're doing?"

Roberto took a large sip from the cup that had been Edward's. "No tea for you? It's excellent, actually. My compliments. But that's enough. Now that we know each other a little better let's cut the bullshit, as the Americans would say."

He jumped up and grabbed Edward's arm tightly. "I presume you drugged my tea. Maybe you were going to kill me. Who knows? Who cares? It's immaterial. But I can tell you this. It won't happen again. Do you understand me?"

Edward twisted out of Roberto's grip and replied sullenly, "Just trying to make tea. You pissed me off by not trusting me, so I reacted. You're way out of line and I have no idea what you're talking about, *Juan Carlos.*"

Roberto spoke in a steely, cold voice. "I'm not Juan Carlos, so you can drop the little game you're playing. Regardless of what you just tried to do, we still have to work together. If we don't, we'll never succeed with this amazing discovery.

"I *don't* trust you. You don't trust me either. We're not going to be friends, but we're going to join forces. It's the smart thing for both of us to do. You're going to show me what you have in the crypt. And I'll show you what's on my side. Don't ever try anything stupid again. If you do, you can trust *me* on this. You're no match for me and you *will* regret it. You want me on your side. Period."

Edward seethed with fury as he cleaned up the tea from the floor with a cloth.

And vice versa, he muttered to himself as he unlocked the door to the basement. *Tea's not the only thing I'll be offering you before we're done, Mr. Sebastian. There's room in the crypt for one more.*

CHAPTER FORTY-TWO

For the next two weeks the men worked as a team. There was no camaraderie, no friendship, no trust, but each had something the project required. Edward had been stymied without a so-called partner in crime. Until now he had had no one with which to share the secrets of the chamber, no one to help him with the details, and no one off whom to bounce thoughts and ideas. Edward decided for now he'd call him Roberto instead of Juan Carlos, even though they both knew who he really was.

Roberto found the eccentric bookseller's intelligence and vast knowledge of ancient history immensely helpful as they tackled the mysteries that lay in the rooms below St. Mary Axe. Edward's side had interesting artifacts and books. Considered individually they were valuable items from Saxon and early Briton times. Together, as evidence that the legendary King Arthur might have actually lived, their value could be immense.

Edward's big secret remained his alone. Roberto didn't know where the bodies were literally buried. The bookseller often examined the floor stones where Curtis Pemberly and his clerk lay. As long as those stones looked just like all the others, nothing would give the secret away.

The men worked in an environment of mutual assistance despite the absence of trust. Once they knew that the wooden door connected Edward's crypt with Roberto's, there was no need to keep trying to open it. Each allowed the other access to his side of the chambers. Edward didn't like having Roberto down there, but he had to give something in order to learn more about the tunnel on Roberto's side. He'd keep a close eye on Roberto whenever he was around.

Since he had to wait for electricity, Roberto flew to Lucerne to spend a few days in the office. These days his work with Ciprian Investments primarily was oversight. Philippe was a master at the investment and money management side of things. Roberto had turned those tasks over to his capable partner.

That week in Lucerne the men had drinks and dinner every evening. It was a chance for interaction Roberto had missed while he'd been away in London. Philippe's feelings were just the opposite. He struggled to appear normal although he could think of nothing but betrayal as he sat with the man he'd believed was his closest friend. For him, the days of easy, casual conversation between friends were over. Now Philippe cared about only one thing. Himself. He listened to his partner to learn things he could use for his own benefit.

Roberto told story after story about the psychotic bookseller. To call him different was a massive understatement. From his strange, awkward demeanor to his startling long gray beard, his penchant for threadbare clothes and his aloofness around those he considered intellectually inferior, Edward wasn't a man one wanted to socialize with. In fact *social* wasn't a word that applied to Edward, unless you used the term *socially awkward.* There were no convivial dinners between the two of them. It would have been a painful exercise for Roberto and even harder for Edward. He was more comfortable alone.

Roberto told Philippe everything about the astounding secrets in the crypt deep below St. Mary Axe. Hearing the tales, Philippe couldn't help but be fascinated. It was an incredible discovery. Swallowing his pride and hurt, he asked if he could come to London and see it.

"Let me broach that subject with my new partner Edward Russell." Roberto laughed. "He plays his hand so close to the vest he can't even see his cards. I doubt he trusted his own grandparents and it was their basement to begin with. I'll see if I can convince him to give you a peek."

They talked about Edward's eccentricities. Roberto summed it up by saying, "Supposedly there's a fine line between genius and insanity. I think Edward straddles that line continually. And he falls to one side or the other frequently. It's up to me to figure out which side he's on when I'm dealing with him. And it's never easy."

When he told about Edward offering the tea, Philippe was aghast. "Are you serious? Do you think he was trying to *kill* you?"

"I doubt it. I think at that point he was on the insanity side of the line. I figure he was going to drug me and force me to tell him what I knew. That's all over and done with. Not saying we're friends, but we are civil to each other and it's beneficial for us to be on the same team. I believe it won't happen again."

Philippe struggled to say friendly words to the partner he now loathed. "Just be careful." Of course he had no idea he was talking to the wet-ops assassin Juan Carlos Sebastian. *Careful* was something that had been ingrained in him long ago. He'd gotten lax lately, but he'd vowed to keep his eyes wide open from now on.

"Don't worry. I'll watch my crazy partner every minute!"

Oh, so you have a new *partner, Roberto. Before, I was your only partner. But that's just a word. To me it meant more, but to you it means nothing. Even crazy Edward Russell's your* partner. *It sounds as if he likes you about as much as I do.*

———

That afternoon in London Inspector Dalton showed up unannounced at Edward's store. He waved as he entered and said, "This is your last chance!"

"Last chance for what?" Edward replied.

Glancing at customers all around, he whispered, "Last chance to show me what's in the room down below."

"And why is that?"

"I'm retiring at the end of next week. Thirty years catching bad guys. It's time for some fishing in Scotland. So how about it? Want to satisfy an old man's appetite for mystery?"

"I'm sorry," Edward replied, shaking his head. "It's just not safe."

Dalton slapped the wiry bookseller on the shoulder and said conspiratorially, "You make me think that's where you have the bodies buried!"

Edward jumped back, startled both by the shoulder slap and the man's words.

He replied curtly, "I suppose that's meant to be a joke. I don't see it as that funny."

The policeman shook his head and smiled ruefully. "You need to lighten up, Mr. Russell. You need to get out in the sunshine more and spend less time here with these strange and esoteric objects of yours. I was just joking. Although there *is* a crypt down there, I believe we decided. I guess that's where the bodies really *are* buried!"

Edward bid the officer good luck in his retirement and sent him on his way, relieved to have the man out of his affairs at last.

On Saturday Roberto returned to London. He'd been promised electricity on Monday, and he was ready to get back to work. These days Edward's bookstore was so busy that the only free time they could work together was on weekends. Roberto got to the shop just as Edward was closing things down. The bookseller was positively exuberant.

"Things have progressed well while you were away. Come on! You have to see this!"

He flipped on the lights and they climbed down into the crypt. "Voila!" He gestured towards the heavy wooden door, now standing wide open. The men could see all the way through the doorway into the dark passage heading south from Roberto's building.

"Good work! How'd you get the door open?"

"It was simple once I had this." He held up a very old and very large iron key, caked with rust.

"Amazing! Where'd that come from?"

"From the leader."

"The leader who holds the key?" Roberto recalled the words carved into the wall by the door.

"The very one!" He continued. "I hope you don't mind I spent most of my time on your side of things. Once the door was open, I was anxious to see what was down there." He pointed to the passageway.

"I'd have done the same thing," Roberto admitted honestly.

Edward said that since there was no electricity he'd bought a spotlight, the kind night fishermen use. Its powerful beam gave him plenty of light for the side walls and thirty feet ahead.

He said he'd walked the entire corridor. It ran fifteen hundred feet and ended at a small opening. One couldn't see through it, Edward said, because heavy vines and undergrowth covered it. There was also an ancient set of iron bars running from floor to ceiling at the tunnel's end. Although he could see nothing through the thick growth, he could hear rushing water down below and picked up the unmistakable scent of the river.

"I reached the Thames. My theory is that the Romans built the tunnel as a burial passageway. They created the entrance from the river and the people who erected St. Mary Axe church in the fifth century added the bars for protection. Today I'm sure it's invisible from the river side, covered with embankment or undergrowth, so it's been hidden for centuries, I'd guess."

"And where did you find the key?"

"I counted forty-six bodies lying on the stone ledges. The oldest are furthest down near the river. They're mostly just bones and ash. You know that many of them have inscriptions beneath them. Once I'd gone all the way, I spent every day while you were gone copying each funerary inscription I could make out. I found poets, orators, teachers, physicians and consuls. But I think one of the very oldest bodies was the most important. His ledge was almost at the end. And interestingly he was laid to rest exactly like the others – no fanfare, nothing special at all."

Roberto was fascinated. "Was he a general?"

"Better than that. He was Sextus Calpurnius Agricola. He was the Roman governor of Brittania, headquartered here in Londinium. I looked him up. His place of burial has been a mystery for centuries. Now there are two people on Earth who know where old Sextus lies. You and me!"

"Incredible! When was he buried?"

"That I don't know – his date of death isn't recorded anywhere I could find. The only dates on his inscription tell when he was governor. 163–164 AD. He probably died not long afterwards."

"So this key was with his body?"

"Yes. Once I found him, I'd cataloged almost all the inscriptions I could read – maybe forty or so. He was the only 'leader' per se. So I rummaged around. In the pile of bones that had once been his upper torso I found this key. I figure it had been around his neck when he was laid to rest. I brought the key back, inserted it, and amazingly it turned on the first try. So now we can pass through the chambers without going out to the street upstairs. Helpful, in my opinion."

"Great job. Good work!"

Suddenly Edward's mind boiled. His dark side emerged. Seething on the inside, he struggled to maintain a pleasant facial expression.

You speak to me as though I'm your obedient dog who's just performed a trick. I'm going to kill you.

Patience. Patience. Good things come to those who wait. And those who plan creative endings to partnerships with rich, pompous asses like this one.

He struggled to mask his hatred of this man. "Thank you. I thought you'd enjoy hearing about what I found."

CHAPTER FORTY-THREE

Edward loved the bookshop, but now he lived for just one thing – the hours after work sitting at his dining table, translating Guinevere's diaries. He was surprised how the pages struck him. It was as though he were watching a dramatic soap opera, its episodes captured in Guinevere's stirring words. Tossed together in her daily entries was a hodgepodge of profound sadness, terrifying fear, hopeful gratitude, the grace of a second chance, the lust of an immature girl, the broken heart of a man betrayed. She wrote of many feelings. More interesting were the feelings that were *not* there – repentance, shame and willingness to change. She was rueful not that she'd slept with other men. What saddened her was that her husband who adored her would find out. What she did caused her no guilt. Her sadness at having cheated resulted not from having done it but simply because Arthur now knew about it. It was clear from the diary that she intended to continue her escapades. She would henceforth be more discreet.

Edward started translating the Queen's next entries.

In the days after she returned home from London, Guinevere kept to herself and consequently stayed out of trouble. The King was on a grouse hunt when they arrived back at Camelot, and she wept tears of gratitude, thankful she didn't have to face him right now. It would happen soon, but she thought it better if Lancelot broke the news to him rather than Guinevere's pretending everything was all right until he learned of her betrayal.

She hadn't spoken to Lancelot since the night he'd caught her in the throes of climax with Lamorak. When he rode away one afternoon, she presumed he was going to find his master and reveal her misdeeds. He'd tell at least one of them – the one involving Lamorak. She didn't expect him to confess his own sins.

Shortly after Arthur's return from hunting, Guinevere's world began to collapse. Lancelot had done the unthinkable. Far more than just a loyal servant, the knight and Arthur had long been very close friends. They confided secrets – private thoughts, plans and plots known to them alone. Until now Lancelot had kept his biggest secret hidden – the fact that he'd had sexual relations not once but dozens of times with the Queen, Arthur's beloved wife Guinevere.

This time the knight had come clean. Lancelot told the King not only about Lamorak's sexual escapade – he admitted he'd done it with her himself. Lancelot, the king's best friend and confidant, confessed he'd had intercourse time and again with the love of Arthur's life.

Most of those at Camelot presumed Arthur already knew his wife was a deceitful, conniving, lying whore who had slept with a dozen men or more since her marriage to the much older king. Everyone in the castle was aware – she was so blatant about it that surely the King knew too. Perhaps he chose to ignore his beautiful, sexual young wife's dalliances – the entire court could see that his love for her was boundless. He treated her with the utmost respect and attention. He was repaid with the same love and affection she also liberally shared with others. Maybe he was willing to accept this because he treasured life with her more than life without.

For a week the King had been back on the isle of Avalon, but this time things were different. Suddenly the royal couple slept in separate wings of the castle and was never together except at dinner. The servers whispered gossip about how they sat at opposite ends of the huge dining table, saying nothing during their meals. It was sad, they all remarked. It cast a pall over Camelot, a place that had once rung with laughter.

The Queen normally saw Lancelot at least once a day here or there, but since the King had returned, Lancelot and Lamorak were nowhere to be seen. For days they'd been absent from the castle and its vast grounds. The Queen dared not ask her husband about them, and her trusted handmaidens could find out nothing. The men had vanished.

One evening at dinner Arthur broke the silence that accompanied their meals.

"I lead the men into battle against the Angles and Saxons tomorrow. It promises to be a difficult time and I pray our soldiers shall have success. We Britons are strong and well trained. Pray, my Queen, that I may have steadfast and firm leadership of the contingent of brave knights who shall accompany me."

What he said next saddened her greatly, her diary reflected.

"Although you have not inquired, I will tell you that Lancelot and Lamorak have been leading an advance party near Bathampton Down, some fifteen miles north of here. Their reports have allowed us to prepare for the offensive we must mount in order to defeat our enemy."

"My darling–" Guinevere began. But he cut her off, raising his hand from his seat at the far end of the table. His voice was quiet and sad but determined.

"Not now, my Queen. If the Lord wills it, I will return. We shall see then what He may have in store for Arthur and Guinevere. Until then I must keep my mind clear and focused for battle."

He rose from the table and left the room. She would not see him again for ten weeks.

With most of its warriors away, the castle was quiet. A small contingency remained to guard Camelot, but daily activities were accomplished without the usual fanfare, laughter and interaction to which Guinevere was accustomed. People performed their duties with heads hung low, speaking quietly to each other. It made Guinevere sad, so she was determined to uplift everyone's spirits. She danced gaily around the courtyards, laughed and joked with her servants and retinues. But nothing worked. They didn't respond. They merely looked at her with reproach, shook their heads and went about their duties.

She approached Merlin one afternoon and asked why everyone seemed upset with her. "Why are they not smiling? I laugh but no one laughs with me."

It must have been hard to write his harsh response in her secret diary. "Foolish girl. The entire castle knows you betrayed your husband and wrenched his best friend from his side. You have stolen his very spirit. Now he and his men – many of them your lovers – have gone into battle, a fight from which none may return. Yet you laugh. You smile. You want things to be as they were. Have you not noticed you are the *only one* who smiles? And of every soul who lives here at Camelot, have you not learned by now that *you* are the cause of their sadness?"

The next words must have been the most difficult.

Merlin said, "Leave me alone. Leave us all alone. Depart from here. Especially from the man who loves you. He deserves better." The king's magician walked away.

———

The diary entries became more subdued and less wordy. It took Guinevere several weeks to decide her libido needed stroking, so at last she again set out on the hunt. Her diary recorded in detail the results of her activities. On each of three days she approached a handsome man who caught her eye. One was a palace guard who conveniently stood watch in her wing of the castle at night. Two others were grooms, working in the king's stables. There were plenty of empty stalls there with all the men off to war, and there was nothing like the smell of fresh hay around naked bodies, she thought with a grin.

But something unexpected had happened.

Each of them had turned her down.

It was done respectfully, no doubt. The men must have been afraid how she might retaliate if she felt spurned. But, Edward thought as he read, each mustered the strength of his convictions and chose the high road. Each man turned down a sexual romp with the lusty, exciting young Queen of England.

Confused and astounded, Guinevere pondered how this turn of events could have happened to her. Naively unwilling to blame herself, she decided their loyalty to her husband and their fear of the war made the men impotent. It must be that – they couldn't perform, so they passed up the opportunity rather than face embarrassment in their Queen's bed.

The sexually charged twenty-four-year-old girl had fantasized for days about each of her three upcoming trysts, but nothing had materialized. She was primed for action but had no partner. So she did the only thing she could think of. After her lady-in-waiting undressed her that evening, the naked Queen seduced the girl instead. It wasn't perfect but, as her diary faithfully recorded, any port in a storm.

CHAPTER FORTY-FOUR

One hundred and sixty miles southwest of London is the ancient city of Glastonbury. Glestingaburg, the town's Anglo-Saxon name, was established in the Iron Age around the time of Christ's birth. It is said Joseph of Arimathea visited here in the first century AD, and the place features prominently in the legend of King Arthur. Ages ago Glastonbury Tor, the highest point in the area, was surrounded by a lake. For centuries it has been reputed to be the actual isle of Avalon. According to legend, Avalon was the location of the magical castle Camelot, the home of Arthur and Guinevere.

No one knows how old Glastonbury Abbey really is, but it is known that Ine of Wessex, a Saxon who became king in 688, expanded the existing church during his reign. By the mid-twelfth century Glastonbury was the richest monastery in Britain and it was replete with treasures of all kinds, including books and artwork dating back hundreds of years.

In 1184 a fire totally consumed the abbey, leaving only two huge walls of the once-great church; those walls still stand today. The monks immediately began to rebuild a portion of the building. While the reconstruction itself is indisputable, there's a story many historians don't accept. What is factual is that monks excavating near the abbey's Lady Chapel in 1191 unearthed a sarcophagus below that contained the bones of two people buried six hundred years earlier. The academic world disputes who those people were, but the monks said they were King Arthur and Queen Guinevere.

Even a thousand years ago, attributing the bones to the monarchs increased tourist traffic to Glastonbury Abbey. According to some, that's the reason the monks actively promoted and even embellished the story. Tourists flocked to see the site where the legendary couple's remains were buried.

In the twenty-first century guides still keep the story alive. They explain how Arthur's and Guinevere's bones were dug up in 1191, displayed for a hundred years then entombed in the Abbey Church in 1278.

Alternate stories abound, including a persistent theory that the Abbot John of Taunton himself whisked away the bones to a secret site. Regardless of the truth, plaques at Glastonbury identify places where the bones were allegedly found and reburied.

After the 1200s the already wealthy abbey continued to prosper for centuries. During the Middle Ages, the abbot of Glastonbury had more power than any other person in southwest Britain and lived in opulence. His friend King Henry VII was the abbot's guest in the late 1400s, but thanks to his successor Henry VIII, by 1539 the buildings that made up the splendid abbey complex were gone. That infamous King presided over the destruction and razing of nearly a thousand churches, abbeys and friaries throughout England as part of a religious movement called the Dissolution of the Monasteries. The king also appropriated all the wealth and assets the churches held.

Roberto and Edward stood inside the towering ruined walls of Glastonbury Abbey. They had seen the plaques, one where the bones of Arthur and Guinevere were disinterred and the other where reburial occurred.

Although they enjoyed the ruins, their visit to Glastonbury Abbey wasn't for sightseeing. They intended to find out if Arthur and Guinevere really had been reburied there. That answer would require ingenuity and subterfuge.

Neither of them had a problem with illegal activities. Even amongst them there was deception – both pretended to be legitimate businessmen – one an occult bookstore owner and the other a wealthy investor. They hid the dark aspects of their lives. One of them was a killer who had two bodies in his basement to prove it. The other was a pay-to-play assassin for governments who hired his services. Each of them could easily step outside the law to accomplish a goal. For this trip they'd created a believable story, one designed to get them answers, and boarded the train to Glastonbury.

They spent two hours at the site then drove their rental car a few miles to the town. They had an appointment with Cameron Shockey, the director of the privately funded Glastonbury Abbey Trust, which owned and maintained the ancient grounds. His biography was posted on the trust's website; they learned he held doctorates from Cambridge and the Sorbonne in Paris and was forty-two years old.

Dr. Shockey was a friendly, outgoing man, slightly balding and considerably overweight. Roberto and Edward introduced themselves and said they were history buffs fascinated with the Arthurian legends. Edward explained, "We're friends who have been blessed with sufficient success in business to allow us to indulge our passion for all this. We're neophytes compared to yourself, Dr. Shockey, but we want to learn everything we can about where Arthur and Guinevere may be buried."

Shockey discussed the legend of the interment of the King and Queen. He was convinced they were real people who had truly been buried at Camelot. He believed Glastonbury Abbey was built on the site of their mythical castle, the bodies were found in 1191 and were removed by monks.

"The bones were discovered beneath the flooring in the Lady Chapel, tucked underneath an old stone sarcophagus. According to the monks who found them, that coffin held one of Arthur's Knights of the Round Table. As I recall, it was inscribed 'Eternal Protector of the King.'"

My God! Edward thought. *He's describing Lamorak's sarcophagus!* He glanced at Roberto, who subtly shook his head.

The administrator continued. "That sarcophagus disappeared in the 1200s, around the time Arthur's and Guinevere's remains were reburied. Its present location is unknown; it likely was accidentally destroyed while they were trying to move it. No one knows for sure."

Edward's skin tingled as he listened to the man confirm so much of what they'd found back in London. Changing the subject, Shockey said how much they hoped to continue excavations around the abbey. There were no current projects – although his board of directors had identified several, funding was tight. For years they'd been unable to do anything but the most basic work.

"There are hundreds of worthy projects in England, but donations have declined so dramatically in recent years we can't do much. Our trust alone could use a million dollars a year. For instance, we want to restore the foundations around Glastonbury Abbey that disappeared in the thousand years between its construction and when Henry VIII took down everything in 1540. And that's just one project that comes to mind – there are a dozen we could begin today if we just had the money."

The administrator was glad the subject of money finally came up. He was pleased to speak with two wealthy gentlemen from London who were obviously interested in Glastonbury, but it was time to see what they could do for the trust. He needed benefactors and hoped these two would help ease the long dry spell without funding.

It turned out the men had one particular project in mind. Roberto asked if they donated, say, a half million dollars, would the trust be willing to disinter the bones of the legendary King and Queen and perform DNA testing to prove their identities?

The man brightened at the prospect of new patrons. "The stories that place Camelot here fuel millions a year in tourism revenue for Glastonbury. It would serve us well to conclusively prove that the legendary couple actually are buried here. However, gentlemen … well, to put it bluntly, this is a bit of a delicate subject. Before speaking further, I must ensure you'll keep our discussion confidential."

He pulled a paper from his desk drawer and handed it to Roberto. "This is our standard confidentiality agreement. If you're willing to sign it, I'll give you some thoughts about the project you envision."

They'd come all this way to find out the answer they needed. Both signed immediately. Dr. Shockey laid the document on his desk and continued.

"The search for the reburial site has been conducted time and again over the last hundred years," he said ruefully. "As you saw today, a plaque marks the location, but confidentially, the bones have never been found. There's absolutely no hard evidence they're buried here and our Trustees wouldn't accept your money for what we are certain would be a fruitless endeavor. There's no telling where they are, if they even existed. But it would be disastrous if the public found that out. We need curious tourists spending their money here at what they believe is the site of Arthur's Camelot."

Perfect.

The administrator mentioned other projects they might consider. They politely declined for now and asked Shockey not to discuss their visit with his board.

"There's no need to raise expectations unless we found something else we'd be willing to support," Roberto explained. Shockey said he'd contact them if anything new turned up regarding the bones of the monarchs.

On the evening train to London they recapped the fruitful day at Glastonbury. They sat in the bar car, speaking in whispers over their drinks. Having never seen the ruins until today, Roberto had thoroughly enjoyed himself. Best of all, they learned the critical thing they wanted to know. Now they knew the legendary King and Queen very possibly weren't reburied at the abbey at all.

There had been the one revelation that really made them excited. Lamorak's sarcophagus had once been at Camelot, now Glastonbury. Sometime after 1191 the stone coffin and its occupant disappeared.

Now they were certain Lamorak's body was in the sarcophagus. That fact in turn supported the theory that the monarch actually existed. So far they had no idea why Lamorak's body had been buried in the crypt of the Church of St. Mary Axe. But it surely was.

Dr. Shockey had said Arthur and Guinevere had originally been "tucked underneath an old stone sarcophagus inscribed 'Eternal Protector of the King.'" What if in 1278 it had happened all over again? What if Arthur's and Guinevere's bones had been secretly brought to London along with Lamorak's sarcophagus? What if they'd been reburied in the same manner as their original interment? What if the King and Queen of Camelot were actually lying below the coffin in Edward's basement?

CHAPTER FORTY-FIVE

Now that the power was on, Roberto's bright floodlights illuminated the ancient Roman passageway more than halfway to its end at the Thames. The men divided responsibilities. Roberto spent his time below ground while Edward continued translating the diaries. Since Lamorak had been moved to London hundreds of years after Guinevere's death, her journals wouldn't explain how he ended up in the crypt. Her diaries had already helped them immensely. Translating them was top priority whether they got an answer about Lamorak or not.

A UPS van snaked down the narrow street, briefly blocking traffic as it unloaded three twenty-pound boxes onto the sidewalk in front of the bookstore. Roberto signed for the ground-penetrating radar unit he'd ordered and carried the boxes through Edward's shop and down the basement stairs. He unpacked them and lowered the contents to the chamber below, taking advantage of the pulley Edward's grandfather had installed years before.

It took about an hour to put the unit together and mount it to its carriage. When he was finished, he had a black box with several gauges that sat on a wheeled tricycle. An operator could move the unit backward or forward while it was aimed at the ground, or it could be swiveled to examine walls and ceilings.

He planned to cover every inch of the two rooms and the long passageway. He'd also try a slant in an attempt to check underneath the sarcophagus. It wasn't likely the slant would work; if it didn't, they'd have to wait until they ultimately moved the heavy stone coffin. The GPR sweep would be slow but the reward substantial if they found new secrets from long ago.

Roberto connected a large battery pack, and lights began to blink on the radar. He had memorized the online instructions before the equipment arrived, so he was ready. He started next to Lamorak's sarcophagus, aiming it at the wall and flipping a switch. A beep indicated the device was ready, so he began with a test. Running it along the side wall of the stone coffin, he immediately got a reading that there was a space and something else behind it. That would be the interior of the sarcophagus and the body of Lamorak. Perfect. He now knew what to expect if he got a hit.

The radar penetrated only straight down or straight to the side. It worked perfectly on floors and walls, but one of the things Roberto considered most promising, a slant search, wasn't possible. The unit wouldn't operate that way. The area under the sarcophagus would have to wait since the machine couldn't go through the coffin and into the floor at a slant.

He started with the walls. For fifteen minutes he explored the ones above the sides and back of the sarcophagus. The indicators showed solid stone with dirt behind – no hollow spaces, no anomalies. He couldn't use the machine on the walls that abutted Lamorak's coffin because the stone sarcophagus was up tight against them. He'd look at those after the sarcophagus was moved.

He finished one wall, moved to the next one, then the third. There was no need to use GPR on the fourth – it separated Roberto's chamber from Edward's via the wooden door. They knew about both sides of that one. So far he'd found absolutely nothing.

He moved to the floor. He was optimistic about this sweep primarily because of the story they'd heard at

Glastonbury. If the bodies of the King and Queen were actually here, he should find them in this room, near Lamorak.

He operated using a grid, pushing the machine back and forth along the floor in a pattern. There were no positive readings, and he was disappointed as he approached the wall that would mark the end of the floor search. Suddenly the dials swung wildly. Beneath the stone and dirt there was an area of loose fill and something solid was buried there.

Jackpot!

Roberto marked an X on the stones that had triggered the radar. He grabbed his entrenching tool and used its pry bar to raise the first stone. He lifted it out of the hole, eagerly grabbed his flashlight and looked down. He saw fresh brown dirt and a sprinkling of white powder. Fresh dirt? What was that about? He used the tool to carefully begin removing the soil. If the bones of the king and queen were here, he didn't want to accidentally hit them with a shovel.

"Exactly what do you think you're doing?"

He jumped, startled to see Edward standing directly behind him. In his excitement he hadn't noticed him come down the ladder.

"You won't believe what the GPR found! Look at this – there may be bones down there! These could be the bodies we're looking for!"

"Unfortunately those aren't the ones," Edward replied softly.

Suddenly everything went black.

CHAPTER FORTY-SIX

Roberto slowly opened first one eye, then the other. He had a throbbing headache. He struggled, unable to move his arms, as he began to recall what had happened.

He was in a corner of the chamber, securely bound with twist ties around his wrists and ankles. He was tied to a heavy sewer pipe in the corner so tightly he could barely move. He knew calling for help was fruitless; the crypt was two stories below the busy store and only he and Edward knew it was there.

Fifteen minutes later he heard a door slam and steps coming down the basement stairs. Finally Edward Russell climbed down the ladder and faced him. The man's eyes darted around the room crazily. His insane personality was in charge of him right now.

"Ah, Juan Carlos, you're awake. Sorry to inconvenience you, but you got a bit too close for comfort." Edward chuckled, mostly to himself.

"What the hell are you doing? And why are you calling me Juan Carlos again?"

"Because that's who you are. I've been ready for you. I knew you'd come eventually; I just didn't expect you to be in the guise of a friend. But then we've never really been friends, have we? We tolerate each other, we bide our time while we learn as much as we can about the secrets in the crypt, but we don't like each other, do we? And you've planned all along to take everything for yourself. For your collection. Right, Juan Carlos?"

From the wild look in Edward's eyes, Roberto knew he couldn't reason with him. He had to talk Edward back into his other persona. And he had to find out how much Edward actually knew about the assassin Juan Carlos.

"Okay, I give up. I admit I've used the name Juan Carlos before."

"I knew it!" Edward clapped his hands like a gleeful child. "You're the collector Curtis Pemberly told me about." Almost as an aside, he gestured to the hole where Roberto had removed the rock from the floor. "That's Curtis down there, by the way."

Roberto's look of astonishment made Edward happy. He laughed and said, "Maybe I'll put you there too!"

The deranged man continued. "So do you admit you're here to steal the things I found? That's it, isn't it?"

Roberto replied in a calm voice. "Listen to me and think about this. I'm not here to steal anything. I really am your friend even though you don't think so right now. You know I was looking for the bodies of Arthur and Guinevere. I told you I was renting a radar unit and you knew I was going to use it. If you had secrets of your own in the crypt, I'm surprised you left me down here alone, but you did.

"I have secrets too. Big ones, like you do. But I really am Roberto Maas. I really am a Swiss businessman. Juan Carlos was me in a previous life, one I left behind long ago. I'm seriously interested in antiquities and I love collecting things – the rarer, more unique and amazing, the better. You're a perfect match as a partner because you have the intellectual background and the academic connections to research just about anything. I don't give a damn what's under the floor unless it's the bones we're looking for. Don't you see? I'm on *your* side. The fact I stumbled upon a secret of yours makes no difference. We're onto something big. We're close to proving Arthur and Guinevere are buried here. I need to keep working because I know how to operate the GPR. And you have a business to run. I can do all this while you're doing your thing. Cut me loose and let's keep going. All I need is a couple of aspirins. What the hell did you hit me with, by the way?"

"A shovel," Edward answered casually. He glanced around the room, then carefully replaced the floor stone. Filling its seams with dirt, he said, "I really wish you hadn't done this. I'm not sure it'd be safe for you to remain alive now."

"If I went to the police, it would be worse for me than for you, trust me. I've killed people too, Edward. I really have."

"Then maybe you'll kill me too. See? You just gave me another reason I shouldn't untie you. I don't like you anymore." He sounded like a child now, saying simple sentences in a singsong voice. At the moment he was totally insane.

We're going to kill him, aren't we?

Maybe. Be patient.

Roberto scrambled for logical thoughts. "I'm sharing secrets with you, Edward. Let's get back to the project. You don't have to like me. I don't have to be your best friend. But I want to help you find these amazing things right here below your store. They're here! I know they are! You do too! We can enjoy them together, even if we don't tell anyone they exist. I don't want fame and fortune. I just need to know I found something no one else has ever found. Don't you want to do that too?"

Edward rocked back and forth on his heels as Roberto talked. He quietly hummed a tune, apparently oblivious to the man tied up in front of him.

He's losing it right this minute and he's totally irrational, Roberto thought. He began to be fearful Edward was going to kill him now.

Finally Edward turned and started up the ladder.

"I'll think about it. I'll come back later. Either I'll bring you something to eat or I'll kill you."

I say we kill him!

CHAPTER FORTY-SEVEN

Edward's mind raged. Two floors below, Juan Carlos was his prisoner. He couldn't keep his mind on work; he was so preoccupied his clerk had to take over a transaction he was trying to complete. She shot him a quizzical look and he excused himself, saying he didn't feel well. He sat at the table in the back room and picked up Guinevere's diary. He wanted to do this now. He didn't want to think about Juan Carlos down in the crypt. He just needed to calm down and read the diary. He picked up the book and started translating. Immediately both his mental state and his countenance changed. His mind transformed. He became his old self again. The bad dark thing retreated to the place he lived in Edward's head. For now.

Guinevere's diary told about the ongoing war near Mount Badon, around twenty miles from Camelot. Messages were carried back and forth from the castle to the front lines. Merlin went to Mount Badon regularly and provided Arthur the benefit of his mystical powers.

One gray afternoon in 500 AD in the sixth week of the conflict, Guinevere watched from her tower window as several mounted riders appeared in the distance. As they got closer, she saw the flag of the Britons; these were Arthur's soldiers accompanying a wagon carrying a wooden box. A coffin. The riders wore black armbands and the neck of the horse pulling the wagon was draped in a black sash.

"Oh God. Oh dear God," her diary recorded. "Please God don't let it be my husband."

Edward stopped a moment and reflected. He was halfway through the last of the three diaries. He had translated every word from Welsh. Exciting words, inciting words, mundane words. He felt he had an insight into the shallow young woman who hopped into bed without shame, embarrassment and apparently without caring who knew. Except for her husband – for some unknown reason she strove to keep hidden from Arthur the dalliances that were an open secret to everyone else. It wasn't out of fear. Arthur likely wouldn't hurt her although God only knew how badly she hurt *him*. But he was truly in love with her. Even the Queen knew, and dutifully recorded, that most of the castle felt his pain when they saw how she returned his love.

Her words said it all.

I have no friends. My retinues are my only comfort and even they merely pretend to care about me. In truth my husband's subjects loathe and revile me. Even the men I bring to my bed merely perform like mere actors on a stage. I suppose I want love from them. I really don't know why I do this. From my sexual partners I get lusty passion, a hard penis and thrusting, grunting orgasms that remind me of the animals in our pens. Only my Arthur is truly my lover, my friend, my confidant, my King. And how do I repay him? I give him sex then go straight to the arms of others. What kind of horrible creature am I?

Edward reflected on her words. He could have written them himself. *I have no friends either. My release isn't sexual – oh, maybe now and then, by myself – but I get my release in a different way. I go to secret places inside my own mind. I can live without friends because I need only myself. I have no friends either, but I'm not pitiful like Guinevere. I'm strong. I even have a prisoner! I'm like ...*

He paused at what he had almost admitted. He'd had these thoughts before. But he hadn't embraced the truth –

hadn't put a name to what he was. But now he could. He wasn't mentally ill, he assured himself. He was simply two people living inside one body.

I'm like Dr. Jekyll. He chose not to think about Jekyll's alter ego, the one who presently held Juan Carlos prisoner in the chamber downstairs.

In an odd way that brief self-evaluation comforted Edward. He turned back to the diary.

Guinevere ran to the courtyard as the horsemen arrived. Tears streamed down her face. She saw the knight Percival, the one who had been chosen to accompany the body home. She realized they were bearing someone important; dozens or hundreds had likely already given their lives but a knight had not accompanied their bodies home. For Sir Percival to be along was a bad sign. She feared the worst. Her heart pounded as she grasped his tunic.

"Is it he? Is it he?" *I was weeping so hard I could not see,* she wrote.

Edward found himself engrossed in her story. The sadness must have been overwhelming. The next words tore at Edward's heartstrings, as they must likewise have done to the Queen.

"I regret that it is, my lady."

I screamed over and over. "Oh my God! Oh my God! My husband is dead."

Surprised and suddenly embarrassed, Percival shook his head. He spoke quietly so others would not hear. "Apologies, my Queen. I misunderstood about whom you were inquiring. The body we bear is that of my brother Lamorak."

Obviously everyone had heard of her sordid tryst with the brave knight. Even his own brother Percival thought her tears were for Lamorak instead of her own husband.

How pitiful, Edward thought.

Edward glanced at his watch. The time had flown. It was almost five and the store would close soon. It had been six hours since he came up from the chamber. He had to decide what to do with Juan Carlos Sebastian.

CHAPTER FORTY-EIGHT

Roberto spent the afternoon trying to escape. He had to admit two things: Edward had done a good job securing him and, despite his background, he hadn't been prepared for Edward.

His hands were so tightly bound with the twist ties that the circulation was almost cut off. His fingers were numb – using his hands to feel around for a solution was therefore impossible. He sat on his butt, feet in front of him on the floor, back and arms roped to the pipe, thinking of a way to get loose. He rocked back and forth, but the pipe was solid. It didn't budge. Nothing else came to mind and he dozed periodically as the hours dragged by.

He thought of using his feet to kick Edward and knock him out, but that wouldn't work. All Edward would do was wake up with Roberto still tied in place, and retaliate.

He spent his waking hours planning how to talk his way out. Maybe that would work with this completely crazy bastard. If it didn't, he'd be the next resident of the new cemetery Edward had created below the floor.

He heard creaks on the stairs, and Edward finally appeared in the chamber, carrying a grocery sack. Roberto looked at his face; the man appeared calmer and more composed than he had earlier. That was a good sign.

Edward put a bottle of water and a sandwich next to Roberto. Then he removed a notepad and a knife.

"I want to finish our project, but I don't see how I can trust you. I'm going to release one of your hands so you can eat, but I may decide to tie it up again when you're done. While you're eating, I want to tell you what I learned this afternoon from Guinevere's diary."

Roberto was encouraged; the fact that he wanted to talk instead of killing him outright just might indicate there was a chance for escape.

Edward reached behind Roberto and sliced through the tie around his left wrist with the knife. Roberto shook his hand hard to restart the blood flow. It was nearly purple.

"These ties are too tight. I'm going to lose my hands if you leave them that way."

Ignoring him, Edward sat on the floor five feet away and read the entire passage he'd translated about the Battle of Badon.

Roberto was a little concerned about eating the food Edward prepared, given his history with the tea. But he was starving, and surely Edward wouldn't spend time explaining what he'd learned from the diary if he was going to poison Roberto right away. As he ate, he listened intently to Edward. The information was intriguing and Edward was as sane as any person alive … at this precise moment. Who knew how long it would last? Roberto had to convince Edward to release him.

"Incredible work. Now we know that the body of Lamorak has arrived at Camelot. I'm hoping the next diary entries will tell how he got to London. You're getting right to the meat of the matter – exactly what we need to know. This corroboration can prove everything. This could be our proof that the Knights of the Round Table were real. We need to do this together. Let's put the past behind us. Cut me loose and let's move on. I can use the GPR to search for the graves of Arthur and Guinevere, and you can continue the translating."

Edward hung his head, contrite. "I shouldn't have hit you. I thought you were trying to find the bodies …"

The bodies. There was more than one person down there.

"But now I've thought it over. I need you alive and I want to continue our project too. Do you give me your word you'll let this go and not retaliate against me?"

"Absolutely. It was an honest mistake. I can see why you were concerned and how it all happened. Thankfully all I ended up with was a headache."

Edward seemed relieved. Roberto leaned forward to allow Edward to cut the twist tie off his other wrist and loosen the ropes. He sliced the restraints on Roberto's ankles and the man was free.

Roberto massaged his wrist and feet, then stood unsteadily. After a few minutes he worked out the stiffness in his joints and looked at his watch. It was six p.m.

Edward put the food wrappers back in the sack and stuck out his hand. "I apologize."

They shook. "Apology accepted. Let's move ahead."

Roberto would deal with all this. Edward's retribution would come.

CHAPTER FORTY-NINE

Edward researched the legends surrounding contemporaries of Arthur before continuing the work on Guinevere's diary. He was seeking more information on Lamorak and his family.

Lamorak's father, King Pellinore, had bravely fought Angles and Saxons from his bastion in Anglesey. Like his father before him, Lamorak had many victories to his name. At least three of his brothers were already aligned with Arthur. After Pellinore's death, Arthur asked Lamorak to join his siblings at the Round Table. The young man eagerly accepted and soon became one of the strongest and bravest of the mighty band.

Edward opened Guinevere's journal, read her description of events in 500 AD, and learned something astounding.

The father of Lamorak, King Pellinore, rests in peace in London, in the graveyard of the tiny Church of St. Mary Axe. I expected Sir Percival to inter his brother there as well. But Percival convinced my husband Lamorak would prefer the beautiful vistas around Camelot. To my surprise, Arthur gave approval for the knight to be buried here, despite his having succumbed to my seduction. His funeral was held weeks ago and today the knights will bear Lamorak's body to the abbey. A special sarcophagus has been constructed for my brave soldier. He will remain at Camelot for eternity. Lamorak, we had only one glorious night. But you were the best of all. And now you rest, the eternal Protector of your King.

Edward was both confused and excited at more and more validation. Lamorak's *father*, King Pellinore, was buried in London? Was the body in the crypt then Pellinore's? Not according to Guinevere – she said Pellinore was in the graveyard and that Lamorak had had a special sarcophagus built for him. The sarcophagus below the bookshop was inscribed "Eternal Protector of my King," just as Guinevere said it was. She'd obviously seen the inscription herself. If that stone coffin started out on the isle of Avalon – in Glastonbury, over a hundred miles away – when, how and for what purpose would it have been moved to London?

If Pellinore's remains were found, it would be one more confirmation of the Arthurian legends. But that was impossible. It was inconceivable that a body buried in a fifth-century churchyard would be found today. The interment was over fifteen hundred years ago – buildings had been erected, razed and rebuilt over the centuries. Today there was no trace of the cemetery Guinevere mentioned. There'd be no way to figure out where it had been, much less find a particular grave.

CHAPTER FIFTY

Something was wrong. He wasn't sure what it was, but something just wasn't right.

Every Friday Philippe emailed the weekly report, the fifty-page spreadsheet Roberto relied upon when he was away from the office. The summary gave him an overview of his expansive portfolio of investments and earnings, deposits and withdrawals, income and expenses. Today Roberto flipped from one page to another and back again, trying to figure out what didn't make sense.

He was a genius with numbers and he knew these accounts by heart. Today something just didn't add up. Every so often there was a line item that he didn't understand. With over three hundred million dollars in play, there were movements of money every single day. Some were significant, others small. Large amounts of dollars, dinars, pounds or yen were routinely transferred into another investment, another country, another currency. The movements were so commonplace Roberto quickly skimmed over most of them. But now and then he checked both sides of a particular transaction just so he'd stay on top of things.

In the latest report he'd picked up negatives in one account or another with no corresponding positives. Money moved out, but there was no offsetting accounting entry showing where it went.

There had to be a simple answer. Philippe had been directing all this for years while Roberto sat across the office from him in Lucerne and he'd never had questions about the mechanics of any transaction. But today four small entries didn't tally. There could be many reasons – a computer glitch, human error, a number inadvertently omitted in the complex spreadsheets. He had no doubt there was a simple explanation and he wanted to believe Philippe would have it.

—

Roberto got a quiet ding and glanced at his phone. There was one word, texted as usual from an untraceable phone in another country.

"Nine."

Today's was the second wet-ops assignment he'd received since he and Edward began working together. The first text message had said, "Two." It came immediately after his confinement in the crypt and it would require a trip to the United States. Roberto declined. He couldn't risk leaving the deranged bookseller in charge of things. He responded to the request for Juan Carlos's services by texting the French word *Non.*

Now there was another request, this time for an operation in Moscow. He hadn't been back there in years, and things had settled down with Edward. His dark side, the dangerous part of him, hadn't peeked out in a while.

Roberto had spent weeks underground cataloging, pushing the GPR device and looking for whatever might be hidden. It was time for a change, some fresh air, some danger. Juan Carlos needed to emerge for a while. So he texted *"Oui"* to accept the job. He would travel to Moscow next weekend and check out the situation.

Roberto told Edward he had to return to Lucerne for several days for meetings. The bookseller assured Roberto things would be fine until his return.

After one quick glance at TrickTracker, Edward knew Roberto was lying.

Edward Russell was a highly intelligent and incredibly eccentric individual. Two people lived inside his head. The one he now compared to Dr. Jekyll was fortunately dominant. The other personality had no name – that one both frightened and excited Edward the times he appeared. Thankfully that wasn't very often.

Edward was determined to learn the truth about his partner. When he had been tied up in the crypt, Roberto said he used an alias and had secrets of his own. He even admitted killing someone. Was all that made up so Edward would free him? He wanted to find out who this "Swiss businessman" really was and what his motives were for teaming up with Edward Russell.

He found a fascinating product called TrickTracker on the Internet. It was marketed to jealous spouses; it allowed one person to spy on another's cellphone. The website promised it was easy to install – you needed another person's unlocked phone for only ninety seconds. Once installed, the app was invisible: it wasn't displayed anywhere on the target phone. TrickTracker let you see the other person's texts, emails, call lists and websites visited – any activity on his or her phone. With GPS technology it also told you where the device was. And you could spy using your computer, a tablet or even your own smartphone!

Don't be the last to know, the homepage blared. *Their secrets won't be safe from you any longer!*

He paid three hundred dollars for the software package at a spy shop in Leicester Square and bought a throwaway cell phone. He put the software on his laptop then downloaded an app. He practiced opening the program on his new cell phone several times. Finally he had it down; he could do it in under two minutes. If Roberto ever left his phone unlocked, Edward could merely press a button on his own phone. Everything would happen automatically after that. It sounded simple. And it had been.

The opportunity came one afternoon as Roberto crouched down in the Roman passageway to examine an inscription. He got a ding and pulled the phone from his back pocket. He glanced at an email then put down the phone. Edward was a foot away, copying words Roberto read from the wall carving. Roberto's phone was unlocked and Edward acted quickly. He pressed a button on his own cellphone, picked up Roberto's and started the process.

A few minutes later Roberto stood and explained the Latin inscription he'd seen. Edward couldn't concentrate – he was anxious to go upstairs and see if TrickTracker worked.

And it did. It had performed exactly as advertised.

On his computer, Edward observed Roberto's phone activity. He saw the recent single word *"Nine"* texted from a blocked number. He saw the response *"Oui."* Edward searched online for the cell number but got nothing.

He was enthused. He'd wondered what his partner was up to and now he'd know. He had already looked into Guinevere's private life. Now he got to peek into someone else's!

Roberto said he was going to Lucerne tomorrow. Edward hoped he'd booked the trip on his phone. And he had – thanks to his new spy program Edward saw the flight itinerary.

The man's excitement was like that of a kid with a toy. He felt like a secret agent and wondered if Roberto might be one too. If Roberto actually *did* have secrets in his life like he claimed, Edward was going to find out what they were!

According to Roberto's reservation, he was going to Lucerne tomorrow. But then Edward saw something interesting. Roberto wasn't going to the office several days for meetings like he'd said. He was spending tomorrow night only. The next day he'd be on the afternoon flight from Zurich to Moscow.

Thanks to his new toy, Edward was in the middle of a mystery. He was ecstatic. *I'll get to Moscow first!*

CHAPTER FIFTY-ONE

It was winter in Lucerne. Philippe and Roberto walked from the office to lunch in a brisk, chilling wind. Rain was beginning to fall; gray clouds turned to ominous thunderheads as the men ducked just in time into Roberto's favorite restaurant, La Belle Fille. As they entered, the skies opened into a torrential thunderstorm that lasted all afternoon.

One great bottle of Puligny-Montrachet led to another as thunder crashed and the rain poured outside. Inside the restaurant an inviting fire crackled. They picked one of the specialty fish dishes for which the chef and proprietor was famous. Afterwards they moved to a couch next to the fireplace for a cognac. It was late afternoon; the owner asked permission to begin preparing for the dinner crowd; soon a vacuum quietly buzzed in the dining room behind them. Roberto was totally relaxed, enjoying one of the most pleasant times he'd had in weeks. Philippe, on the other hand, struggled to maintain an appearance of normalcy around a man he no longer considered even a friend. A man he now hated. He masked the knot in his stomach as he forced a smile.

Roberto talked about the diaries and the trip to Glastonbury Abbey. "The good news is there's no proof Arthur and Guinevere are buried there. After getting us to sign an NDA, the administrator of the trust admitted he and his board don't think they are. Since 1278 no one's been able to find the bodies, but the town has done a great job ignoring that fact. They want tourists to keep coming to see where the bodies are today. Even though they're not there!"

Despite his feelings toward Roberto, he found the story fascinating. Thoughts of betrayal still simmered just below the surface, but he couldn't mask the excitement at what Roberto was doing in London.

"I'm surprised you've been able to keep these discoveries quiet," he reflected.

"Neither of us has motivation to reveal them. I eagerly anticipate everything we do every day – you just don't know what's going to turn up next – and Edward, as odd as he is, looks forward to it too. He and his grandparents should have involved the antiquities people ages ago but didn't. I don't think he'll do it now. At the moment he has nothing to lose by keeping quiet. Neither do I. Some day that may change, but that's the plan for now."

"I hope I get to see it soon," Philippe mentioned again, as he had done before. "It certainly sounds intriguing."

Once again Roberto ignored the less-than-subtle request for an invitation. "It is for sure. And here's something else you'll find interesting – a modern addition of sorts to the historical aspect of all this."

Roberto had wrestled with revealing that there were bodies Edward had buried. He decided Philippe was his partner and there was no harm telling him. Without mentioning he'd been Edward's prisoner, Roberto told about how the GPR accidentally led him to something much more recent in the ancient crypt.

"They're still using it for burials today?"

"Yes and no. 'They' aren't using the crypt anymore – there've been no sanctioned burials in a thousand years. But someone is."

"Don't tell me it's Edward. This guy vacillates from scholarly wimp to calling me with threats to offering you drugged tea. What's going on with him?"

"It is Edward. I've decided he's schizophrenic – sometimes meek, sometimes maniacal. I guess all of us have something to hide, but he tells me there are bodies – plural – buried in the crypt. I can't investigate while he's there every day, and I'm also not going to ruin everything by calling the authorities. Not with our knight's sarcophagus sitting right there in the same room. If the police considered the place a crime scene, then we'd lose everything that's there."

Roberto further explained that if there actually were bodies, they'd have to deal with them once they were ready to bring in the antiquities people.

Changing the subject slightly, he instructed Philippe to exercise the option he had on the vacant building and buy it outright. He explained, "I don't know where this is all going, but I need to be the owner, not a tenant. Put it in the real estate trust that we established in Mauritius."

As they lingered over coffee, Philippe casually said, "You're here for only one night. Where are you off to tomorrow?"

"I've got a quick trip to Moscow. I've reconnected with an old friend from Zurich who's based there now. He's come up with a telecom opportunity that might prove lucrative."

"Moscow, eh?" Philippe's mind raced as he thought of everything the Russians had told him. "Have I heard you speak of this friend before? I don't recall a telecom connection ..."

Philippe's tone this afternoon concerned Roberto. The man seemed uncomfortable and distant. Now he was challenging and distrustful. A tinge of concern crept into Roberto's mind. He hoped what he saw in Philippe had nothing to do with the discrepancies he hadn't brought up yet.

Roberto chided his partner. "Come on, Philippe! Don't get paranoid on me. No secrets anymore – right?

You've never heard of this guy. I hadn't thought of him myself in years until the other day when he dropped me an email. I'll be sure to keep you in the loop this time."

Philippe lowered his head, angry at how smoothly his former friend could lie to him. *Keep me in the loop? Right. You haven't told me the truth yet. Whatever this trip's about, it's not about investing in telecom. That's for sure. You haven't researched a new investment idea in two years. That's* my *job. Everything you're telling me is a lie. Why are you* really *going to Moscow? And who are you* this *time? Slava Sergenko? Juan Carlos Sebastian? You're a killer – a man with something to hide yourself – and you're trying to say that Edward Russell killed people and buried them? If there are bodies buried, I'd bet they're* your *dead bodies. Edward may be crazy as hell, but he's not a murderer. You, on the other hand, are.*

There was a period of uncomfortable silence. Roberto cleared his throat then brought up the last thing he had to discuss – the accounts. He'd waited until the end on purpose, and he tried to sound upbeat. Until and unless he found out otherwise, there was no need for concern.

"I have a few questions about the last weekly report. I found a few entries I can't understand. I guess I've been away too long; maybe I'm losing my touch!"

He studied Philippe's body language. Despite Roberto's initial reluctance to think his partner was involved in wrongdoing, he saw Philippe stiffen imperceptibly and lean away slightly.

There's something going on.

Philippe forced himself to remain calm. He'd prepared himself for this and he was ready. But he was nervous; he'd never done this to his partner before and it made him uncomfortable.

Today was the first time in months Roberto had asked even a single question about the vast sea of numbers he received weekly. It was also the first time there actually was something wrong with them. His partner was sharp and on top of the financials – that was certain. But everything was completely under control. This was not a problem – it was a test. It was a critical part of Philippe's plan for the future.

"I'm glad to help. Do you know offhand which entries you're asking about, or should we go over everything at the office?"

Philippe's discomfort was more and more evident, but Roberto still wanted there to be a simple explanation.

"I hardly expect you to know a thousand transactions by heart! I'll email you my questions so you can show me what I'm missing. It's not a big deal – not even big money involved. It's just something I need to understand."

At home that evening Philippe poured a nightcap. He looked at Roberto's email for the tenth time and relaxed. His boss had immediately picked out the few small errors. Philippe wasn't surprised at Roberto's diligence – the man was a genius. But he'd learned something – he had to be extremely careful. The good news about all this was the one large transaction Roberto *hadn't* caught. That one had been hidden much deeper than the others. His boss had missed that entry at the moment, but Philippe would wait a couple of weeks to be sure. Then that two hundred thousand dollars would be transferred to his offshore account. Even two hundred grand was a pittance in Ciprian Investments' vast holdings. The transaction would easily go unnoticed as long as Philippe was careful.

So far so good; make this work and there'll be much more to come!

That evening Philippe called the Russian and told him about Roberto's upcoming trip to Moscow. He didn't know the travel details, but his new associate seemed pleased with the information.

"Keep me advised," he told the Russian. "I want to know what happens."

His so-called "partner" wouldn't leave Philippe in the dark any longer.

———

Philippe's email quickly explained the four errors Roberto had caught. Expecting this level of scrutiny, Philippe actually *did* create offsetting entries – in different amounts and different currencies just to muddy the waters – and funds had been deliberately moved into incorrect accounts. Philippe explained there had been a few mistakes made by people in the accounting department. Nothing was missing and he pointed out the offsetting entries that made things match up.

The trial run had gone perfectly. Four obvious little mistakes caught, one huge error overlooked.

———

After a candid self-assessment the other day, the man had chosen a clever nickname for himself.

The Bad Man.

He didn't know why he hadn't thought of it before. He was very good at keeping secrets and a master at ensuring none of those around him knew what and who he really was. All the outside world could see was the façade. Nobody knew the Bad Man was inside. Only an unlucky few ever saw him emerge.

He'd keep the Bad Man secret, of course. He wouldn't even say it to himself. Only his alter ego could call itself that name.

Today he sat in business class on the Moscow flight and sipped a glass of champagne. He had a tough project ahead. With decades-old information, he wanted to learn about a boy who disappeared long ago. There was much to learn in order to see what he was up against. This person was creating a problem today – years after his disappearance from Russia – a situation the Bad Man intended to correct.

———

Edward stayed one night at the Aerostar Hotel a few miles from Moscow's Sheremetyevo Airport. Since he would be standing at International Arrivals the next evening, he chose a hotel nearby. Presuming Roberto's itinerary didn't change, Edward would switch to the National Hotel next to the Kremlin tomorrow. That was where Roberto would be staying.

The next morning Edward checked his phone. TrickTracker revealed an update from the airline. Roberto's flight was delayed a half hour and would depart from Zurich's Flughafen Airport at 1:30 p.m. Thanks to the GPS feature on Roberto's cellphone, Edward could see he was already at the airport.

At 7:10 p.m. Moscow time, Swissair Flight 441 landed and taxied to the gate. Edward stood at a barrier separating the passengers exiting the secured arrivals and customs area from a crowd who waited to meet them. He watched as GPS tracked Roberto's progression through customs and immigration. Finally the exit doors swung open and the man came through, briefcase over one shoulder and rolling a carry-on bag. Roberto passed within twenty feet of Edward and looked directly at him. Edward smiled broadly at the man who couldn't see him.

Edward was dressed head to toe in a black burqa. A veiled slit for his eyes was the only thing anyone could see. He was a Muslim woman, just one of dozens milling about the busy international airport.

He congratulated himself on being clever once again. Any attempt to change his appearance would have to have included shaving his long gray beard. That would require an explanation when Roberto returned to London. So he decided to go in costume instead. No one ever talked to Muslim women; they were basically treated as if they weren't there. That was perfect.

———

After Juan Carlos checked in and went to his room, the front desk clerk placed a call to the number on his computer. When he had brought up Juan Carlos Sebastian's reservation, the clerk couldn't miss a notice emblazoned on his screen. The FSB – the Russian security service previously called the KGB – wanted to know when the man checked in. No one failed to obey the FSB.

———

Edward knew Roberto had a dinner reservation at nine p.m. at Skorpio, a quiet place around the corner from the hotel. It was for one person, TrickTracker told him. He saw no need to waste an evening. He'd pick up his quarry in the morning.

Once Roberto was at dinner, Edward checked into the hotel using his own name and passport. He had no alternative and figured it didn't matter anyway. As long as he didn't run into Roberto, no one would ever know he was staying here. As far as Roberto knew, Edward was in the crypt doing his fieldwork.

At seven the next morning, Edward sat in the lobby wearing the burqa. There had been nothing on Roberto's schedule for today, so Edward had planned to follow Roberto using GPS. That had all changed around 6:30 when he woke, went to the bathroom then crawled back in bed with a cup of coffee. He checked GPS and was astonished to see Roberto had left the hotel. He'd missed him!

At first he thought of going outside to find Roberto, but at this early hour it was too risky. There were few people on the streets, he figured, and his prey might spot either Edward himself or the woman in disguise he'd created.

Instead he put on the burqa, sat in the lobby and followed Roberto's movements until he returned. Around nine he walked back into the hotel.

What the hell? What had he been doing for over two hours? Edward cursed to himself for possibly missing an opportunity. It was essential to know what Roberto was up to, and he'd completely blown what might have been a chance to find out.

He watched Roberto come through the massive front doors, walk through the lobby and enter an elevator car. Edward waited a few minutes, saw no movement on GPS and figured the man was now in his room. He went upstairs himself.

Roberto had been wearing a jogging suit but wasn't out of breath. On the surface that wasn't significant – he could have spent the last half hour cooling down from an exhausting run. But had he been jogging at all? According to GPS, Roberto hadn't gone more than twelve blocks from the hotel during his entire two and a half hours away. And he'd been stationary much of the time. So he wasn't out jogging. What the hell *had* he been doing?

Frustrated, Edward jotted down two addresses where Roberto had stopped along his route. He had no idea what they were, but both were nearby. He'd see for himself where Roberto had been so early.

———

When he awoke today, Roberto had become Juan Carlos. When that happened, his entire being – his mind, actions and movements – transformed into those of the assassin. His alarm woke him at six a.m. He dressed totally in black – ski cap, gloves, T-shirt, jogging pants, lightweight jacket and running shoes. There were similarly dressed joggers in the lobby and outside under the porte cochere. It was drizzling and the temperature was in the forties – he was chilly, but after running only a couple of blocks, Juan Carlos's system was warmed up and in high gear.

Last evening before dinner he'd picked up a cheap cell phone with prepaid minutes from a street vendor. He used it to dial a number he'd memorized long ago. Thirty minutes later he received a text message. He jotted down the information he needed; then he took the phone apart. This morning as he ran he dropped its pieces in one trash can after another along his route.

The text message told him everything he needed to know about the target – who he was, where he lived and worked, what his routine was. Armed with this information, he was ready to reconnoiter the area.

Juan Carlos ran through massive Red Square, the colored domes of St. Basil's Cathedral behind him and the glittering GUM department store on the right. It was oddly reassuring to see the lone sentry guarding the Tomb of Lenin outside the forbidding walls of the Kremlin. Every time he'd been here he'd seen the guard, twenty-four hours a day.

He ran once around the square then back to the east, slowing to a walk in Nikolskaya Street that ran alongside the huge GUM store. Nineteenth-century buildings lined the picturesque avenue; before the Russian Revolution, the area was home to the Enlightenment and had been a center of learning and culture.

At the far end of the street there were imposing three-story structures that once had been mansions for wealthy industrialists in the early and mid-1800s. After the fall of Communism in the 1990s, the houses had been converted to condominiums for a new generation of wealthy Russians – the former government elite who had been in the right place at the right time. When the Soviet Union collapsed, they grabbed what they could, made use of extensive political and social contacts, and transformed easily from Communism to Capitalism. The only difference now was that they were free to accumulate wealth publicly, at least until their activities caught the negative attention of someone more powerful than they. Today the condos housed wealthy foreigners from many countries.

Juan Carlos slowed as he passed number twelve, the most elegantly restored of the former mansions. He glanced up and to the right. The third-floor flat to the south was awash in light. Excellent. He wouldn't have to wait long.

At seven Juan Carlos walked into Cappuccino Express across the street from number twelve, ordered a nonfat latte and a croissant. As he waited, he read a copy of the Russian-language newspaper *Izvestia.* At 7:50 a trim Arab in his late thirties dressed in a tailored dark suit, white shirt and red tie entered the shop. He ordered, pulled rubles from the pocket of his Burberry trench coat, paid and walked out.

Juan Carlos followed him at a comfortable distance. Given the considerable foot traffic on the sidewalks around Red Square, he was unlikely to be spotted, especially by a target who had no idea he was being tailed. Besides, Juan Carlos knew exactly where Sami Terzi was going.

Terzi walked several blocks before turning onto Mokhovaya Street. Thirty feet down the street he entered a gleaming, modern high-rise with Arabic and English above its doors.

البنك الدولي من سوري

THE INTERNATIONAL BANK OF SYRIA

Juan Carlos watched through the bank's enormous front windows as Terzi flashed his badge to a guard then walked to the elevators.

Sami Terzi was the bank's primary money-mover. He was an expert in creating huge transactions that stayed under the radar of the world's money watchdogs. ISIS, the militant Islamic State of Iraq and Syria, kept its ownership of the bank a closely guarded secret. Almost no one knew the International Bank of Syria was Terrorism Central – no other institution on earth funded more atrocities worldwide. Sami was starting another routine day at work. By day's end he personally would have facilitated the transfer of a hundred million American dollars from a huge Saudi conglomerate's secret bank account directly into the waiting arms of the brutal group of kidnappers and executioners called ISIS.

Hope he enjoys his day, Juan Carlos thought grimly as he walked back to the National Hotel. *He has so few left.*

Typically Juan Carlos kept his political persuasions separated from his job. But this time there was a tinge of pride. Soon he would rid the world of a person who funded murderers, rapists and torturers – men who killed not only their enemies but also their own people. As the redneck joke went, "He needed killing" sometimes truly was a justification for homicide.

Juan Carlos walked into the hotel lobby at nine. Ever alert, the assassin took in the surroundings as he walked to the elevators. The public area was busy – couples were heading to breakfast, men at tables were engaged in earnest conversations, fashionably dressed women were preparing for shopping in the area's high-end boutiques.

Out of the corner of his eye he noticed a figure dressed in a black burqa. She was seated by herself, apparently waiting for someone, perhaps her husband.

Something about her ... what was it? An alarm in his brain said something wasn't right.

He got off the lift only one floor up. On the second floor a balcony circled the huge lobby below. Juan Carlos walked to the railing and looked down.

The woman in the burqa was gone.

CHAPTER FIFTY-TWO

Edward stayed in his room for a while. It was risky venturing out – TrickTracker showed nothing on Roberto's calendar for today and that was troublesome. With no itinerary there was no telling where and when he might go. The GPS feature was all Edward had, but at least he could stay several blocks away from his quarry while keeping up with his activities. The burqa was a good disguise, but it was hot as hell and a lot of trouble – he kept tripping on the bottom of the flowing robe. But he donned it one more time and walked through Red Square on his way to Nikolskaya Street.

Edward stopped in front of number twelve, a beautiful old building and the spot where Roberto had spent an hour earlier this morning. With the exception of a coffee shop on the corner across the street, this area consisted of nothing but old, stately structures that had been converted to upscale housing. A discreet sign offered two-bedroom condos for sixty million rubles – around a million US dollars at today's inflated exchange rate.

Chastising himself for sleeping when his quarry was already out on the street, he tried to imagine what could have kept Roberto here for an hour. The coffee couldn't be that good – there were a dozen other shops much closer to the hotel than this. Finally he gave up, looked at the map he'd pulled up on his phone and walked to Mokhovaya Street, the second of Roberto's stops. He arrived at the address where Roberto had spent twenty minutes and gazed at a soaring skyscraper.

What the hell had he been doing at the International Bank of Syria?

He had little time to ponder the question. TrickTracker suddenly sprang to life – Roberto Maas was on the move again.

—

Juan Carlos spent his day on the Sami Terzi project. Entering the banker's condo had been child's play. A dingy service entrance in the back, an unlocked door and a dusty sign in Russian saying "Freight Elevator" made it almost too easy. Once upstairs, a lock pick was all it took. If the man's alarm had been set, Juan Carlos would have simply left. But it wasn't. This was a safe, secure building with a concierge and a locked front door. People got lazy. It happened all the time; human carelessness was a weapon in the assassin's arsenal.

The condo yielded nothing of interest except two tickets to Alexander Pushkin's most famous play, the drama *Boris Godunov*. It happened to be one of Juan Carlos's favorites. With the tickets was a receipt that contained Sami's address, the last four digits of the credit card he'd used and, most importantly, his cell phone contact number.

On a Friday night in two weeks two people would be at the Bolshoi Theatre. All Juan Carlos needed was to find out who they were. He called Sami's number.

Sami Terzi's phone rang. He glanced at the number but didn't recognize it.

"*Da?*"

The caller said in Russian that he was with the Bolshoi Theatre. "We appreciate your attending the play *Boris Godunov* soon. If you and your guest would enjoy a bottle of champagne before the performance, I'd be happy to offer you a nice French one at a fifty percent discount."

At a price of less than fifteen American dollars, Terzi couldn't refuse. He thanked the man and laughed. "My girlfriend will enjoy that very much."

Bingo. Sami was going to the theater with a date. Juan Carlos would be there too.

He was standing across the street when Terzi left the bank around three. He followed him home and waited until Sami went out for a jog. Roberto left him at that point and returned to the hotel, comfortable with the plan that was almost finished.

The woman in the burqa had preyed on Juan Carlos's mind all day. What was it? At last he remembered. He'd noticed another woman in a burqa, covered head to toe and with the same veiled eyes, when he arrived at Sheremetyevo Airport yesterday evening. Nothing special on the surface, but the woman looked almost identical to the one in the lobby today. Height, weight, everything. But again, a burqa was a burqa. That woman at the airport was apparently waiting for someone just like the person in the lobby this morning. So she'd disappeared as soon as Juan Carlos came through – no big deal.

His brain kicked into overdrive when he returned to the National Hotel at four p.m. Sitting in the same chair in the lobby was the woman! Suddenly every instinct – every red flag in his being – went on high alert. The assassin had learned from experience there was no such thing as coincidence.

He walked nonchalantly through the lobby to the elevators and went to the second-floor balcony. He watched for a few minutes until he saw the woman get up and head for the lifts. He pressed the button to go up and waited to see if things would work as he hoped. And they did.

Within seconds a ding indicated one of the three elevator cars was stopping. The doors opened; the only occupant was the woman in the black burqa. She shifted to one side as Roberto entered the car. Now it was time for a little test.

He noted which floor she'd selected, a higher number than his. He surreptitiously pulled a white handkerchief from his pocket then swooped his hand to the floor next to the woman.

"Excuse me, is this yours?" he asked the woman in Arabic as he showed her the cloth.

Startled to have Roberto suddenly so close, Edward reflexively jumped and muttered, "Shit!"

"I'm sorry if I surprised you." Again in Arabic.

No response. She merely shook her head and turned away.

Juan Carlos got off on his floor. He knew that many Arab women simply ignored strangers. He wouldn't have been surprised if she had said nothing. But this one knew the word *shit* in English.

In a male voice. A voice he knew well.

CHAPTER FIFTY-THREE

Damn the luck!

Edward had gotten flustered when Roberto suddenly showed up in the elevator car. He tried to be unassuming, but the damned man had surprised him with the handkerchief. He'd said *shit* before he even knew it had come out. Dammit. Now it was possible Roberto, or Juan Carlos, or whatever he was, knew Edward was the woman in the burqa.

He'd followed Roberto this afternoon and stayed far out of his way. GPS on Roberto's phone made it easy to know his every move. Edward saw him go into the building at 12 Nikolskaya Street, across from the coffee shop where Roberto had spent an hour yesterday. In ten minutes he came out again and went over to his other destination yesterday, the International Bank of Syria building.

At three p.m. a man came out of the bank, and Roberto appeared to spring to life, following him back to the same building on Nikolskaya Street! Edward had no idea what Roberto was doing, but he appeared to be interested in the Arabic-looking man from the bank.

The banker went into his building while Roberto waited outside. There were few people on the street and it wasn't safe for a burqa-clad woman to be here. Edward would easily be noticed; he decided to call it quits for this afternoon. He went back to the hotel lobby and waited for Roberto to return, which the man did at four.

Even though Roberto had surprised him in the elevator, one thing continued to be his salvation. TrickTracker was incredible. Edward saw Roberto's reservation on the morning flight tomorrow from Moscow to London, so he booked a later flight on Alitalia from Moscow to Rome, connecting to London. He'd land five hours after Roberto's nonstop on British Airways, plenty of time to avoid an accidental face-to-face encounter. And from now on, as long as this lasted, he couldn't run into Roberto again.

TrickTracker showed him something else interesting. Two weeks from now Maas would return to Moscow, arriving on Thursday afternoon and staying again here at the National Hotel. He'd be back in London Saturday.

He's back in two weeks for only two nights? What's that all about?

It took only a moment to find out more. Using the name Juan Carlos Sebastian, Roberto purchased an online ticket for Alexander Pushkin's play *Boris Godunov* at the Bolshoi that Friday night.

The man's coming back to Moscow as Roberto Maas. He's flying for hours all the way across Europe just to go to a play*? And Juan Carlos, an alias he said he hadn't used for a long time, is the man going to the theater. Intriguing!*

Edward decided to come back too. This was getting really interesting. It was a mysterious adventure he wasn't about to miss. He'd be more careful and he'd keep quiet about all this when they were together again in London.

He booked one night at the Metropol, a few doors down from the National Hotel. That was safer than risking running into Roberto, and there was no need this time to stay extra days. That Friday night at the theater appeared to be the only reason for his visit – Roberto was back to London the next day.

Edward was giddy with anticipation.

Just call me Bond. James Bond.

———

"Alison, this is Roberto Maas. Is Edward there?"

The helpful clerk at The Necromancer's Bookshop said, "Sorry, Mr. Maas. He's away for a few days, but he didn't say where he was going. I'm sure you can reach him on his mobile. You have that number, right?"

"I do. I just hadn't heard from him in a day or so. Do you think perhaps he's ill? I don't want to bother him if he is."

"Oh, I don't think so. He seemed fine when he left. Maybe he ran up to Oxford for a few days. He does that sometimes."

Next Juan Carlos walked to the hotel's front desk and asked, "Can you tell me if Edward Russell from London is staying here?"

The clerk checked his screen and said, "Yes, sir, he is. Would you like to go to a house phone and I can ring his room?"

"That won't be necessary. Thank you."

CHAPTER FIFTY-FOUR

As he was leaving the hotel the next morning, Roberto glanced around the lobby for Edward, but he wasn't there. He called Philippe from the airport lounge. His partner's phone rang once and went to voicemail.

It's unusual for Philippe not to have his phone handy. He left a message that he was checking in and asked his partner to call if he needed anything.

As Roberto waited for the plane to depart, he began to finalize plans for Sami Terzi's last night on Earth two weeks from now. There was no remorse for his upcoming victim. Instead, his underlying thought was how much he'd enjoy seeing the play *Boris Godunov* again. This murder would be timed so Juan Carlos could watch the entire performance first.

Three hours after Roberto's flight left Moscow, Edward was in Alitalia's departure lounge. This TrickTracker program was the key to his domination over Roberto. Now that he could see everything on Roberto's smartphone, he had a powerful secret weapon. *A weapon for your mass destruction, Juan Carlos.*

The Bad Man was satisfied with his trip to Moscow. He had accomplished what he needed to do, and the next steps would be put in place shortly. It was hard to believe he'd be here again in two weeks. He made a few notes and a call, then picked up a newspaper. Soon his flight would be called for departure.

CHAPTER FIFTY-FIVE

Edward planned his strategy as he flew back to London. It was very possible Roberto knew the burqa-clad woman was him, but there was nothing he could do about it. He'd said *shit* out loud through his burqa, but maybe Roberto hadn't even heard it. Whether Roberto knew it was him or not, Edward's involvement in the crypt project was critical for several reasons. Roberto wouldn't hurt him, at least for now. Edward concocted a plausible story in case Roberto confronted him. And whenever he saw Roberto today, he'd know immediately if the man was onto him. He'd be ready.

Edward had looked forward to resuming Guinevere's diary last evening. Instead, jet lag took its toll; he fell into bed exhausted and slept soundly for nine hours. This morning he was refreshed and ready to go. He was at the shop two hours before it opened, the diary on the table in front of him. With a cup of tea in hand he began to read. When he stopped ninety minutes later, things were beginning to all come together. Everything he read made the picture clearer and brought them closer to the answers both men wanted.

Edward heard footsteps on the wooden stairs. The basement door across the room opened and Roberto came in. He'd entered the crypt on his side, walked through and come up on Edward's.

Everything's completely normal, he coached himself. "You're back," he said in as nonchalant a voice as he could muster. "Would you like some tea?"

Roberto didn't accept drinks from this lunatic any more. "Not a chance."

He wanted to interrogate Edward about Moscow, but that had to wait. The most important thing right now was the crypt project. Edward's work on the diaries was key to solving this mystery.

"Did you learn anything new while I was in Lucerne?"

Lucerne. Right. Edward relaxed, confident that Roberto wasn't aware he'd been in Russia. "I do have some news from the diaries. But first, how was your trip and how's Philippe? Did you and your partner get caught up?"

"Absolutely. We knocked out the business things first; then we took Friday afternoon off and went sailing on the lake. It was very relaxing."

Roberto had decided to pretend everything was normal until the time was right. Edward had been in Moscow and therefore knew Roberto wasn't in Lucerne Friday afternoon. Now as Edward warily watched Roberto, Roberto did the same to him. He noted how Edward reacted to his lies. All this came easily to Roberto – after all, there was one professional in this room and only one. It wasn't Edward.

Edward's face was impassive as Roberto continued. "So tell me what you've learned since I was away."

His face suddenly brightened with excitement. "Sit down. I need to read you Guinevere's latest entries! This is getting really good!"

Edward opened the journal to the pages he'd read before Moscow. He skimmed the notes that said King Pellinore was buried in the St. Mary Axe graveyard and his son Lamorak at Camelot. Then he turned the page and began to read the words he'd translated this morning.

———

Camelot, 17 August 500

My husband's heart is hardened.

At this point he never speaks to me. Upon his victorious return from the battle at Badon, someone, probably that old man Merlin, told Arthur about my attempts to seduce the stable hands. The magician had warned me earlier to leave Camelot. But I am the Queen. Even he, my husband's trusted advisor, cannot force me to leave. But I am fearful every day. By rights my husband could have me hanged. Perhaps he still loves me, as I do him. However, I will understand if he cannot stay with me now. I am a bad person. My lust overpowers my conscience, my devotion, my love. Why, I do not know. I cannot stop pursuing forbidden things. In doing so I hurt the man who loves me.

Once again as before, Arthur and I are together only once a day at dinner in the dining hall. No words are spoken; we eat in silence. Anything I know I learn from others. I know that Lamorak, who betrayed his King by having sex with me, will not be allowed to rest in peace within the walls of Camelot after all. Merlin convinced Arthur it must not happen. Thanks to the words of this cunning magician, my husband's heart was hardened and he issued new orders. Lamorak's body and his sarcophagus are banned from this castle.

25 September

An entourage left the castle this morning. I watched from my bedroom window in the tower where I have lived since I was banished from my husband's bedroom. There were horsemen accompanying two heavy carts, each drawn by stout horses. The first cart bore a sarcophagus of thick stone, its lid inscribed with a carving of a knight in helmet and holding a staff. The other cart carried a wooden coffin inside which lies my Lamorak.

I am told they are taking him two miles from here to the small abbey near Avalon's eastern shore. His sarcophagus will be placed there.

I pray that he rests in peace forever.

———

Edward closed the diary. The two enemies, bound together by an incredible discovery, sat in silence for a few minutes, each lost in his own thoughts. At last Roberto spoke. He asked how much of the final diary remained to be translated. Edward said there wasn't much left. He'd looked briefly and noted other people wrote the last two pages. The handwriting was totally different than the Queen's. The next-to-last page was in Welsh like the rest of the book, but the final page was in old English.

Edward didn't reveal one important thing – he knew who authored both pages. Although he hadn't translated the last pages yet, he'd read the writers' names. And these were fascinating too. They only added to the intrigue. He still didn't know the story's ending, but he had ideas simply because he knew the final author's name. He had forced himself to wait – to finish the diaries in order and not skip forward. There wasn't much left to translate now and he wanted to read it in order.

He would reveal everything only after his translation was completely finished. One had to be careful about wrapping things up. Once Roberto didn't need his services any longer, Edward was certain something bad might happen to him. He had some planning to do before he would tell his partner the end of the story.

The men went over what they'd learned so far. In 500 AD Lamorak was buried at Camelot, now Glastonbury, in what was later called the Lady Abbey. Now it was downstairs.

According to the administrator of the Glastonbury Trust, Arthur and Guinevere were also buried in the Lady Abbey underneath Lamorak's sarcophagus. In 1191 monks discovered the bones of the monarchs and kept them on display until 1278. At that point the story got murky. There was no mention of Lamorak after 1191, so that was an unsolved piece of the puzzle. Another was the final burial site for Arthur and Guinevere. A marker at Glastonbury Abbey showed where they were reinterred in 1278, but the trust administrator confided that it was likely they'd been buried elsewhere, that location eventually forgotten.

They still didn't know why Lamorak's corpse was here in London. The movement of his body obviously occurred centuries after Guinevere's death, so it was unlikely her own diaries would reveal anything. Except for those last two pages of her diary, written by others. That was Edward's little secret for now.

Sometime long ago the sarcophagus had been relocated to the crypt below the bookshop. That was a fact. The only thing left was to solve the mystery of how and why it had been moved.

CHAPTER FIFTY-SIX

Edward tossed and turned all night long. The person who revealed Guinevere's diaries would achieve instant fame and fortune beyond his wildest dreams. Surprisingly, the reclusive bookseller eagerly anticipated the public acclaim and recognition that would soon be his. Finding the sarcophagus of a Knight of the Round Table was unprecedented. But this was real, it was Edward's and his alone.

He'd made several errors. It had been a mistake to bury those two bodies in the crypt. At the time it seemed like a good idea, but now Edward had to do something about Curtis Pemberly and the young shop assistant. They had to move out so the archaeologists could move in. And he couldn't handle it alone.

He'd made a mistake bringing Roberto Maas into his confidence, and now he had to do even more. He had to tell Roberto his darkest secrets. He'd also made a mistake in Moscow – Roberto might know now that he was the burqa-clad woman. Regardless, he had to move ahead.

Like himself, he knew Roberto had two personas, one public and one shadowy. He didn't know exactly what the man was up to, but he was determined to find out. Striking at him first – hitting him without his retaliating – would be tricky, but Edward was a clever man, smarter than anyone. Because *he* had two personas too. He had Dr. Jekyll and that other one.

By the time he fell asleep, a plan was developing. He had to have help with the bodies; in exchange he'd keep Roberto fed with information from the diaries. Shortly he'd take care of Roberto, aka Slava, permanently.

CHAPTER FIFTY-SEVEN

Something in the financials still wasn't right. Every Friday when he printed the voluminous report, Roberto immediately shredded the prior week's copy. But he'd held on to the one with the errors for three weeks so far, looking at first one page, then another. Something bothered him and he was frustrated he couldn't figure it out. It wasn't the other little errors he'd found. Those could have happened to anyone, although Roberto couldn't remember even a small mistake before. Philippe was very thorough and prided himself on accuracy. Understandably he didn't personally prepare all the numbers – a couple of accounting people crunched the data and created the spreadsheets. But Philippe compiled it, reviewed it himself and vouched for its accuracy. It was his baby and his responsibility. Roberto frequently asked probing questions and Philippe had always been right on top of everything. He had never missed a beat. Until now.

Something *was* different. At the moment it was simply a feeling, but he'd learned to trust his gut. This morning he sat in his hotel room, poring over the old report once again. His eyes were tired – he was ready to give up and admit his feelings were wrong – when he saw it.

Two hundred thousand dollars.

There was no discrepancy here like the small issues earlier. This one was a routine payment for real estate services, one of a dozen more posted here and there – so ordinary it could be easily overlooked. He finally picked this one out only because he didn't recognize the name of the project associated with the payment – *Parmenter.* He flipped to the last section of the report that contained an index of the real estate his trust owned. The list had three columns per page for six pages, showing every property in his worldwide portfolio. The offsetting entry for the two hundred thousand dollars would be in the Parmenter account. But that name didn't appear in the index. No wonder he hadn't recognized it. There wasn't a property named Parmenter.

The weekly summary was simply that – a summary – so he sent a brief email to Christian Braud, the man in his accounting department who created these entries. He asked for a detailed accounting on Parmenter, including its income and expenses. That would show him everything tied to this particular project.

His requests were always top priority at the office in Lucerne. When the boss asked, people responded quickly. Roberto waited – if the man was at his desk, he should have an answer in five minutes. It was a simple matter of emailing an Excel spreadsheet back to Roberto.

But the spreadsheet didn't come.

Roberto grabbed his phone, putting aside the doubt creeping into his mind. He called the accountant's direct line.

"Mr. Lepescu's office."

What? Roberto hesitated for a moment.

"Hello?"

"Elise, this is Roberto Maas."

Her voice was perky and bright. "Good morning, Mr. Maas. How may I help you?"

"I was trying to reach Christian Braud in accounting. I thought I dialed his number, but perhaps I made a mistake. Can you transfer me to him?"

"Certainly, sir. One moment."

He heard a couple of rings, then an answer. "Mr. Lepescu's office."

"Elise, it's me again."

"That's odd. For some reason Christian's calls are auto-forwarding to Mr. Lepescu's line. I'll check into it and have him call you back. In the meantime do you need to speak with Mr. Lepescu?"

Roberto declined and asked that the accountant call as soon as possible.

Five minutes later his phone rang. He glanced at the name on his phone. It was Philippe.

"Good morning. I didn't expect to hear from you. I'm waiting for a call from the accounting people."

Lepescu responded smoothly, "Is there something I can help you with?"

Suddenly alarms clanged in Roberto's brain.

"I want to speak to Christian. Is he there?"

"He's not, actually. He, uh … he resigned this morning. Something about going back to finish his education. He'll be missed, but we'll replace him easily, I'm sure. I'd be glad to help …"

Philippe's words came fast and clipped. He was nervous as hell.

"What's Parmenter?"

Philippe paused for a moment. He replied shakily, "Parmenter? I'm not sure. Is it a name?"

"I'm referring to a real estate project in the financial report."

"Must be a small one. I don't recall it. Are you looking at this week's report?"

"I'm looking at the report from three weeks ago – the one that had the small discrepancies I asked you about."

"Right. Give me a few minutes to look this up and I'll call you back."

"One more question while I have you, Philippe. When a lower-level accounting employee resigns, do you always have his phone calls routed to your desk?"

"Of course not." Philippe's laugh sounded forced, unnatural. "That's some kind of mistake by the IT people. I'll get that corrected. I'll call you back shortly."

Shit.

Philippe walked to a bar discreetly hidden behind a wall panel ten feet from his desk. He poured a brandy and tossed it down.

After his explanation of the small errors, Philippe had relaxed. He waited two more weeks to be sure Roberto didn't catch this big mistake. If he had, Philippe was ready. He'd created a fake Parmenter realty account for an obscure property in Jordan the trust had owned for years. The money was all still here, everything was fine. Just another little error someone had made.

And until last week that would have worked, because the money actually *was* still in-house and Philippe was prepared to explain away the error. But he'd decided enough time had passed. Roberto had surely shredded the old financials by now – he'd received three more weekly updates and he never kept an older one. Last Friday Philippe had confidently transferred the two hundred thousand dollars to his personal offshore account.

And he'd brazenly done it again yesterday. Another two hundred thousand was gone this week. He had to undo that transfer fast. He had two days to make that happen before the next financial report went to Roberto. Worse, he had to explain the first two hundred thousand dollars – the Parmenter transaction – fast. And he had no idea how he'd do it.

While Philippe fretted in his office, Roberto made another call.

"Celia," he said to the young lady who sat next to Christian in the accounting room at the office, "this is Roberto Maas."

"Good morning, sir! How may I help?"

"Is Christian there?"

"He's out this week, Mr. Maas. He's in Austria skiing with friends. He'll return on Monday. Is there something I can assist with?"

"I had a minor question for him, nothing that can't wait. Thanks for your help."

The call ended. Roberto had to go to Switzerland. Immediately. This morning.

A half hour later he was in a cab, briefcase in hand. He'd left Edward a voicemail that he was making a quick day trip to the office. Edward's glance at TrickTracker confirmed that was exactly where Roberto *was* going.

When Philippe returned Roberto's call, he had no idea his boss was in Swissair's departure lounge.

"Sorry it's taken me so long to respond. The Parmenter thing is a bit of a mystery. I see the entry you mentioned, but I can't find it listed in the projects spreadsheet. I don't want to think anyone downstairs is at fault" – he was referring to the accounting department – "so before I answer, I need a little more time to look into this."

Roberto told his partner to take his time. It made no difference now what Philippe said. Roberto would be there in three hours to find out for himself what was going on.

Philippe was a man of habit. Every day at one he took his lunch, usually in the same quiet, expensive restaurant he and Roberto had visited a few weeks back. Roberto timed his arrival when Philippe would be at lunch. He used his access card to enter the building, went directly to the office he shared with his partner, and greeted Elise.

"I'm surprised to see you, Mr. Maas! When we spoke this morning I didn't realize you were coming today. I'm sorry Mr. Lepescu's at lunch; shall I ring his mobile and let him know you're here?"

"No, don't do that. There's no need to disturb his meal. I'll see him when he returns."

Roberto closed the door and sat down not at his own desk but at Philippe's. He shuffled through papers, an appointment book, then the desk drawers. He didn't know what he was looking for, but he'd know when he found it.

And there it was. Two wire transfer confirmation slips lay in the back of the middle desk drawer. Two hundred thousand dollars wired to a numbered account in the Seychelles last Friday and an identical transfer to the same account yesterday.

He leaned back in the chair, deflated. He hated this – in his varied, exciting life he'd never dealt with embezzlement – moreover by a friend, a trusted associate, a partner. He'd made Philippe a wealthy man by including him in deal after deal. And the man repaid his generosity by *stealing?*

He was still staring at the two confirmations, hardly able to believe it, when the office door burst open.

CHAPTER FIFTY-EIGHT

"What the hell?" Philippe abruptly stopped halfway across the room when he saw Roberto sitting behind his desk.

"My thoughts exactly. Come on over and sit down, Philippe. It appears we have some things to talk about."

Roberto had been betrayed and he made no attempt to hide it. He spoke quietly, more in sadness than in anger, his words echoing how he felt inside. Philippe sat across from Roberto, who was in Philippe's chair behind the desk.

"What's going on? I just spoke with you a few hours ago. Why are you here–"

Roberto interrupted. "I need some answers." He pulled out his smartphone, flipped to voice memos, hit record and put the phone on the desk in front of him. Their conversation would be recorded.

Philippe suddenly became aggressive. He stood and shouted, "Are you spying on me? Going through my desk? Maybe there *is* something we need to talk about, *partner*!"

Roberto merely held up the two slips of paper. "Where did this money go, *partner*? You took the first two hundred because I failed to notice it. Did you decide yesterday it was safe to take more? I have no bank accounts in the Seychelles. Whose account did four hundred grand go in – yours, I presume?"

Philippe glanced away. He was trapped and had to think quickly. He'd spent ninety minutes over lunch unsuccessfully trying to come up with a plausible explanation for the original Parmenter money. Suddenly he was caught – confronted with the two thefts he'd committed. He had no time, no explanation, nothing. It was over.

Resigned to his fate, Philippe straightened in his chair and decided to control the situation if he could. "Right. It went into my account. You've never been my *partner.* You've been the boss and I've been your little errand boy. That's become more and more obvious lately. I do all the work while you play archaeologist in London. I make everything happen. I keep my hand on the rudder. If it weren't for me, you'd have far less wealth than you do. I deserve more. I deserve it and I decided to take it."

During the two-hour plane trip, Roberto had determined what he'd do if the worst were true. The time for anger and accusations was over. He spoke calmly. "I want to tell you what's going to happen next. I'm going to call the police and you're going to sit here until they come. If you choose not to do that, I'll ask the security guard downstairs to detain you." He picked up the desk phone's receiver.

The man sitting across the desk from Roberto had only one remaining card to play. It might work, it might not. There was absolutely nothing to lose now.

"Put the phone down, Juan Carlos."

CHAPTER FIFTY-NINE

Roberto paused with his hand on the receiver.

"What did you say?"

"I said put the phone down, Juan Carlos. You're not calling anyone."

Roberto put the receiver back into its cradle. "My, my, Philippe. What have you been up to? Is there anything you haven't poked your dirty little nose into?"

"I have information. Not only do I know about Juan Carlos, but I know about Slava Sergenko too."

Roberto snapped to attention. *No one* knew about Slava Sergenko. Suddenly his calm, resigned tone of voice turned to unrestrained fury.

"You're on very dangerous ground, my friend. Where did you hear that name? Tell me now or I'll …" He stood so quickly his chair flew backwards and banged into a credenza. "You damned bastard! You have no idea …" He came fast around the desk.

Suddenly Philippe realized he'd made a crucial error. He'd gone too far; now he was genuinely afraid for his life. He'd been told that Juan Carlos and Slava were murderers, but the Roberto Maas he knew wasn't like that. He was a businessman, not a cold-blooded killer. For the first time, he saw the other side of his partner. Philippe cringed in his chair as Roberto approached. He shrank back, raising his hands defensively in front of his face.

"Wait! Don't hurt me! I'll tell you! Just stop and I'll tell you everything!"

Roberto grabbed the man by the lapels and lifted him easily. Philippe was surprised how strong he was. Roberto threw him back onto the desk and slapped him hard across the face. "Oh, you're right about that, you goddamned thief! You'll tell me everything and then I'm going to cut you into pieces and feed you to the fish in the lake!"

Suddenly the phone on the desk buzzed quietly. It was Elise, the assistant whose desk was just outside the door. She was probably concerned about the noise – she couldn't have missed hearing something. Roberto answered the phone with one hand, holding Philippe down on the desk with the other.

Calmly he said, "Everything's fine, Elise. We'll be in conference for a while. Just hold our calls and don't disturb us."

"Yes, sir," the concerned assistant responded, unsure what was happening in the next room. Whatever it was, Mr. Maas certainly was angrier than she'd ever seen him. He'd never even raised his voice – today through the door she could hear muffled shouting.

Over the next two hours a cowering Philippe Lepescu told his partner everything. He related the visit from two Russians who told a story of a child prostitute turned murderer and blackmailer, a wealthy bartender in Prague who had a penchant for antiquities and doubled as a CIA assassin. The Russians were working for one or more of the people Slava had blackmailed and they were intent on capturing, torturing and eliminating him.

"Why didn't you tell me about them earlier?"

"I was fully prepared to. I was going to call you in Greece – you said you were going on holiday there – remember? Then Edward Russell called and told me you were in London. I asked you about it and you confirmed you'd been lying to me. That's when it all changed. That's when I knew I couldn't trust you and you didn't give a damn about me. I thought you were my friend. My business partner …" Philippe began to shed tears.

Usually totally in control of his emotions, Roberto's rage surprised even him. He shuddered with anger as he interrogated this man he'd trusted. The usually calm, collected assassin had never been this furious. He could barely control the urge to kill Philippe with his bare hands. He slapped him again, harder.

"You learned that I, your boss who owes you absolutely no obligation to disclose my personal life, misled you about my whereabouts. And that indiscretion made you decide to keep quiet about two men who were out to kill me? Then you implemented a systematic program to steal my assets. Did you plan to help the Russians find me? Was that the plan, so it didn't matter now if you stole from me or not since I'd be dead?"

Philippe's words gushed forth. "You don't know how hard it was. You were the first real friend I ever had. I thought we were more than boss and employee. You called me your *partner*. That one word was the most important thing I'd ever heard. Someone wanted me to be his *partner*. I thought we were good friends. I wanted to share with you, to laugh with you, to have a real friend for the first time in my life. But everything you told me was a lie. I found out from the Russians that your entire life was made up. You aren't really Roberto Maas at all. You weren't even really Juan Carlos Sebastian. You're a teenaged boy whore from Russia who killed someone and blackmailed a lot of others. Are you proud of that, Roberto? Are you proud?"

Roberto said nothing as Philippe voiced the betrayal he felt. He understood completely – he felt exactly the same way. First it had been Edward. Now it was Philippe. He'd decided years ago to trust no one. Ever. What happened today made him feel even more isolated. Like Philippe, he also never had a friend, nor had he ever felt comfortable and safe enough to let his feelings emerge. And this was precisely why. The hard veneer of Roberto Maas remained solidly in place.

The last thing he got from Philippe was contact information for the Russians who wanted to kill him. He'd watch security camera footage from their visit to see what the men looked like. And he'd be prepared.

He held out his hand and said, "Give me your cell phone." Philippe handed it over. It belonged to the company anyway and he'd get another this afternoon.

"Unlock it and give me your passwords."

He watched Roberto's fingers fly first over the phone's keypad, then the computer on Philippe's desk.

"What … what are you doing?"

"I'm locking you out. No email, no contacts, no anything. It's over."

"You're treating me like some kind of …"

"*Criminal?* Is that the word you're thinking? Because that's the word *I'm* thinking. You son of a bitch! You stole four hundred thousand dollars from me after everything I've done for you. You started here with nothing and now you have a lot of money, thanks to me. But that wasn't enough, was it? You had to steal even more. You're a damned gypsy – I guess I should have believed what I always heard about you people. Thieves. That's what everyone called you gypsies. And I guess it's true, isn't it? You're nothing but a gypsy thief just like your father was."

The words stung harder than anything Philippe had ever heard. They burned to his heart. Any remorse he might have felt was gone – washed away by the overflowing hatred that now permeated every pore of his body. Roberto had impugned his family – his father's heritage. A rotten thief – that was what Ciprian Lepescu's killers had called him – and now Roberto was calling Philippe and his father the same thing.

Philippe's face revealed how deeply the words had affected him. It made no difference now to Roberto. The damage was done and the man had been caught red-handed.

Whatever semblance of friendship there had been was gone forever.

"Get out. Keep the damned four hundred thousand dollars you stole from me. Consider it your thirty pieces of silver – your payment for telling me about the Russians. I'd better never lay eyes on you again. You're truly lucky, Philippe. What you know about me only scratches the surface – I should kill you for what you've done, but I'm going to let you live. For now. But listen to me closely – if you mention anything, if I see you, if I hear anything at all about you – you're a dead man. You'll never run far enough to escape. And you'll have to look behind you every minute because I'll hunt you down and kill you."

Philippe was shaking from pent-up rage. He took a deep breath, forcing himself to remain calm.

"I understand," he said quietly. "Can I get my personal things …?"

Roberto slammed his fist into the desk and screamed, "Are you *insane?* I'm not sitting here while you clean out your desk! Elise can box up whatever I say you can have. She'll arrange to meet you somewhere to hand it over. Now get out. Get out!"

Alone in the office he had shared with Philippe, Roberto turned off voice memos on his cell phone. The entire conversation had been recorded – it was as damaging to him as it was to Philippe, but he'd keep it just in case. He walked to his own desk, linked the phone to his computer and downloaded the voicemail to a secure file. Then he erased the recording from his phone.

The conversation was deleted. Except for TrickTracker.

The rest of Roberto's afternoon was spent with the security director for Ciprian Investments. Locks were changed, video footage was reviewed and an astonished Elise was briefed on the departure of her dishonest boss.

For hours Philippe Lepescu sat alone in his apartment as afternoon turned to night. His hands were clenched, but he kept the seething rage bottled up. Undoubtedly the employees at Ciprian all had been told he was a thief. They had no idea about Roberto's own secrets. Somehow, some way, Philippe would correct the injustice. No one shamed a gypsy without retaliation. He would have revenge. For his father and for himself.

Across the street from Philippe's house, the man stayed in the shadows, avoiding pools of dim light cast from gas lamps lining the quiet residential street. A pedestrian strolled past now and then, unaware of the figure dressed completely in black who was standing nearby. He watched the two-story house and especially an upstairs apartment he knew well. He'd been to the flat several times; he knew exactly what he was waiting for.

At 10:30 the lights on the south end of the second floor were extinguished. The man watched a second set of windows – the single bedroom. Its light remained on until nearly eleven, then the flat went totally dark. He maintained his post for an hour just to be sure his quarry was asleep. There was no one on the street at midnight when he walked to the front door of the apartment house, used his trusty lock pick and entered quietly.

Avoiding an old lift he knew from experience was noisy and creaky, he took the stairs one quiet step at a time. The pick worked again, but when he opened the apartment door, there was a small flimsy chain hooked to the door jamb on the other side. Years of practice taught him ways to do almost any task soundlessly. He pulled a heavy-duty wire cutter from his jacket, made one clip and unhooked the chain. He was inside.

He walked to the bedroom and through an open door. He pulled a silenced .22 pistol; for close-range work this gun was perfect – a bullet would enter the brain but not exit. Instead, it bounced around doing maximum damage and ensuring the death of the subject.

His quarry lay in bed, covered by a blanket. The assassin walked quietly to the bed, aimed the pistol and fired two shots.

The figure didn't flinch.

Juan Carlos jerked the blanket back, realizing he'd been the victim of the oldest trick in the book. Pillows were arranged to resemble a body. Before he left, he glanced at the lamps and saw the timers that had automatically switched them off. Obviously his quarry had locked the front door with its security chain and left through a window. The entire time Juan Carlos had stood outside no one had been there.

Clever, Philippe. You've eluded me but not for long. Just watch your back. I'm coming.

Philippe *would* be careful. He now knew what to expect. Thanks to a simple nanny camera he'd installed high in one corner of the bedroom, he watched his attempted murder on his smartphone.

You underestimate me, Juan Carlos. You think I'm weak. That will be your downfall.

CHAPTER SIXTY

The recording lasted for more than two hours. Edward sat transfixed and listened to every word of the heated exchange between Roberto and Philippe.

The longer he eavesdropped on the discussion, the more exciting it got. It started out as an employee caught stealing four hundred thousand dollars, a great deal of money. Edward could hardly wait to find out what was going to happen next. Would Roberto kill him? Maybe! After all, Roberto had killed other people and this was a big deal! That would be exciting – Edward wondered if he'd hear gunshots on the recording.

Then suddenly everything changed. Edward heard Philippe say, "Put the phone down, Juan Carlos."

So Philippe knew about his previous life!

This was a crazy mystery, like listening to an audiobook novel. He leaned closer to hear Philippe say a Russian name – Slava Sergenko – that obviously made Roberto furious. There had been a scuffle, a hard slap and a phone call from someone named Elise, probably an assistant who heard the noise.

He listened to Roberto's life history. He knew everything now. He also knew why Philippe stole from his friend and his boss. Philippe was a partner scorned by a rich man who cared nothing about him.

It's exactly the same way Roberto treats me. Maybe he needs to learn to be a little friendlier. Maybe those Russians will teach him a lesson in the social graces! That made Edward smile.

The dark side weighed in. *Maybe I should just kill him.*

Edward chose to ignore that. The bad one seemed to have had more and more input to offer lately, and Edward was afraid to feed his desires too often. The dark side had to stay under Edward's control.

Philippe gave a phone number and an email address – contact details for the Russians who wanted to kill Roberto. Edward wrote them down. It would be a lot easier to let these people take care of his enemy than to dirty his own hands. Let the professionals handle everything. It was a simple solution he'd keep in mind for when the time was right.

Edward deleted the recording and turned off TrickTracker. The money he'd spent on that little program had certainly been worth it. *Now* I'm *the only one with secrets, Roberto,* he thought to himself. But not for long. It was show-and-tell time for Edward too. He had to tell Roberto about the two bodies in the crypt.

After that can we kill him?

CHAPTER SIXTY-ONE

Since Edward knew everything about Roberto Maas, he should have been very afraid of him. But more often these days Edward's dark side controlled his twisted mind. The bad one continually reassured Edward he was smarter, wilier and more cunning than the professional killer who was his partner. He created scenarios in Edward's head on how to eliminate his adversary. But Edward resisted.

We need him right now. But then we're going to kill him, right?

Yes, but not now.

Roberto was leaving for Moscow on Thursday. As usual he had lied, saying he was going to spend the weekend with friends in the south of France. Also as usual, Edward knew where he really was going. He'd be there himself on Friday.

But now it was time to get rid of the two bodies buried beneath the floor in the crypt.

On Saturday afternoon he and Roberto sat in the back room as Edward prepared for confession. He'd run this conversation in his head a dozen times. First he'd ask Roberto some questions – things Roberto didn't realize Edward already knew. He wanted the man to be invested in the secrets between them before he told him everything about the bodies.

"I have something to tell you, something involving the crypt that I hinted at once before. This is difficult for me; I need to reveal something very confidential. First I want to ask you something. When I tied you up in the crypt, you said you'd killed people. Were you telling the truth, or were you just trying to get me to cut you loose?"

Roberto answered smoothly, "I'm not proud of it, but it's true. I worked for a governmental agency – one you've heard of – but I can't say more than that. I've killed more than once. Why are you asking about that now?"

"Very soon we have to involve the antiquities people in the discoveries we've made, don't you agree? This is all becoming too big to keep quiet. At first it was less complicated. We had a fifth-century body in the basement. Now we have the diaries of the wife of King Arthur himself, the possibility their bodies are also buried here, and a Roman passageway dating back almost to the time of Christ. As much as I wish it didn't have to happen, I don't see how we can keep this to ourselves any longer."

"I totally agree. I've been thinking the same thing; every diary entry you translate makes me more and more sure. What's down there is unprecedented – earthshaking from a historical standpoint – and there's no way to keep it under wraps much longer. What are you thinking?"

"I have to know I can trust you. I know there are things both of us did that created mistrust, and I understand that. Secrets are secrets and everyone's got them. But now I need some help and I have to tell you a big secret. Do you swear to keep this to yourself?"

Roberto assured Edward the secret would remain sacrosanct.

"I'm thinking …" He paused for effect – Roberto could see the gleam in his eye. The demented bastard was obviously enjoying the mystery of all this.

Edward took a breath and continued. "All right. I'm thinking I need your help to move some things in the crypt. Remember the things the radar picked up in the floor? The, uh … the bodies? I shouldn't have buried them there."

"No problem," Roberto said reassuringly. He knew where this conversation was headed. If there were bodies, they had to go before the archaeologists arrived. By now they both were convinced the crypt had to be examined by professionals. Roberto was certain he could work things out so the items in the crypt remained theirs. Money talked, even with the authorities. Archaeologists were always underfunded. A few million dollars would keep things on the right track.

Roberto answered, "I'm willing to help. I just want to know something. How many bodies are down there, and who are they?"

Edward told him. Roberto knew the name Curtis Pemberly – he'd spoken with the man before Edward killed him. The assistant shopkeeper was a surprise, but the deaths only reinforced the fact that Edward was psychotic and couldn't be trusted for a moment.

To gauge his reaction, Roberto casually said, "So you've got a couple of kills under your belt."

Edward didn't respond. In order to move two dead bodies, his dark side would have to emerge for a while. That one didn't like Roberto laughing at him. He did have these two kills, but also there was the matter of Edward's grandparents. He'd suppressed that whole episode so far back in his brain it rarely surfaced anymore. His bad side assured him it didn't matter. What he'd done to his grandparents was part of the plan. Anyway, they were old and sick. Everyone died sometime. He'd just helped them along.

Edward's "Dr. Jekyll" side didn't like thinking about that. He'd loved his grandparents and they'd been good to him.

But neither of his personalities liked Roberto, the cocky bastard. His dark side spoke quietly in Edward's psychotic mind.

He'll be dead soon. We're going to kill him slowly, make him suffer. I can't wait!

By the time they quit for the day, they'd lugged fifteen bags of topsoil to the basement. At dawn Sunday they began to dig. It had been years since the two bodies were buried. Edward hoped this wouldn't be a smelly, nasty operation; he told Roberto that he'd put them in heavy-duty zippered plastic bags, the kind used for construction debris, and he hoped those bags remained intact.

Wearing latex gloves, they brushed away the lime he'd sprinkled in case the bags ripped, removed the dirt covering the bodies, and tugged them out of the hole. Everything was fine – not even a whiff of odor – until curiosity got the best of Edward and he suddenly unzipped one of the bags. Roberto wasn't surprised – this man was the strangest he'd ever encountered and he'd have put nothing past him.

Curtis Pemberly's corpse was gray and had a fine coating of mold where skin was exposed. There was the putrid smell of rot and decay. Edward quickly zipped the bag.

Edward was surprised how matter-of-factly he dealt with the whole thing. There wasn't a tinge of guilt – instead, he found himself irritated at these two men who caused him the inconvenience of digging them up. They set the body bags in one corner of the crypt.

The topsoil went into the gaping hole that had held two bodies. They smoothed everything out and replaced the floor stones. They swept and rearranged, and by five p.m. everything was back to normal. They agreed a visitor would have no idea the floor had ever been disturbed.

They had time to kill, so to speak. They went to a Chinese restaurant in Soho, had dinner and waited until it was quiet on St. Mary Axe Street. Roberto noticed throughout the entire exercise that Edward remained cool and calm. The man had absolutely no remorse. All he cared about was accomplishing a task – removing two people he'd murdered from their graves in his basement. Roberto was sure now that the bookseller was completely insane. He wasn't a trained assassin like Juan Carlos. Edward was a homicidal maniac with no conscience and multiple personalities. He was unpredictable and dangerous.

At nine they returned to Edward's store and used the winch to raise the bodies from the crypt to the basement. With considerable difficulty they tugged and pulled each one up the stairs and dragged them to the front door of the bookshop.

Edward walked to a parking garage on Leadenhall Street, picked up his car and drove back to the now-deserted street. He double-parked in front of the bookstore, put his flashers on, and they brought the bags out. One went in the trunk, the other in the backseat. They left without encountering anyone.

For two hours the men drove west. Finally they arrived at a remote site in a forest where Edward's grandparents had sent him to camp one awful summer. He'd hated every minute of it – he didn't enjoy interaction with the other kids one bit. He knew this place had been shut down for many years. When he was a kid, there had been a deep well that he hoped no one had covered, and he was in luck. It was still there, a circular pile of stones marking its location. They dumped the bodies down the shaft. They heard the first one hit water maybe thirty feet down. The second thumped on top of the first. Roberto admitted Edward had found a good hiding place. Surprisingly for an amateur, he had planned and executed this entire project well.

They threw stones into the hole until it was full, gave it a last look and drove back to London. At close to three in the morning a sleepy attendant waved them back into the parking garage.

In bed around daybreak, Edward reflected on what they'd accomplished. He was exhausted because his bad side had been out all day. It had to be that way; sometimes he experienced regret. But the dark one always helped him get over that. So he'd let it stay out, not that he had much choice today. It had been a struggle all day long to keep his feelings and urges in check. Every few minutes the bad side developed a new way to kill Roberto. One time he almost gave in – the voice said *Pick up the shovel and kill him now.* But that was stupid, irrational. It would only compound the problem. There would be three bodies to deal with and no one to help him. Now wasn't the time. He told the bad person to be patient. But the dark one didn't like to be patient.

Now the bad side reminded Edward that only one person knew his secret about the bodies.

We have to kill him.

We will. But for now you just have to wait.

Don't make me wait too long. Or I may just take care of it without asking you. I want to kill him soon.

That was strange, Edward reflected uneasily. This was the first time his dark personality had ever threatened to take charge on its own.

Do these conversations mean I'm crazy? Or is everyone like this?

He fell asleep without answering those questions. He was a little concerned that the bad side might start acting on its own. If he ever lost control of it, things could get really dangerous.

CHAPTER SIXTY-TWO

Roberto and Edward met early the next morning around the table in the back room of the shop, coffee and tea in their respective hands. Each had more reason than ever to distrust the other, yet each of their skills was required to piece together what they'd discovered.

Edward said, "Thanks for your help yesterday."

"Congratulations on an excellent, well-executed plan. I couldn't have done it better myself."

Edward smiled while contradicting thoughts boiled in his head. He hated this man with every fiber of his being. Despite that, he enjoyed the praise. Since his grandparents died, he'd gotten none and it felt good.

For a moment he thought perhaps he and Roberto might continue to work together as partners in the future. That thought was shattered as quickly as it came by what Roberto said next.

"Now that I know all about your little secret in the crypt, I want to ask you something."

"Certainly. Go ahead."

"How'd you know I was in Moscow last week?"

He'd only been half-listening, still basking in the positive feedback from Roberto. The question jolted him back to reality.

"I … uh, I don't know what you're talking about." Edward fidgeted and squirmed, his face a contorted jumble. One second Roberto saw fear – the next it was unbridled malice. Edward's two personas were emerging simultaneously – battling for supremacy – before Roberto's eyes. In other circumstances it would have been fascinating to observe. Right now Roberto needed to be very careful. He had to push for answers, but there was no telling what might happen if he pushed too hard.

"You know exactly what I'm talking about. I just helped you dispose of two bodies. That little job could send us both to the death chamber. I did that for one reason. I wanted to see for myself if you're as crazy as I think you are. And I wasn't surprised. You actually *did* kill two people. Now you're going to answer me. How'd you know I was in Moscow?"

There was a battle in Edward's mind as his two personalities struggled. Edward responded meekly, "I really don't … I really don't understand. You were in Moscow last week? I thought you were in Lucerne …"

I'll take over now.

Suddenly Edward's eyes blazed and he screamed, "Screw you, you bastard! I don't owe you answers! You think I'm afraid of you? You think you'll kill me like the others? Not a chance! I'll kill you first! I can murder people too and you know it!" He started to stand. His eyes darted around the room, and Roberto saw he was going for a kitchen knife on a counter two feet away.

Before Edward could get up, Roberto turned over the table between them. Coffee and tea flew everywhere as the table hit Edward in the chest, knocking him backward out of his chair to the floor. The assassin walked to him, planted a boot on Edward's chest and said evenly, "Talk or you're a dead man. Got it, *partner?"*

CHAPTER SIXTY-THREE

Edward struggled as Roberto's boot pushed harder and harder into his chest. It was hard to breathe – he began to panic.

"Hey! Hey! What're you doing? Stop … I can't …"

"You were in Moscow. You were following me. How?"

"Okay," Edward gasped. "Let me breathe …"

Roberto pulled back, leaving the man writhing on the floor, gasping for air. "You have thirty seconds."

Using the chair for support, Edward pulled himself up and sat. His chest burned and he was wheezing. "Give me a minute …"

He felt dampness. He looked down and saw the front of his pants was wet with urine. That infuriated the dark one. "You bastard!" Edward screamed. "Look what you've made me do!"

Roberto's leg lashed out and connected solidly with Edward's knee, knocking him backward. Within seconds he was back on the floor, Roberto standing over him.

The bad side retreated. Edward meekly said, "I wasn't in Moscow …"

"Bullshit! You have two options. You talk or you die. If you lie to me again, I have interesting ways to convince you to talk. You'll talk; then you'll die. I've done this many times and my victims usually complain a little about the pain involved." He stopped to let that sink in. Edward began shaking, obviously terrified.

"This is it. It's confession time and it'll either be easy for you or very, very hard. Your choice."

"Just let me sit up ..."

"You're staying there. I can hear you loud and clear. You have ten seconds. After that you *will* talk – my way."

Edward tried desperately to pull up a credible story, but he was so afraid he couldn't think of anything. His voice trembled as he attempted to divulge as little as possible.

"All right. I followed you to see why you lied to me."

"I saw you in a burqa at the airport. You were there before I was, so you knew when I was arriving. How'd you know that?"

Shit. He scrambled for an answer that didn't involve TrickTracker. Roberto would be infuriated to know the extent of the bookseller's invasion of his personal privacy. Edward was as good as dead if that came out.

"You ... uh, you left your phone unlocked in the crypt one day. I ... I looked through it and saw your reservations."

Roberto paused a moment. Although the crazy bastard could have learned Roberto's flight plans that way, it was a stretch to think he could do it in the brief time he'd have had. It would have been highly coincidental to find exactly what he needed before Roberto missed his phone.

"Okay, you've had your chance. You're still lying, so this is over!" He grabbed Edward's shirt and hoisted the man up easily. The bookseller probably weighed 140 pounds and Roberto was in excellent physical shape. He tossed Edward into the chair like one of the sacks of topsoil. He turned away slightly then jerked back and hit him hard in the face. Edward's head recoiled and his nose began to bleed. He looked up at Roberto in terror, tears streaming down his face. He tasted blood from a cut on his lip.

Roberto unplugged the steaming teapot with a jerk and held it in front of Edward. As he tipped it slightly, some of the scalding liquid fell on Edward's arm.

"God! That's boiling!" He screamed in pain as Roberto poured a little more. Edward tried to move and Roberto splashed a generous dollop on his pants leg.

"Shit! You're scalding me! I'll talk! I'll tell you everything! Just don't burn me."

"You didn't fly to Moscow to see if I was lying to you. What were you there for?"

"I've known all along you were Juan Carlos. I told you that when I first met you. You wanted the things in the crypt because you're rich and you collect ancient artifacts. And you have some kind of secret life. I wanted to know what it was. I … I guess I got caught up in the intrigue of it all. I'm just a bookseller …"

"Keep talking."

Edward's fear subsided just a little and his story flowed more easily. "There's nothing very exciting in my life …"

"Yeah, everyone I know has killed two people and buried them in the basement," Roberto said sarcastically.

Edward was ready for this part. His explanation was also the bad side's justification. "Of all people, you should know that wasn't exciting. Those killings were necessary. I didn't shoot them or anything, and it isn't like I'm a paid assassin. Isn't that what you are? Aren't you some kind of hired killer?" He tried to change the subject and take control of the conversation, but Roberto would have none of it.

"What else?"

"That's it. I wanted to see if your other life, your 'Juan Carlos' life, was like James Bond. And I wanted to know why you're going back …"

Roberto's head darted up and he moved close to Edward, his fist inches from the bookseller's face. He said menacingly, "Why I'm going back *where*?"

Shit. I shouldn't have said that. That was a stupid mistake.

Edward was trapped. "To Moscow on Thursday."

How the hell does he know that? Roberto had grossly underestimated this maniac. Fortunately he'd caught things in time.

He took the sharp kitchen knife on the counter and brought it up close to the soft skin under Edward's ear. "Tell me more," he whispered, "or I'll slit your throat."

Edward's mind struggled to create something – anything. But it was too late. It was over. Edward could only hope Roberto would keep him around because of his value to the project. A lot of Edward's contributions could be done by no one else.

Don't worry, the bad side of Edward's mind reassured him. *Tell him everything. Then I'll kill him before he kills us. Trust me.*

"Have you ever heard of a program called TrickTracker?"

CHAPTER SIXTY-FOUR

Half an hour later Roberto Maas understood what was happening. TrickTracker was a simple but effective program that gave its user a major advantage. Whoever had it could stay a step ahead, and Edward had done exactly that. The assassin had been bested by a simple but ingenious program designed to catch cheating spouses.

As he was forced to demonstrate TrickTracker's capabilities, Edward was thankful he'd deleted the voice memos recording. With that, Roberto would have known that Juan Carlos and Slava Sergenko were secrets no more. Edward had kept that one part of TrickTracker's success to himself, and Roberto had no idea this crazed individual knew his entire background.

"You've put me into a dilemma," Roberto commented at last after hearing and seeing TrickTracker's demonstration. "You've spied on me, lied and plotted behind my back."

Edward's position was improving by the minute. He knew Roberto's dilemma well – it was the same one he faced. The psychotic side of him wanted to kill Roberto Maas. It was all Edward could do these days to keep the bad one in check. He needed Roberto until the project in the crypt could be finished. And Roberto needed him.

"I guess we're even," Edward replied. "You lied to me from the very beginning. You sent your partner to buy my building and you really were Juan Carlos the antiquities collector just as I thought. I have no doubt if you could manage without me, I'd be just another notch in your assassin's belt. But you can't. And believe me when I say I feel exactly the same way. The best day to come for me will be the day you're gone – out of my life – one way or another. If you're dead, I couldn't care less. But for now I don't see any way except to continue working together."

"You're a fool if you think you can beat me. I'm a professional ..."

Edward was becoming overconfident. He began to change. His eyes became cold, his jaw hard and set. His words were clipped. The dark side took over.

"You have to admit, Mr. Professional Killer, that I've done a good job of staying ahead of you so far. So what's next? You know I've spied on you. You know I saw you in Moscow. And I know you're going back to see a play on Friday. Which is total bullshit. What *are* you going for? Another one of your little jobs? Got to run to Russia and kill somebody?"

He began to shout, his arms thrashing crazily about. "I will kill *you* when this is over! You know it and I know it. Me, the meek bookseller from London. I'll kill all of you, Juan Carlos Sebastian, Slava Sergenko and Roberto Maas! I. Will. Kill. All. Of. You. Slowly, so it hurts."

He stopped talking, sat back with arms folded and smiled. *I enjoyed that a lot. Talking like that felt almost erotic – as good as it gets, aside from when I get to kill him!*

Roberto was an intelligent man dealing with a raving lunatic who could not be underestimated. Edward's schizophrenia manifested itself more often every day. The evil part of him yearned to be free. That side of his personality was the killer of two people and maybe more. Who knew? That dark side of Edward Russell was unpredictable and dangerous. The day Edward could no longer control the maniac within his head would be the day he'd strike.

He couldn't drop his guard for a moment. At this point he had to move the project along as quickly as possible, engage archaeologists to explore the crypt, and see it to completion. He'd already developed a plan for the crypt. He needed a plan for Edward too, but one couldn't plan logically for a crazed lunatic. There was no logic to Edward's dark side. That one did no rational thinking. It was simply evil.

The best course of action for Roberto was to assuage Edward's psychotic mind, to calm him so they could move ahead. The one thing that always evoked a positive reaction in Edward was what Roberto had to use now. Compliments.

"I have to reluctantly admit you beat me."

His bad side told Edward not to smile, but it happened anyway. "Glad to see we agree on something."

A few minutes later the two had decided to continue their tenuous working relationship. There was no discussion of the future after the project in the crypt. Each believed he could overcome the other. The problem would be getting the upper hand. Timing would be everything, and as the archaeological endeavors drew to a close, the time for action would be nearer and nearer. Then it would happen.

Roberto stood and walked to the door. He looked at Edward and said, "I'll kill you. You know that. Stay out of my business or I'll kill you regardless of how important you think you are." He turned and left.

It had been two days since Edward last saw Roberto. He knew the assassin was going to Moscow tomorrow for the second time in as many weeks. Edward had planned to be there too, to learn what was going on, but things had changed. Roberto knew what Edward was up to and he'd threatened to kill him.

Edward had no doubt what Roberto would do to him someday. But Edward would strike first, when things were right. Strangely, even though Roberto had scalded him with boiling water, that didn't make him as angry as having pissed his pants in front of Roberto.

He was frustrated that he'd been caught after things were going so well. Nothing had changed – he'd still figure out exactly what Juan Carlos was up to. The dark side kept assuring him they would beat this assassin, but after their encounter, Edward had lost his primary aid. TrickTracker hadn't functioned for days. Roberto had destroyed his phone and bought a new one.

Edward mustered courage and suppressed his fear. Roberto was far, far more than he appeared. He was a dangerous professional, but Edward forced out the negative thoughts.

I'm dangerous too. Especially when my other side comes out. That's the one that'll beat Juan Carlos Sebastian. That's the one that killed the others, and Juan Carlos will be his next victim.

His face broke into a malicious, evil grin as the other one emerged.

You're right, Edward. I'm glad you realize how dangerous I am. It's time for you to let me kill him! It'll be really fun – more fun than the others. This time we won't use poison. We'll make him suffer. We'll cut him *and boil* his *skin. He'll beg you for mercy. Then I'll kill him!*

You'll have your turn soon, I promise. It won't be long now.

It was almost laughable how much his bad side wanted to come out and play, Edward reflected with a smile. It really wouldn't be long – all he needed was the right time and place.

CHAPTER SIXTY-FIVE

The clock chimed midnight. Edward lay in bed wide awake, the translations almost finished. Only a few pages remained in the last of the three ancient diaries that bore the initials G.P. on their covers. He returned to the final pages of Guinevere's diary.

---

14 November in the year of our Lord 502

The country grieves at the news of the death of their beloved monarch this morning. No one is more saddened than I. I have lost my husband, the man for whom I was the one true love. My tears are those of regret for so many wasted moments, so many lost hours, so many times I could have loved him back but chose other men instead. My tears are for the loss of a man whose death I caused.

I left my husband, my castle, my kingdom, to go with another. Lancelot – my husband's best friend – took me away and I went willingly. I did not deserve the respect and love of my brave husband, but Arthur loved me anyway. He came to Wales and laid siege to Lancelot's castle. As it ended, I returned to Camelot while my Lancelot was banished to France. But Arthur would not rest; he wanted revenge. I begged, I cried that he stay, but he went to France in search of Lancelot, in order to slay him. Instead my Arthur is gone.

My shame at my actions is overwhelming. I fear I cannot bear it. But I must. For tomorrow I shall be crowned Queen of Britain. I will assume the throne my dear Arthur held for these many years. I am not worthy, but there are many before me who likewise were not worthy, and many shall follow after my reign is completed.

Merlin will be my adviser as he was for my husband. I know the hatred he bears toward me. He loved Arthur more than I myself did. He hates the sadness I gave my Arthur. He despises me for the flagrant indiscretions right before the King's face, even in the royal bedroom itself, and even the one with Lancelot that caused Arthur's death. Merlin would much rather have me on the gallows than on the throne. But God works in His own ways. And tomorrow, God willing, I shall be Queen – this time not as the wife of a King, but in my own right.

I pray to God that I will reign honestly, steadfastly and in the interest of our brave nation. My Arthur's knights shall protect me and our land as long as I shall live.

You shall be buried at Camelot, dear Arthur. Goodbye, my King. Goodbye, my darling. I truly did love you. More than I loved any other man. Not with my body as much as with my heart and soul. Sweet dreams as you rest in peace, your battles well fought, your journey complete.

With your death and my ascension to the throne, I close my journals forever. I dedicate them to you, my husband Arthur Pendragon.

Edward stopped. She'd written her last entry, but there were two pages left. He knew a little of what was next. Right now he had to process what he'd read so far before continuing.

He was amazed to find that Merlin was still alive. He'd been an old man when Arthur took the throne. He was always depicted in stories as a sorcerer with a long white beard and a tall pointed hat. He must have been over ninety by then, a ripe old age for those times. Apparently he was still going strong, an advisor to royalty and a man who was never afraid to speak the truth, even to the Queen he despised.

The single page of vellum he'd just translated would rank in this country's history as one of its most important and significant documents. It was a handwritten account in medieval Welsh by Queen Guinevere recounting the death of her husband Arthur on November 14, 502. Once the diaries were authenticated and carbon-dated, the lives and deaths of this legendary couple would become reality once and for all. And forever linked with King Arthur's legend would be its famous discoverer, Edward Russell!

He glanced at the clock. 1:30 a.m. No matter. There would be no sleep tonight until this enchanting tale was finished. He turned the page. There were two more entries, each written in a different hand. Knowing who the authors were made it more exciting. On the next-to-last page he began to translate the Welsh words before him, prickles of excitement making goose bumps on his arms and scalp as he read.

———

3 January 503

It is left to me, Myrddin, to complete the dead Queen's journals. I have read every page of her blatant sexual exploits, her thoughts and desires, her cheating, despicable actions against the man who loved her more than life itself. I disliked her before, but her diaries, her words of deceit, disgust me to my core. I cannot pity her. I harbor too much hatred to have pity. I can only be thankful her miserable life is over.

Who shall reign next, I do not know. What matters, sadly, is that the era of Camelot has come to an end forever, thanks in no small part to the actions of the Queen.

As usual she chose to ignore my advice. She interred her husband in the abbey below Lamorak's sarcophagus. Even in death the brave knight will forever protect Arthur, she blithely told me. But the "brave knight" was in fact a cheater, a thief who stole the wife of his King. The people forgave Lamorak, blaming the Queen for his indiscretion.

When she buried her husband next to her lover, the insolence was too much. The people considered it one more slap in the face of their beloved King Arthur and they were infuriated. But as usual Guinevere chose not to see their ever-growing hatred for her.

Truly it matters not where one's earthly remains lie. The people revered Arthur and even Lamorak. They detested Guinevere, but she refused to believe it. The people thought she had gone too far – she paraded her sexuality too publicly. Even a royal cannot be forgiven for breaking the heart of a good man. And she broke the beloved King Arthur's heart not once but often. Her death is a relief to her subjects.

The successor to the throne will not come from Camelot. Its time is finished. A man from some other place will lead our nation. Here on the isle of Avalon it is my task to dispense with the staff and close the castle. And it is left to me to bury the Queen.

Although she does not deserve it, I will have her body laid to rest next to her husband. That is what Arthur would have wanted, and therefore it shall be.

With this final entry the journals of Guinevere, Queen of England, are closed forever.

Once again it was a wrap, yet a final page of writing still remained. Edward could hardly contain himself. This was exactly like the thrilling end of a good book, the climax just a page away. But tonight Edward forced himself to slow down. He paused to reflect on the words he'd just finished before turning the page and reading the last entry in the ancient volume.

Myrddin. When he saw it earlier, he had easily recognized the Welsh name of the author. His name in English was Merlin. The legendary sorcerer – the man whose dislike of the adulterous Queen was known to everyone, including Guinevere herself – wrote these words in his own hand.

Edward paused, thinking about the significance of these pages. *I may be looking at the only handwritten words by Merlin the Magician that exist on Earth – words that prove the mythical figure lived just like Arthur and Guinevere.*

This is one more exciting discovery to go along with all the others, Edward thought to himself. *My fame will be larger than I imagined.*

He turned at last to the final words. *Let's see what the abbot of Glastonbury wrote to end the Queen's diary.*

The last few words were in medieval English. There was no date and only two sentences.

I, John of Taunton, abbot of Glastonbury, do attest that I have arranged the movement of the sarcophagus of the knight Lamorak from the abbey to the Church of St. Mary Axe in the City of London. The others rest with him.

The others! Arthur and Guinevere! Their burials were tied to Lamorak's all along. It had to be them. The final pieces were falling into place!

It was time to use one more resource, something that had lain unattended for years. Edward had another way to verify the information he'd learned from the diaries. He had no idea what it contained, but now was the time to find out. He'd go to the bank tomorrow morning.

CHAPTER SIXTY-SIX

Roberto spent most of the flight to Moscow thinking about what to do about Edward. This was far more complicated than the wet-ops work to which he was accustomed. Like some other things he'd let slip recently, he admitted he'd underestimated his partner. There was no way to know how much Edward had learned through TrickTracker. At the very least the man had followed him to Moscow and knew Roberto was back there again today. He'd considered changing his plan, but this entire job was tied to the theater performance. It had to come off tomorrow – everything was set. This time there would be no mistakes. He'd keep his eyes wide open for his psychotic partner.

The truth was that the crypt was the most exciting thing Roberto had ever experienced. He'd bought amazing rarities from places all over the world. But this was completely different. There was a story – a legend – accompanying this discovery. There were relics – some from Roman times but others that he now believed would confirm the existence of the legendary King and Queen of Avalon. These relics had surrounded a King – not just *any* King, but Arthur himself. These were things no man could have ever expected to own.

Edward was an integral part of all this, and Roberto couldn't do it without him. The man was a paranoid, schizophrenic maniac. He had discovered parts of Roberto's background, and he had to be dealt with eventually. For now Roberto had to be realistic. The man owned the St. Mary Axe crypt, he'd translated almost all of the three diaries, and he possessed the other fifty-plus books found in the chamber. Who knew what new secrets *they* might reveal? Moreover, the man was a history scholar and a translator. He had to have Edward's skills until they understood it all.

Shortly Roberto would eliminate Edward. For now he had to keep the man under control.

———

Edward swallowed his pride. Like Roberto, he was amazed and astounded by the things that lay in the crypt below their adjoining buildings. Until now his entire existence had been dull and drab, the few exceptions being when his alter ego popped out and did an exciting, scary deed or two. For his entire adult life he had been just two things. First he was a student; then he became the proprietor of an occult bookstore. For the first time things were really exciting. The bodies had been moved so now they could bring in archaeologists. His time for fame was approaching quickly and he was enthralled.

He needed Roberto. It was an unfortunate fact of life that he couldn't do all this without him. Roberto owned the ancient Roman burial passageway next door; it was a key part of the archaeological discovery they intended to disclose to the public. He also knew Edward's secrets; Edward knew his too, of course, but Roberto was a professional killer. If Edward told anyone about Juan Carlos, he'd be a dead man.

Edward would deal with Roberto soon. Once the discoveries were public and the artifacts dealt with, he'd surprise Roberto Maas one day.

I can beat him at his own game. He laughed to himself.

That's exactly right, Edward. We'll kill him!

Roberto was on a plane to Moscow this afternoon. Edward had a ticket for the same flight tomorrow. He placed a phone call, assuming Roberto's new cell phone had the same number. He didn't know if Roberto would answer, but Edward had to tell him what he knew. As much as part of him hated his partner, this news was just too exciting to keep to himself.

When he heard the familiar greeting, he left a message.

I've confirmed our two royal friends are in the crypt with Lamorak. Call me if you want to talk about it.

CHAPTER SIXTY-SEVEN

The house lights dimmed precisely at eight p.m. Juan Carlos sat in the packed first balcony of the Bolshoi. An hour later act two of Pushkin's *Boris Godunov* ended and the curtain went down for a brief intermission. The assassin applauded enthusiastically along with the rest of the crowd.

Sami Terzi and his date had arrived early, ready to enjoy the half-price bottle of champagne he'd been offered by the theater. Sami was angry that no one knew anything about it, but he didn't want to appear cheap in front of his girlfriend, so he paid full price for a bottle. He wrote off the experience as just like everything else in Russia – a bureaucratic mess with lots of talk and no results.

The actors were masterfully performing the dark play about a tormented czar in the early 1600s. Juan Carlos loved it – obviously Sami and his girlfriend were enjoying it too – Juan Carlos watched her give him a peck on the cheek. Like many young Russian women, she was strikingly attractive. Her white sweater accented her shoulder-length jet-black hair.

When Juan Carlos broke into Sami's flat, he had seen the tickets and noted the seat numbers. He reserved a seat two rows behind the couple. He was so close he could touch them. Everything was in place for the murder of this terrorist financier, but he'd promised himself he'd watch the entire play first.

The final curtain went down at 10:30. The cast received a standing ovation that went on for five minutes. Bows and curtsies were followed by a bottle of champagne for the famous Russian who'd played the lead role. Soon the attendees began to file out, pushing and shoving as Russians do.

Juan Carlos timed things perfectly. He moved slowly towards the aisle and stepped out directly behind Sami Terzi, who carried a peacoat while guiding his girlfriend up the stairs ahead of him. The aisle was packed with exiting patrons, so no one noticed a thing when Juan Carlos plunged a tiny needle into Sami's leg. There was just a prick; in all the shoving and bustle even Sami didn't notice.

At the top of the stairs Sami hesitated, teetering uncertainly as Juan Carlos and a dozen Russians pushed past him. The assassin glanced back and saw Sami fall into one of the empty seats, his girlfriend looking concerned while patrons hustled past without a glance or an offer of help. By the time Juan Carlos was outside, the man would be comatose, and before help could arrive, he'd be dead.

The National Hotel was a ten-minute walk from the theater. Juan Carlos enjoyed the crisp twenty-degree weather as he strolled, thinking how much he'd enjoyed seeing the play once again. The man he'd just murdered never entered his mind. He casually glanced around him but saw nothing out of the ordinary. There was no one watching him.

The Bad Man didn't know what was going down tonight, and he couldn't risk going into the theater for fear Juan Carlos might see him. He waited near the Bolshoi. Once Juan Carlos arrived, the Bad Man had dinner in a restaurant directly across the street. He'd picked it out earlier – heavy curtains shielded patrons who sat in front window tables, but he could pull them back and see the doors of the Bolshoi forty feet across the broad avenue. He stretched his dinner to nearly two hours – an easy feat in Moscow, where fine dining was an event. Precisely at nine the theater's doors opened and dozens of Russians in greatcoats poured out to the sidewalk for a smoke. Intermission came and went with no Juan Carlos. After the second act began, the man killed another hour with coffee and a brandy, then paid his check and walked outside to wait. The play would be over shortly.

When the crowd finally streamed out, the Bad Man was in the shadows across the street. Cabs and ostentatious limousines crowded the avenue; it was hard to see faces especially with everyone's coats and hats. At last he saw Juan Carlos Sebastian exit, turn left and begin walking. It was clear the man was on alert – he glanced from side to side, then behind him, as he walked. The Bad Man stayed far out of the way since he was virtually certain where Juan Carlos was going. Large groups of people were heading to the same place – they wanted a nightcap. He watched his quarry go inside the National Hotel, waited five minutes to ensure he didn't leave again, and walked back to the Bolshoi Theatre.

The Bad Man heard sirens. That wasn't unusual – they blared constantly in this enormous city. Back at the Bolshoi the crowd of patrons was gone. Now several police cars and an ambulance blocked the street in front of the theater. He moved closer and stopped an officer who was directing traffic with one gloved hand while holding a cigarette in the other.

"English?"

"Some," the cop replied.

"What happened?"

"A man had a heart attack after the play. I guess Boris Godunov was too much for him!" He laughed and turned away, diverting cars from the blocked street.

From a distance the Bad Man watched for fifteen minutes. He saw two paramedics come out of the theater, rolling a gurney. A white sheet covered a body. A distraught girl walked alongside, sobbing as the body was hoisted into the ambulance. Siren and flashing lights off, it drove silently away.

Had Juan Carlos done this? Did he just witness Roberto Maas the assassin at work? This was no coincidence. Juan Carlos didn't come all the way back to Moscow just to see a play. He had killed this man.

This changed everything. He'd confirmed firsthand that his partner was a cold-blooded murderer who could kill, then stroll nonchalantly back to his hotel. Instead of ending up as one of the man's next victims, he'd turn the tables.

The predator will become the prey.

The Bad Man considered his evening very successful. Things were finished here and he'd be back home tomorrow. No one would ever know he'd been in Moscow.

CHAPTER SIXTY-EIGHT

The Council for British Archaeology directed the frequent, often complex projects constantly underway in the City of London. Every time excavations began for a new building, ruins of Roman Londinium inevitably were found a few feet underground. These discoveries got top priority – time was money on enormous construction projects. Even then there were too few people to handle everything. More things got reburied or destroyed than got seriously examined by archaeologists. It was a sad fact in the ancient City.

Roberto submitted a proposal to the Council, confident they'd deny his request. He asked for money and archaeologists for further examination of some things they'd found. A scant few paragraphs described the situation: he and the adjoining property owner in St. Mary Axe Street had discovered an old crypt from the Middle Ages and a burial ground from ancient Londinium. All this was interesting on the surface, but to the Council for British Archaeology, it was simply more of the same thing. Old crypts and Roman burials were everywhere. They had no time for this rather routine project, so it was denied without discussion.

Roberto had deliberately left out a few key facts that would have caused the Council to spring into action. He omitted the names of the occupant of the sarcophagus and some of the personalities in the Roman passageway. He wanted the project rejected – a denial gave him the right to continue without their oversight. They weren't interested, and that was exactly what Roberto had planned.

Next he went to the British Archaeological Guild, a privately funded nonprofit that engaged archaeology students and professors from local universities. The Guild focused primarily on sites outside of London. They'd uncovered some important things near Stonehenge and Avebury in western England; now they were on the coast near Brighton, digging to see if the Romans had built a port there.

His proposal to the Guild was totally different and irresistible to its archaeological staff. Roberto would underwrite the entire project if the Guild would begin immediately. That was no problem – within two weeks a team was ready to start in the crypt. They were delighted to have both a fully funded project and one in London, close to home instead of out in the countryside for once.

Roberto added a requirement – he and Edward would be part of the Guild's team. This was a privilege his funding bought that wouldn't have happened had the government been in charge.

CHAPTER SIXTY-NINE

Edward opened the safety deposit box and removed the only thing it held, the ancient book that in handwritten Latin described the Battle of Badon. For years it had sat, as so many other things in the crypt seemed more important. A simple military history, even one mentioning King Arthur, paled in significance to the diaries of Queen Guinevere. But now this book was crucial. It could independently corroborate the diary entries about Lamorak's death and burial.

Its words were easier to translate than the Welsh of the diaries. This one was in Latin, a dead language in which he was fluent. In a day he skimmed the entire book, stopping here and there as relevant passages arose. According to the anonymous eyewitness who wrote it, Lamorak did indeed die in 500 AD. The knight's brother Percival accompanied his body back to Camelot, where a sarcophagus would be prepared.

So far this book and the diaries tallied perfectly.

Most of the story was a monotonous, tedious description of medieval warfare. He'd found nothing of benefit except the validation of Lamorak's death. He stayed with it to the end, just in case. After all, the last was best in Guinevere's diaries.

This book was the same. As in the Queen's third diary, the final two pages of this book were the astounding parts. These words were in old English, not Latin.

These last two pages completed the puzzle.

Today is the fifth of June 1278. I, John Taunton of Glastonbury, am responsible for the removal of the remains of the three.

Since their discovery by the monks almost a hundred years ago, the bodies of our King and Queen have lain in the abbey, awaiting a final resting place. I had hoped they could remain here where ancient Camelot once stood. But that cannot be. Edward Longshanks, our King and Protector, valiantly defends England against both the Welsh and our enemies to the North. If either of those prevails against us, they will surely ransack the abbey and our city as well. Its longstanding ties with King Arthur's reign make it a prime target for enemies who would destroy our culture and heritage.

Edward stopped reading and turned to his computer. He knew the name Edward Longshanks – it was the nickname for King Edward I, ruler of England from 1272 to 1307. He had put down rebellions in Wales in 1276–77 and would permanently defeat them in 1283. The book's mention of "our enemies to the North" was a reference to the Scots, with whom Edward I was engaged in an ongoing battle that Scotland would temporarily win in the 1290s.

He was excited to see the entry written by John of Taunton, who was abbot of Glastonbury from 1274 to 1291. The same man had written the final entry in Guinevere's diary, saying he'd "arranged the movement of Lamorak" and "the others rest with him." This book was the final nail in the coffin; he laughed to himself at the comparison.

John Taunton's name had also been mentioned when Edward and Roberto visited Glastonbury Abbey. During their tour, the guide had spoken of an old rumor. "Some people say the abbot whisked away the bodies of Arthur and Guinevere." He laughed derisively. "But that's not true, is it? Look here." He pointed down to a marker. "This is the site of their reburial in 1278. End of story!"

The sad truth was that the guides spewed out the lies that kept tourists coming. They assured visitors that Arthur and Guinevere were still around.

Edward returned to the abbot's final words.

At the direction of my King I have prepared the sarcophagus and the bodies for the journey to London. The knight will be buried in the crypt below the Church of St. Mary Axe, near the graveyard where legend says his father Pellinore lies. Longshanks has impressed upon the Archbishop of London the requirement of secrecy. No one will ever know that the knight's sarcophagus hides the secret resting place of the beloved monarchs of Camelot.

In the crypt with their bodies I will place the books our monarchs loved. I personally prepared the boxes that will protect them from the elements. All that remains is for me to add this final book to the last box and seal it. That I shall do before we leave.

Caledfwich has been prepared as well. May it guard our King as it has for almost eight hundred years.

Edward stopped again. Caledfwich? It was a word he didn't recognize – Welsh, almost certainly, but what was it? He googled the word and looked at the screen. Suddenly he became light-headed. His hands slipped from the keyboard and he fell from the chair onto the floor in a dead faint. Moments later he awoke, dazed and dizzy but with adrenalin rushing through his system. His head almost burst with the amazing knowledge he now possessed. He stood and looked at his computer again to be sure he'd seen it correctly.

Caledfwich was the Welsh name for Arthur's sword. The screen also showed the name in English.

Excalibur.

King Arthur's sword is buried in the crypt too.

There's a relic that'll make history for its discoverer.

With shaky hands Edward returned to the book.

A special place in the crypt has been prepared for the bodies where a heavy wooden door separates it from an ancient Roman tunnel. The three will be safe for eternity and free from harm, God willing.

The book ended with three simple sentences.

Tomorrow we shall begin our journey. God be with us and protect our revered King, Queen and knight. God protect our country and our brave monarch Edward Longshanks.

In an old book about a long-forgotten battle, the abbot of Glastonbury wrote that he personally accompanied the bodies of three legendary figures from his abbey to the crypt at the Church of St. Mary Axe. Guinevere's diary had been one piece of the puzzle, but this book nailed it. Here was the proof.

In addition to three bodies, the abbot had also moved a sarcophagus, books and a legendary sword named Excalibur. Everything fit together perfectly with what was in the crypt. If the sword actually were there, it would be an overnight sensation. It would rank among the most important relics of England's historic past. If there had been nothing but Excalibur, its discoverer would still have the fame Edward sought. But he had the sword and much, much more.

Although the book never mentioned them by name, there was absolutely no doubt who the "beloved monarchs of Camelot" were. No other royals had ever been linked to Camelot and Avalon. It was the home of just one – King Arthur himself.

Pellinore, the book said, was the father of the knight buried with the monarchs. That was the name of Lamorak's father. Case closed.

At long last Edward knew the incredible history that surrounded the burials in the crypt. He knew why, how and when the bodies were moved. During the week of June 5, 1278, Arthur, Guinevere and Lamorak were laid to rest in the crypt of St. Mary Axe. This book made it all clear. And Edward was sure it was all true. King Arthur and the naughty queen Guinevere lived, reigned and died. And they were buried in the basement along with Excalibur, the most famous sword in history.

Amazing. Truly amazing.

And his alone.

Can we kill him now? Can we? Can we?

It was getting harder and harder to keep him at bay. And less and less necessary to do so.

CHAPTER SEVENTY

The Bad Man had waited until the long passageway was quiet, devoid of the activity that had been going on all day. It was after midnight and he easily gained access through the skylight on the roof of the vacant building.

Both Edward and Roberto had intended to repair the skylight Edward had slithered through weeks earlier. In the excitement of their discoveries, both had neglected to have it fixed. That was a good thing tonight. It was a perfect entryway. He could easily have gone through one of the front doors, but he avoided the street because of the security camera. The Bad Man didn't want his partner knowing he was paying a late-night visit to the crypt.

This time all he did was look. He noted everything and prepared his final plan. There was one thing to do before he'd be ready to fix things once and for all. To right the wrongs, the injustice. His partner was going to pay for what he'd done. It was finally time.

He stood in front of the sarcophagus of Lamorak for several minutes, gazing on the fully armored body lying before him. A bronze helmet and faceplate covered the knight's head. A shield nearly four feet long, surprisingly free of adornment, covered his torso. His gloved left hand was wrapped around an impressive sword. The word *Lamorak* was lightly etched on its golden handle.

The Bad Man loved history. He'd spent hours at one museum or another, staring at suits of armor and coats of mail. But none of those seemed real like the one before him. Seeing a stone coffin in a crypt was breathtaking in itself. It was even more so when one considered this knight served under Arthur, King of the Britons.

He knew how much his partner coveted the things that had been found in this crypt – the books, the knight, the possibility of a connection with Arthur and Guinevere. Roberto had been a different person since he'd begun working on the project here in St. Mary Axe. He was full of wonder, full of excitement, full of anticipation. He didn't care about anything else anymore. He was passionate about the discovery here.

All that made it more satisfying to know his partner would never have these things he coveted so much.

So close to success, *partner*, and yet so far.

The Bad Man left the building the way he'd come in, through the skylight onto the roof. He was pleased how well everything was falling into place.

It would all happen very soon now.

CHAPTER SEVENTY-ONE

Over the past few weeks there had been more activity in the narrow lanes of St. Mary Axe than at any time since merchants hawked their wares here in the Middle Ages. The British press eagerly reported the discovery of what appeared to be a fifth-century knight's tomb. For the moment the connection with King Arthur remained a secret. Roberto and Edward would confirm the truth before creating a firestorm of rumors. Once they saw the bodies and told the world, everything would change. St. Mary Axe would become one of the best-known lanes in the world.

Today tourists streamed to The Necromancer's Bookshop to see the site where the ancient things had been discovered. Huge double-decker tour buses that had no business turning into the tiny street tried anyway, failing and tying up traffic for hours. The police had finally blocked both ends of the street and made it solely pedestrian. Edward hired additional people to work in the store while he and Roberto used the first floor of the vacant building next door for the Guild archaeological team's command center.

The archaeologists had been here nearly a week. They'd developed a routine – every workday ended with the team sitting around a table for a wrap-up meeting. There were three conservators, a photographer, Edward and Roberto. The daily recap, recorded for transcription later, summarized the accomplishments of the day and laid out the plans for the next day's work. Every evening after the crew left, Roberto and Edward went back down into the crypt for a few minutes. These two enemies forced into partnership held a short daily recap of their own.

For four days the crew worked on Lamorak's sarcophagus, getting it ready to be removed from its niche in the wall. Yesterday it had happened – the stone coffin now sat in the middle of the room. The heavy winch and steel wires that had been used to move it were still in place. Photos and videos were shot from every possible angle; then the knight's shield and sword were lifted out. They carefully snaked six straps underneath Lamorak's body and slowly raised the corpse a couple of inches with the winch, just enough to slide a sheet of plastic under it. Lamorak was gingerly raised from his coffin for the first time since 1278, the year he'd come to London from Camelot. His corpse now lay on a table in a corner of the crypt. In a few days it would be transferred to a laboratory at the British Museum.

Today's work on the body and armor had been the most critical so far. The sarcophagus lid was considered important too, but Edward had broken it earlier. The pieces were already at the museum, where experts would reassemble the lid for study.

The coffin's front carvings had been carefully photographed because of the chance of its destruction during removal. Luckily that hadn't happened. The ancient sarcophagus remained as solid now as it was centuries ago when it made the long ride from Glastonbury Abbey to St. Mary Axe.

Edward and Roberto stood looking at the space where the sarcophagus had been. When it was moved, a three-by-four-foot hole in the floor underneath it was revealed. Dirt filled the hole completely to floor level.

"I just can't believe it," Edward said in a hushed voice. "Everything I read – it's … it's all true!"

"What you read? What are you talking about?"

He hadn't told Roberto until now. "I translated one of the books we found in the metal boxes. It's about King Arthur and the Battle of Badon. It appeared to be a routine military history book, significant only in confirming Lamorak died in 500 and was buried at Glastonbury in this sarcophagus. But then came the last couple of pages. They were the best of all." He stopped and smiled.

"Are you going to tell me what you found out?"

"Curious, are we?" The bookseller grinned like a schoolboy and taunted, "Want to know more, *partner?*"

My God but this man was crazy. Roberto went on alert. Edward was changing personalities. The psychotic side would be out soon – Roberto wanted to know what Edward had learned, but he had to hurry. Edward was quickly transforming.

"Of course I want to know more! You're the scholar here. Enlighten me!"

Edward clapped his hands excitedly, the compliment keeping him sane for the moment. "You're not going to believe this! On June the fifth, 1278, at the direction of King Edward I, known as Edward Longshanks, the abbot of Glastonbury himself moved three bodies from there to St. Mary Axe. Right here."

Amazed that Edward had withheld this critical information from the archaeologists, Roberto nonetheless held his tongue. "So this book confirms that Arthur, Guinevere and Lamorak were put into the crypt?"

"Not by name, but there's no mistaking who they are. It talks about the sarcophagus of the son of Pellinore, below which are buried two monarchs. You know the metal boxes of books my grandparents found? The abbot put the books in the boxes and brought them here too. The book I read even describes the Roman burial passageway underneath your building. It's … it's the final piece of the puzzle – the last thing we need."

Roberto shook his head in disbelief. "What were you thinking? Did you plan to let the archaeologists in on your little secret? Did you intend to tell them you know for certain who's buried down there?" He pointed to the dirt-filled hole.

"Maybe and maybe not," Edward replied. His eyes began to narrow and he tilted his head cockily. "Maybe I'll keep it quiet and let it be a surprise. Imagine how exciting to find the bodies and maybe even a relic of the King too!"

Roberto's head snapped around. "What relic?"

"Oh, now he's interested, isn't he! Maybe you have to wait too! I have a secret … I have a secret …" Suddenly he jumped up and down excitedly. "I have to tell you! I hate you, but I can't wait to tell someone! Excalibur's down there too!"

"For God's sake, Edward! How do you know that?"

"It's all in the book. Excalibur's called Caledfwich – that's its name in Welsh – and the book said it rests with the King. The sword's there too! How about that!" He danced a jig around the room, his face contorted in a maniacal grin.

Despite the man's personality shift, Roberto was infuriated. "You damned idiot! Why didn't you tell us today? Don't you think this information is critical to the project? Don't you think the archaeologists need to know this before they start indiscriminately shoveling dirt around? What the hell …"

As Roberto yelled, Edward suddenly stopped dancing. Within seconds his face and his demeanor were calm, quiet. The dark side went away for the moment. Without answering Roberto, he turned to the hole where the monarchs were buried.

They stared at the grave in silence, each lost in his own thoughts. Edward had spent the entire week planning and plotting, ensuring this discovery would be his alone. He'd help the Russians finish Juan Carlos Sebastian's career once and for all. That plan was already in place. He didn't know when they'd strike, but he knew it was going to happen soon. He'd been promised he could have everything so long as they got revenge against Juan Carlos, nee Slava Sergenko of Russia.

Roberto thought of the future without this lunatic, a man whose psychotic interludes had caused bizarre problems time and again. The original plan had been that they would be partners. For a brief time the idea made sense. Very early on he realized that could never happen. There was no room for the two of them. Especially when one had a maniac living inside his head. Roberto would take care of things. Very, very soon.

Each pondered the significance of what lay ahead. They had found the burial site of the mythical King and Queen of Camelot. The King's relic – the sword Excalibur – was in the grave with its owner. Words couldn't adequately describe the once-in-a-lifetime discovery.

Suddenly Roberto raised his head, a quizzical look on his face, and sniffed the air.

"Do you smell smoke?"

"Look!" Edward yelled, pointing at the ladder. Smoke was pouring down into the crypt through the hole from the basement of the bookstore.

"Fire! We have to get out of here!"

By now thick smoke made climbing the ladder impossible. They ran next door to the Roman crypt below Roberto's building and saw an identical situation. Heavy black clouds poured down the hole from above, and visibility was getting bad quickly. The rooms were already getting dark and cloudy – within seconds they would be full of dense smoke.

"What the hell have you done? Did you set the buildings on fire? Have you gone completely crazy?" Roberto couldn't believe Edward would sacrifice the entire project. Lamorak, Arthur and Guinevere were still here, and fifty ancient Roman citizens were entombed in ledges along the ancient passageway. But the man was insane; there was nothing rational about his thought process.

Edward merely smiled. This was the work of the Russians. He wasn't sure of their plan, but it was fine. He'd be fine. They'd promised him that.

But as he smiled, he had one slight, nagging fear. *What if his dark side had started the fire? What if the bad thing inside him had gotten free without his knowledge?*

His smile was the last straw for Roberto. "Goddamn you, you maniac! You did this, didn't you? You set this fire yourself!"

"Or perhaps *you* did," Edward screamed, speaking in an accusatory, childlike voice. "Maybe *you're* the crazy one!" He began to cackle hysterically and dance around. He coughed as the smoke became thicker.

Roberto ran down the long passageway toward the old iron bars that led to the Thames River. Immediately he noticed a problem. The air rushing through the opening at the far end by the river created a strong draft. It propelled the dense smoke quickly throughout the tunnel. Within minutes it too would be engulfed in smoke. There was almost no time to escape.

As he reached the end and gripped the heavy iron bars blocking access to the river, Roberto could hear faint sirens in the distance. They'd be of no benefit to the two men trapped down here. He sank to the floor as clouds of black smoke overhead drifted lower and lower. Soon the tunnel would be full from ceiling to floor and there'd be no air left to breathe.

Closing his eyes to keep out ashes, Roberto tugged and pushed at the iron bars, but they held firmly. He moved to the gate's edges and tried again. No luck. As old as the bars were, they were still solidly in place.

Suddenly something gripped his ankle tightly. Startled, he lashed out with his leg and heard Edward scream.

"Shit! You kicked me in the face! Get me out of here!"

Billows of smoke engulfed the men lying by the iron gate, so close to freedom yet so far away. Life-giving air lay just beyond the bars that held them prisoner. But they couldn't break through the ancient barricade; that precious air might as well be a mile away.

Behind them down the long passageway Roberto could hear crashing and groaning as three stories of wooden building began to collapse into the crypt. His eyes burned and ash stung his eyeballs. He forced them closed and continued to try anything he could. Keeping his fingers tightly wrapped around the iron bars, he pushed with all the strength he had left. His lungs were quickly filling with sooty ash; time was running out.

Roberto felt Edward's hand still clutching his ankle. Coughing hard and trying to breathe, he said, "Crawl up here by the gate! There's a little air coming in and maybe we can breathe!"

There was no response. As he lay next to the gate and sucked in smoky air, he felt Edward's hand go limp. The air became heavy with ash, so thick he could see nothing. He gave the iron bars one last thrust as everything began to fade away.

CHAPTER SEVENTY-TWO

The narrow two-block street of St. Mary Axe was a difficult place for vehicles to maneuver. Big tour buses couldn't do it and neither could forty-foot-long fire trucks. A ladder truck might have extinguished the roaring inferno; instead it sat idling helplessly on Leadenhall Street a block south of the blaze. It was simply too long to turn the corner. All night long three engine trucks poured streams of water. They worked at first on the two burning buildings, one vacant and one housing a bookstore. As the fire grew stronger, the trucks were forced to move. The buildings were so close to the street that the towering blaze threatened to engulf the engines themselves. The firemen moved down the lane, working to save nearby structures while those two burned themselves out.

The sun rose the next morning over a ghastly sight. The firemen had lost the battle; an entire block lay in blackened ruin. Eight ancient wooden buildings from the 1500s, each an important example of Middle Ages architecture, had burned to the ground.

The Guild archaeologists arrived for work and were shocked at the loss of the things in the crypt. They told police that a major archaeological site ran below the two buildings where the fire had occurred and off southwards to the Thames. They explained how they'd moved Lamorak's sarcophagus and discovered what they assumed was an ancient gravesite beneath it. Today's plan had been to excavate that grave.

How could this have happened? Was it deliberately set? No one knew. Fire investigators would spend days sifting through the ashes but never arrive at a definitive answer.

The Guild told authorities about their two benefactors, the eccentric Edward Russell and the Swiss businessman Roberto Maas. They were gone, presumably perishing in the fire. It would take months, maybe years, before the rubble could be removed and the crypt reopened. And it might never happen. The extent of the damage caused when two three-story wooden structures implode into their basements, collapsing tons of burning lumber into the ancient chambers below, was unfathomable. The buildings themselves were gone, a quaint sorcerer's shop was destroyed, and two men had vanished. The knight Lamorak's body and the possible burial sites of King Arthur and Queen Guinevere were buried beneath thirty feet of smoldering ashes.

There were many questions but no answers as to what happened and why.

Perhaps, the Bad Man thought, *I went a bit overboard.*

**The Crypt of the Ancients and
Ghost Train (books two and three of
The Crypt Trilogy), are available now on Amazon.
A new Brian Sadler Archaeological Mystery will be
released in 2019.
Want to be first to know when it's out?
Just go to
billthompsonbooks.com
and click "Sign Up for the Latest News"**

Thank you!

Thanks for reading The Relic of the King, the first book of The Crypt Trilogy. If you liked it and have a few minutes, **I'd really appreciate a brief review on Amazon, Goodreads or both.** Even a line or two makes a tremendous difference, so thanks in advance for your help!

To get advance notice about upcoming books please sign up at billthompsonbooks.com.

I won't share your email address and you can unsubscribe at any time.

Please join me on:

Facebook

http://on.fb.me/187NRRP

Twitter

@BThompsonBooks

Books by Bill Thompson

The Crypt Trilogy

THE RELIC OF THE KING

THE CRYPT OF THE ANCIENTS

GHOST TRAIN

Brian Sadler Archaeological Mystery Series

THE BETHLEHEM SCROLL

ANCIENT: A SEARCH FOR THE LOST CITY OF THE MAYAS

THE STRANGEST THING

THE BONES IN THE PIT

ORDER OF SUCCESSION

THE BLACK CROSS

TEMPLE: THE PROPHECY OF THE HIDDEN TREASURE

Apocalyptic Fiction

THE OUTCASTS

The Bayou Hauntings

CALLIE

FORGOTTEN MEN

Teen fiction

THE LEGEND OF GUNNERS COVE

Made in the
USA
Middletown, DE